# WHITE LILAC

# WHITE LILAC

A SARA VALLÉN THRILLER

## CECILIA SAHLSTRÖM

**Translated from Swedish by Emma Ericson**

Podium

SAGA

EGMONT

Podium

# WHITE LILAC

# 1

He was walking on top of the old city wall that ran along Gyllenkroks Allé and through Lund City Park, on his way to Mejeriet. His walk was slightly uncoordinated—typical for a boy who has yet to become a man. The determined yet insecure youth found himself somewhere between adulthood and childhood. He wasn't able to fully distinguish where the line between boy and man was drawn, but he was completely convinced by his greatness and unique personality.

His shoes were brand-new and white. He was humming a melody—happy, and totally at peace.

The sun was rising in the east. The sky above the horizon was pink and red, while the sky above his head was still dark blue.

He left the old city wall and headed into the park, skipping over a puddle. The park was in full bloom and leaves crowded the branches of the bushes, creating a network full of secrets. The boy, gangly youth personified, strolled into the park—without haste and filled with confidence in life.

Here and there, the roots of the different trees and bushes had created cosy and cave-like structures, big enough to sit in. *That would be a great place to sit with a girl*, he thought, and sighed. He loved summer. Summer break was upon him.

He had shaved his head and now his hair was only a couple of millimetres long. His stubble was dark, almost black. A thin white line on his scalp glistened in the light from the rising sun. A long time ago, he had fallen from a tree. He ran his hand over the scar. It was smooth and hairless.

The boy suddenly froze. He stopped humming and his heart skipped a beat. Out of the corner of his eye, he had seen something white. Something that looked out of place in all the greenery.

He turned his head to the left. A foot, it was a foot. He was sure of it. He suddenly felt slightly nauseous, but he forced himself to look at the cave-like hollowness in the large rhododendron bush where he had seen the foot.

The boy wasn't sure what to do, but he carefully took a couple of steps towards it and squatted down to get a better look.

A girl was lying on the ground in front of him. Her body was curled up in the foetal position and her left leg was outstretched.

Her chest moved slowly up and down.

He stared at her while desperately trying to find his phone. Something trickled out of her mouth, turning her chin almost black. *Blood*, he thought. *That must be blood*. His fingers trembled as he dialled 112, the Swedish emergency number.

"Pick up, pick up," he breathed heavily.

"Emergency services, this is Stefan speaking. What's your emergency?"

When the boy heard the calm and friendly voice of the man on the other end of the line, he gasped for air and said, "There is a naked girl in Lund City Park. Just next to Mejeriet."

"Okay. Can you please give me some more information?" The voice kept calm.

"Just between the old city wall and the path leading away from Mejeriet. You have to hurry. She is breathing strangely. Slowly. And blood is trickling out of her mouth. A lot of blood."

Johannes kept looking at his watch. The girl was still breathing. Slowly. She wasn't moving. He didn't dare to touch her.

Suddenly, Johannes saw a shadow.

He leaned forwards and squinted his eyes. Then he saw a dark silhouette against the greenery. Johannes froze.

# 2

He ran. His body felt light and his mind was clear and sharp.

*Zigzag,* he thought. *Confuse them.* He ran like a gazelle through the park. Along the footpaths and then over the grass, through the trees, past some bushes, and out on the footpaths again. He ran as if the ground was on fire.

Once he reached the beach, he turned around and ran up onto Svanegatan and along it, still light on his feet and as quietly as he could. He turned left on Grönegatan.

His breath pounded inside of his head. *Could it be heard as loudly from the outside?* he wondered to himself. *What did she think? That she would get away? That she could choose her moments?* As he thought about her, his heart started beating faster. It almost felt like he was suffocating. *She was nothing more than a simple whore,* he thought. The flower, the white lilac, had been a good idea. It smelled lovely. And it covered up the smell of the dead body. Nobody would ever understand what he had done for her. That he had saved her from the devil's grip.

He stopped in front of one of the entrance doors to an apartment building and walked up to the landing. *Confuse them,* he thought again. He took a big leap to the right and landed between the door that he had just approached and the one next to it. He stayed close to the wall and tiptoed his way over to the next entrance door. There, he took his shoes off. He caught his breath for a moment, focused, and sneaked in through the door. Then he closed it silently behind him. He had done this before. The courtyard was quiet and the black windows looked like eyes, staring suspiciously at him.

Quietly, he knocked on one of the doors.

"Look at the state of you. Come inside."

He walked into the flat without a word. He was covered in blood. He undressed and stepped into the shower.

When he came out of the bathroom, he was alone. He slipped into the tracksuit that someone had laid out on the bed.

# 3

Sergeant Malva Gran was in charge of the night shift and was busy washing vomit off the back seat of the patrol car. Peter Matsson's reckless driving had made a drunk man named "the Rat" throw up all over it. Peter ate his hot dog as if nothing was wrong. Malva's anger seemed to amuse him.

When they had first met, Malva found him attractive. He was both handsome and strong. After knowing him for a while, she had changed her mind though. Peter was a smug idiot who could be quite aggressive at times. The poor souls who crossed Peter Matsson's path when he was in a bad mood would definitely pay for it.

Malva was just about to wipe the seat down one last time when they heard the radio.

"Three-nine-ten, from seven-zero."

"Three-nine-ten, garage, over," Matsson replied.

"Immediate action required in Lund City Park, entrance from Mejeriet. A guy will meet you there. His name is . . ." the emergency call operator said, then paused for a moment before continuing, "Johannes. Step on it, three-nine-ten. Over and out."

Malva immediately reacted to the serious tone of the operator's voice. Peter Matsson put down his hot dog and Malva threw the stinking cloth to the side before they both got in the patrol car.

The sirens and the flashing lights made Malva's heart rate rise. She looked over at Matsson and could tell that he was feeling the same way as she was. When it came to speed, she had to admit that he was one to count on.

A couple of minutes later, Malva radioed the emergency call centre to tell them that they had arrived in the park. She reached for her mobile phone in the glove compartment and rushed out of the car.

*The path between Mejeriet and the old city wall*, she thought, but couldn't see anything in that direction. The park was silent. The sun was still low in the sky and hadn't made its way through the trees just yet. Not a single person in sight.

"Hello?" Malva called out. "Hello? Anybody there?"

Peter walked up behind her.

"What the fuck is this?" Peter almost looked disappointed.

"I don't know," Malva said before she suddenly shushed Peter. "Did you hear that? It sounded like a moan. It came from that direction," she said, and pointed to one of the footpaths. A bit further ahead, they spotted someone lying flat on the ground. Malva rushed over. It was a boy.

She heard the sound of the ambulance closing in. The sirens of their patrol car would tell them where to go.

"He's alive!" Malva shouted.

"I saw him. He punched me," the boy whispered, and pointed towards the rhododendron bushes ahead. "There, there she is."

Peter Matsson and Malva Gran both walked over to the opening in the bushes.

"Oh my God," Malva exclaimed. "Oh my God."

Peter squatted by the girl's head. "Holy fuck, this doesn't look good," he said. He felt her slow pulse and saw how shallow her breathing was, but he didn't know what to do.

Next to Peter, Malva's phone camera went off, and flashes lit up the cave-like structure in the rhododendron bushes. The scene was grotesque. Malva Gran shielded herself behind the camera.

The ambulance staff came running and rushed the girl off to the hospital. Malva noticed how they shook their heads. *That didn't look good*, she thought.

"Seven-zero to all units in Lund," emergency call operator Stefan said over the radio and listed the number of patrols available that night.

"Seven-zero to all units in Lund. We are switching to channel 60. All units to channel 60. Over."

*It's probably too late*, Malva Gran thought once she had deployed all the patrols. The park was completely open and there were a lot of ways one could disappear quickly.

Johannes was still sitting on the ground. He was holding a flower in his hand, a white lilac. Its scent was intense. Peter squatted next to him.

"He was really tall. He looked huge. Big hands. I think. It was so dark. I'm not sure. I think he had . . . I don't know. He was big," Johannes said. "At least he was bigger than me," he continued.

Peter could tell that Johannes was really trying.

"Where did you get that flower?" Peter asked.

"I don't know. It must have been that guy, the one who punched me."

"Where did he punch you?" Matsson asked.

"In my stomach. That's all I know."

When Malva saw how Johannes was shaking, she walked over to the car to get a blanket. *It's probably the shock*, she thought.

"Seven-zero from three-nine-ten, over."

"Seven-zero here, over." Stefan's voice. *Good, he is always calm*, Malva thought.

"We need forensics out here. And we need the on-call inspector as well, over."

"Roger, three-nine-ten, K-9 on its way. The duty officer will get back to you."

# 4

Chief Inspector Sara Vallén was tired after a long and intense day at work. Lately, she had been forced to solve all her problems on her own as her mentor was on sick leave. She was exhausted.

She was on call, but she was rarely called out in the middle of the night. She was ready to go to sleep, but her spinning head and aching jaw kept her from it. She took an allergy tablet that made her a little drowsy and around 2 a.m., she was finally able to fall asleep.

She was standing in the middle of a room. A door was open. Behind the door, her father stood with an axe in his hand. A snake slithered in through the door. She couldn't move. Suddenly, her father jumped out from behind the door and started swinging the axe at the snake's neck. The snake closed in on her and didn't seem to care about the axe. It hissed at her, and she noticed that it had two ringing bells attached to the tips of its whipping tongue. She pressed herself against the wall, but the sound grew louder and louder. She woke up with a jerk and picked up her phone.

"Vallén," she answered, and took a deep breath to try to shake off her dream.

"Hey there," said the voice that belonged to Duty Officer Kjell Stigsson.

"Yes?" Sara sat up straight in her bed, shook her head, and felt wide awake within seconds.

"A girl has fallen victim to a very violent crime in Lund City Park. As I understand it, her wounds are bad, possibly life-threatening."

"Lund City Park? That's just around the corner from me. I'll call the forensics team. They should be there within an hour. I can be there within ten minutes, I think."

"Good. We're sending a K-9 unit as well," Stigsson said. "The perpetrator fled the scene when a passer-by spotted the girl. Let's hope she pulls through. Good luck!"

Sara was already getting dressed. She always had her clothes prepared on a chair next to her bed. Sports bra, sweatshirt, and trousers. Sneakers on the floor next to the chair. Normally, she was quite messy. Her wardrobe was an absolute war scene. But there were two different sides of her: police officer Sara and private Sara.

Sara Vallén got into her patrol car, an old Saab 900, and got inspectors Jörgen Berg and Rita Anker on the phone.

"Lund City Park. Get there as soon as you can. I'll brief you while I drive," Sara said to her colleagues.

Sara had been given the go-ahead to handpick the members of her major investigation team, and it felt natural to pick her old colleagues from years back. They all felt a bit lost in their new roles. They had gone from working closely together for years to being split up between different police districts and jurisdictions. Nothing was the same anymore. It created a certain amount of insecurity but in a situation like this one, Sara knew exactly what needed to be done.

"I'm not far away from there," Rita said. She lived close by, on Grönegatan.

"I'm already dressed. I'll be there in fifteen minutes. I'll leave home in three," Jörgen said.

Sara shared the little information that she had with Rita and Jörgen.

"See you down there," she said, and ended the call. Then she repeated the procedure with her colleagues Jonny Svensson and Torsten Venngren. They both belonged to Malmö police district now. When she hung up the phone, Sara started feeling anxious. *Were the girls home when I left?* she thought to herself. She hadn't even checked before she rushed off. *What if it's one of them?* She picked up her phone again and dialled the number to one of her daughters' mobile phones. A couple of seconds later, she heard a sleepy voice over the phone. Once she had been assured by her annoyed daughter that both she and her twin sister were at home, Sara felt calmer. She hung up the phone and stepped on the accelerator.

She stopped the car outside of the perimeters and ran towards the flashing lights by Mejeriet.

A beautiful young woman came walking in her direction. She wore her hair in a ponytail. Considering the situation, she looked surprisingly calm.

"Sergeant Malva Gran," the woman said, and put her hand out.

"Chief Inspector Sara Vallén."

"Let me show you the scene," Malva said. "We might already have a suspect. He has been taken into custody. It was the prosecutor's call. Someone at the station will conduct the first interview. Then the prosecutor will decide how to move forwards."

"Great. Do we know who the girl is?" Sara said, and tried to hide her fear of it being one of her daughters' friends by sounding as professional as possible.

"No, not yet. The ambulance had to take her straight away. She was bleeding a lot . . . her tongue had been cut out."

Sara Vallén pulled a disgusted face.

"What kind of a crazy person is this?" she said. "It must have been horrible!"

"Yes, truly horrible," Malva Gran said. "It wasn't the whole tongue, but a big portion of it."

"What a sick world we live in," Sara said, and shook her head. Although she had been working major crime for years, she still couldn't help feeling horrified every time she was presented with the cruel and twisted face of violence.

"Her tongue was on the ground next to her."

"So this is the crime scene?"

"It looks like it. But we can't be sure. Hopefully, the forensics team will tell us soon," Malva said.

Sara nodded.

"The girl was holding a lilac branch. It looked creepy, as if it had meaning somehow. It's hard to know what to think about the tongue on the ground, let alone the lilac . . ."

"Yeah, of course. But there is probably a message there," Sara said.

She followed Malva back to the perimeter a bit further away from the rhododendron bushes where the girl had been found.

Everything had been cordoned off and there was a silent tension in the air. All they could hear was the occasional crackling from their radios.

"Oh, and the boy who found her was also holding a lilac branch," Malva said, and looked away. Suddenly, she looked horrified.

Malva took a deep breath.

"His name is Johannes Vallén."

# 5

Sara felt the ground disappearing beneath her feet. She turned away. She wanted to escape. She pulled herself together and dug her heels into the earth for support.

"That's impossible," she said, and started walking away from Malva.

"We will keep working as if we know nothing," Malva shouted after her.

"Of course," Sara said. "My son could never have done something like this. Do you understand?"

Malva looked at Sara Vallén with respect as she walked off. She was impressed with how strong she came across, but she couldn't help wondering whether she might also be the mother of a violent criminal. She clenched her fist and reminded herself that the most important thing for her now was to stay objective.

Virro sniffed his way out from the rhododendron bushes. A harness was strapped around his chest. From the harness, there was a long leash that connected him to his handler Judging by the way that the dog held his head quite some distance above the ground, the tracks were still fresh. He ran back and forth and it didn't look like he could pick up a distinctive scent. Fredrik, the dog handler, muttered something to himself. Too many people had walked across the tracks. He moved the dog a bit further away from the bushes to the place where the perpetrator seemed to have taken off in flight. There were clear marks from fleeing feet in the gravel.

Virro picked up a scent and started running. The dog's nose was closer to the ground now.

Nobody knew how long it had been since the perpetrator had run along there, but the dog's reaction showed that there was still a scent to track. Fredrik followed the dog. The dog took off over the grass towards Svanegatan. Then he stopped to sniff the ground for a moment, just like he was supposed to, before he kept going. The dog handler followed his dog quietly.

Virro suddenly changed direction again and walked out onto the gravel path, towards the beach. Then he stopped, again. Then he carried on. The trace seemed to be zigzagging everywhere and the dog was hard at work. The varying quality of the ground made it even more difficult for Virro to pick up the scent, but now he continued out towards Svanegatan.

Except for the harness that jangled around the dog handler's hips, all they could hear was the dog's panting. Virro suddenly stopped. Then he made a quick turn and started moving along the footpath towards Högevallsbadet, an indoor pool close by. The dog kept his nose quite a bit above the ground as he ran past the pool and turned right, towards Svanegatan.

*Asphalt*, Fredrik thought. *Not good. That means the trace will end soon.* But Virro seemed to have found it again. Now his nose was closer to the ground and he eagerly turned onto Grönegatan. Virro stopped in front of an entrance door. He smelled the ground for a bit but seemed confused. The trace was too weak here, and the dog couldn't pick it up again. He stuck his tongue out and stared at his handler. Then he smelled the wall next to another entrance door, lifted his leg, and urinated. Fredrik pulled at the door, but it was locked. Something crossed his mind briefly, but he let it go. Virro had lost his trace. Too bad. The dog handler was used to this and knew that both he and his dog had done their best. This was the way the cookie crumbled in his profession. Sometimes you succeeded, sometimes you didn't.

"Seven-three-ten to three-nine-ten." The dog handler radioed Sergeant Gran.

"Talk to me," she answered.

"The dog lost the track. We're at the beginning of Grönegatan."

"Roger that."

# 6

He is seventeen years old, and his summer break is about to start. We can't ground him. You must understand that? Also, he is not a violent kid. This is a mistake, Göran. I have requested the assistance of a solicitor," Sara finally said before hanging up.

"My ex-husband," she said apologetically to Malva, who was standing next to her.

Malva turned to Sara and shook her head. Her posture told her that she had distanced herself from the current events. Once again, Malva thought about Sara Vallén's strength.

"Of course, the real perp disappeared within a couple of minutes," Sara said.

She spoke quickly and blinked repeatedly—her eyelids seemed to have taken on a life of their own. It always happened when she was struggling with puzzling things together, and she knew that it made her look pretty arrogant.

Johannes kept popping into her head and it threw off the balance between rational thinking and her emotions. She had two voices in her head: one that assured her it was impossible for her kind and friendly Johannes to do anything this horrendous, and one that introduced a sliver of doubt in her heart—even if she knew that her son had nothing to do with this crime. It was simply out of the question.

Sara turned her head and felt relieved when she saw Rita Anker and Jörgen Berg running towards her. Shortly thereafter, they heard a car park close by and saw Jonny Svensson and Torsten Venngren step out of it.

Sara told her team what had just happened. She hesitated at first, but then she told them that her own son might actually be a suspect. Her colleagues looked at her, confused.

"But then you shouldn't take the lead on this case," Jonny Svensson said.

"We don't have anyone else right now. But it will be fine because Johannes hasn't done this. Period." Sara gave them a stern look. There was nothing more to say about this for the time being. Everybody realised that.

Jonny didn't look happy, but he lowered his gaze and gave in. He lit a cigarette and told himself that there was no point in arguing about this. That was something he had learned after years on the job.

They stepped over the perimeter together and treaded carefully towards the crime scene. Malva followed them and Sara turned to her.

"Make sure to keep the perimeter secure and send someone up to Grönegatan," she said, surprising herself with how confident she sounded.

"On second thoughts, I will send my own people," she said a moment later, and put a hand up to stop Malva, who had just picked up her radio to send a unit to Grönegatan.

She pointed at Rita and Jörgen. Rita looked eager. She wanted to go right away. As always, Jörgen followed, and the two of them left the crime scene.

Then Sara nodded towards Jonny and Torsten.

"You two, take Svanegatan and Gyllenkroks Allé," she said.

Once they had left, two members of the forensics team approached Sara. She pointed at the crime scene.

"Great, you're here. Unfortunately, there have been quite a lot of people walking around in there. But I know that there are shoe prints that stand out from the rest. They are slightly longer at the front, as if someone took off in a hurry."

The forensics technicians nodded. They were used to this.

"Also, there are probably quite a few footprints from police officers and ambulance staff. As always, it's hard to avoid it," she continued.

"Anything else we need to know?" asked the head of the forensics team, Ove Ovesson.

"Yes, the dog lost track of the scent by a door on Grönegatan."

"Then that area must be cordoned off immediately," said his colleague, Bengt Karlsson. "There might be evidence there that will be relevant to the investigation."

The forensics team entered the area carefully. Karlsson put a camera on a tripod and started photographing the crime scene from all possible angles.

Their white overalls looked like clouds among all the greenery.

# 7

Sara's brain kept spinning. *Johannes*, she thought. *Completely insane.* She flinched when Ove "The Shadow" Ovesson sneaked up behind her. He really earned his nickname.

"We have found quite a lot," he said. "The crime scene is outdoors in an area with a lot of foot traffic. Yeah, you know . . . And I think it's probably best if we collect footprints from all the ambulance staff and all the officers on-site, just like you said."

Sara nodded.

"We'll take care of that," she said quietly and decisively.

She felt very comfortable with all the technical work and knew exactly what needed to be done. She simply found it easier to navigate the practical aspects of her job than the rest.

"The medical examiner will examine the girl, of course."

Sara turned to Malva Gran.

"Have we heard anything from your people by the perimeters or the team knocking on doors?"

"Yes," Malva said. "Negative. Nothing so far. Also, I want to mention that both my colleague and I went into the bushes. Life-saving measure, of course."

"Okay, let's get your colleague's shoe prints too," Ovesson said. "I can see that your feet are small. So let's not create unnecessary work for us all. Is your colleague a smoker?"

Everybody knew that Ovesson hated smokers and that he hated smokers within the police force most of all. They always caused problems. Cigarette butts everywhere, sometimes even at crime scenes.

"No, he is not."

"Great, then we don't need DNA from you guys, only your shoe prints."

Sara waved at Deputy Sergeant Matsson, who walked up to her. Without introducing herself, she nodded towards his big feet.

"Make sure to get your shoe prints to forensics," she said, and pointed towards the team of technicians.

It sounded more like an order than a friendly request. Peter Matsson nodded his head and, even if it went against his instincts, he didn't protest—although he had a feeling that he had just looked like an idiot in front of Sergeant Gran.

He shook his head and walked off to sign the protocol that he had just drawn up. He had written numerous protocols like that during his career and knew that their purpose was to make it easy to follow the decisions taken and actions performed during the first stages of an investigation. He knew how important it was to get everything right from the beginning. It was hard to reconstruct certain things at a later time. Also, the document would be part of the preliminary investigation and he knew that it would be reviewed carefully. Therefore, he decided to add in the fact that his shoe prints would be part of the preliminary investigation. A crooked smile played on his lips just as the dog handler came back.

"What are you smiling about' he asked Peter.

"Oh, nothing. It's just the chief inspector. She is a feisty woman."

"Oh, really? I've heard that she is nice and very competent," the dog handler said.

Matsson's mouth turned into a thin line and the dog handler felt satisfied. Matsson was a nasty piece of work. Everyone who had ever worked with him knew this. The dog handler was no exception. He turned around and walked in Malva Gran's direction.

Sara turned to Ove Ovesson. She knew there were still many questions to be answered, and that she wouldn't get all the answers at this point. Still, she couldn't stop herself from asking.

"Were there any signs of a struggle?"

"No, not really. But there has been some movement in the area, obviously. I have a feeling that she was taken out pretty swiftly. I'm not sure, but that's what it looks like. We will see if the girl has any defensive wounds. Also, we haven't found any potential weapons in the area."

"Great," Sara said, and felt slightly hopeful.

"Great?" Ove Ovesson said, looking confused. "Are you okay?"

"I haven't mentioned this to anyone except my closest colleagues, but the boy who found the girl is my son. He has been brought in for questioning. He is a suspect, I assume." Her lower lip trembled slightly.

"What? Are you serious?" Ovesson exclaimed.

"Yes, I know. It's impossible. That's why it's great that we haven't found any weapons. That would have strengthened the suspicions for now. Before we get all the DNA, I mean."

"Yeah, I guess that's true," Ove said. He wasn't sure if he agreed with Sara's reasoning but decided to leave it for now.

"But . . . Should you really be here?"

"Yes, Johannes's father is with him now. I will go there later. And I will make sure that we get a new chief inspector on the case. But until we do, I am the one in charge."

# 8

"Should I really be the one questioning Johannes, considering you're my colleague?" Torsten Venngren asked Sara when he returned from Svanegatan. Another colleague assisted Jonny Svensson.

"Yes, we don't belong to the same district anymore," Sara Vallén said. "And so far, I'm still the chief inspector on this case," she added.

She knew that she came across as more decisive and unaffected than she felt. Emotionally, she was a wreck. Her heartbeat was faster than normal and her stomach ached. Still, she managed to think rationally. Her psychologist had once told her that her rational thinking was her strongest defence. She thanked her lucky stars for that today. Torsten was the only one she could fully trust. He had the ability to make people tell him everything, without being offensive or disrespectful. That was what made him the best interrogating officer she had ever met.

"Okay. I'll call you as soon as I have anything to tell you. Don't worry, everything will be fine," he said, and gave her a concerned smile.

*Sweet Torsten*, Sara thought. Then she nodded and got back to work.


Inspectors Jörgen Berg and Rita Anker knocked on a door on Grönegatan. They knew the importance of acting quickly. The entrance door where the police dog had stopped was cordoned off. On top of that, a police officer was stationed outside the door. Neither Jörgen nor Rita would be able to step foot in there before the forensics team was done. The uniformed police officer by the door told them that nobody would be able to sneak out anyway, as there were no back entrances.

Every case that wasn't solved within a couple of weeks risked turning into a cold case. There were plenty of them in the archives down at the station. Jörgen and Rita worked as quickly as they could—Rita somewhat quicker than Jörgen—but they both felt the pressure and wanted things to move even faster. One after the other, the residents in the building opened their doors. They were all tired and dressed in robes. All except one. Evert Karlesson was fully dressed at 4 a.m., wearing track pants and a T-shirt made of some kind of silky material. He told them that he was going for a jog as his shift started early and he wanted to squeeze in his exercise before he went to work.

"The mornings are so light this time of year. Perfect for a run," he said.

Rita gave the man in the doorway a sceptical look. He flexed his upper arms and pushed his chest out. She wasn't sure if he did it consciously or not, but she instinctively knew that she didn't like him.

"You haven't seen anyone pass by here?" Rita asked. "Your window is facing the street."

"No, no. I guess it's way too early for people to be out and about," the man said. "Has something happened?"

It was understandable that he asked, but Rita's instinct told her not to answer him. Jörgen Berg, on the other hand, didn't seem to think that there was anything suspicious about the man at all. Instead, he looked at him with an open and interested expression on his face. Rita tried to get Berg's attention, but something told her that he was more impressed by the size of the man's muscles than in what she had to say.

"A girl has been badly wounded and the perp seems to have made his or her way up Grönegatan," he said.

Rita pinched Jörgen in the side. He turned around and shot her a sour look before taking a step away from her.

"That's horrible," the man said, and Rita studied him carefully. He seemed very full of himself and he annoyed her. Something about the expression on his face didn't match his words. She even thought she saw him smile for a millisecond. Or was she mistaken? She looked at him again, but what she thought had been a smile wasn't there anymore. Alarm bells rang in the back of her mind.

Jörgen Berg nodded seriously and shook the man's hand.

"Thanks for your time," he said.

Rita nodded but didn't say anything. The man closed the door and they walked back out on the street.

"He seemed harmless," Jörgen said.

"I recognise him," Rita said, and thought about it for a moment. "But maybe that's not all that strange. We do live on the same street, after all. But harmless . . . I'm not sure. I have a feeling that he was acting. That's why I pinched you like that, to stop you from telling him too much. But no, you didn't pick up on it. Instead, you told him everything as if he was the most reliable person in the world. Did you learn nothing from your fifteen years as an investigator?"

"I didn't think about that. Do you have to get so worked up about it?"

Jörgen Berg shrugged his shoulders and thought to himself that he would probably never really understand women. But still, he and Rita were probably more alike than he and many of his male colleagues.

"What did he look like?" Sara asked when they called her up with their report.

"Tense," Rita said. "And athletic. He said he was working in construction and that he needed to be at work at 6 a.m. That's why he was going for a jog now. If you ask me, there was something strange about him, something unnatural and unpleasant."

"Do you think you can tell me what it was?"

"No, not really . . . Something in his eyes maybe? Anyway, he said that he hadn't heard or seen anything strange."

"Okay," Sara said.

"How are you feeling?" Rita was more worried about Sara than about Johannes. She knew the Vallén family and was convinced that Johannes was innocent.

"I'm not worried, I know he is innocent," Sara said. "But I don't want to talk about that now. Let's talk about it later. How did Jörgen feel about that man?"

"Jörgen didn't notice anything strange, so maybe it's all in my head." She paused for a second. "Here he is, going for his jog. So at least he didn't lie about that," Rita said when she saw the man running down the street. Even if she didn't really want to, she had to admit that it was pretty impressive to go out for a run this early in the morning.

# 9

I will drive up to the hospital to try to identify the girl," Sara said to Malva, who was busy talking into the radio.

Sara looked at the forensics team. She knew that she could leave them without having to worry. Brown paper bags stood next to them containing clothes, as well as smaller paper bags containing cotton swabs covered in sperm and blood. The lilac branch was in a separate bag. The tongue had been transported to the hospital. The men dressed in white walked silently among the bushes, looking for clues on the ground.

Malva nodded towards Sara while she listened attentively to the radio.

"When the forensics team is ready, you can remove the perimeter closest to the crime scene," Sara Vallén said as she headed for her car.

The moment she closed her car door, tears started running down her face. She leaned against the steering wheel and clutched it until her knuckles turned white, crying like a baby. She screamed quietly and hoped that nobody outside could hear her. After a couple of minutes, she sat up, aimed the rear-view mirror towards her face, and ran her trembling fingers across it. She was pale, so she pinched her cheeks to regain some colour. She collected herself and started the car.

"The girl has been subjected to serious trauma, or multiple traumas. Therefore, there are multiple doctors involved," the nurse said seriously, and looked at Sara Vallén.

"What's going to happen now?" Sara asked.

The nurse sighed.

"After the initial life-saving measures, the girl was sedated. Then she was examined by a surgeon, a doctor, and a gynaecologist. Then a neurologist, an orthopaedist, and an ENT had a look at her. But first, we had to stabilise her, of course."

"Can I see her?" the chief inspector asked.

"Well, if you come with me, we can stand outside her room for a bit. Maybe you will catch a glimpse of her."

Sara nodded.

"Do we know who she is?"

"No, no," the nurse answered. "There was no time for that. Also, she was naked and we didn't really have anything that would help us get an ID."

Sara followed the nurse as she walked quickly towards A&E. Through a small window, Sara saw a group of doctors and nurses working around the girl. A female doctor stood behind the girl's head, pressing slowly on a plastic balloon that was connected to the girl's throat with a tube.

"What's that?" Sara asked.

"A resuscitator," the nurse said. "It's a device that blows air and oxygen into the girl's lungs."

"Right. What will happen next?" Sara suddenly felt very uneasy. She had left her worries about Johannes outside the hospital. Now she was only there as an officer of the law.

"Multiple things will happen at once," the nurse said with a friendly voice. "She has already had a cranial CT scan. The doctor is assessing the x-rays now. They might have to operate. Next, she is headed for Neuro ICU. The gynaecologist has examined the injuries to her genitals. As you hear, this will take time. The girl has sustained a lot of injuries."

Sara Vallén sighed and turned away from the window.

"Is she in pain?"

"No, not right now. She is heavily sedated. We sedated her, even though she was already unconscious when she arrived."

The nurse patted Sara on her shoulder.

"Even the most experienced police officers and nurses find this kind of event pretty hard to handle," she said.

* * *

When Sara left the hospital, she felt how tired she was. Her whole being was exhausted. She would probably be able to squeeze in an hour or two of sleep. *Better than nothing,* she thought.

# 10

Johannes Vallén sat in a cell. His elbows rested on his knees and his head in the palms of his hands. He had no idea what was going on or what he was doing there. As he had been at the scene where the girl was found, they told him that he needed to be questioned. But why was he sitting in a cell that reeked of urine and vomit if he was a witness?

His stomach hurt, and the back of his head. Wave after wave of anxiety washed over him and before he knew it, he was throwing up on the floor.

"Help!" he shouted. "Help!"

A guard came running and opened the door.

"What the fuck are you doing?"

"My head is killing me," Johannes whimpered. His gangly body started to shake and the guard rushed off.

After what felt like an eternity, the cell door opened again and a man dressed in a white doctor's coat stepped into the cell. He looked at Johannes with friendly eyes. Then he turned to the guard and ordered him to make sure that someone came to clean up the cell.

"You might have heard about the UN Commission on Human Rights?" he said, and the guard took off.

The doctor examined Johannes and ordered another guard to call for an ambulance.

"The kid needs to go see a doctor for an x-ray," was all he said.

* * *

"Dad," Johannes said when Göran Vallén came into his hospital room. "I'm not sure what's going on. I haven't done this. I promise."

"Of course you haven't," Göran said, and tried to hide how worried he was.

Torsten Venngren got up from his chair by the window.

"Torsten Venngren, we've met before. A solicitor will be with us in a moment," he said, and shook Göran's hand.

"But I didn't do anything. I would never hurt anyone. I hate fighting and I could never do anything like that. I don't even know who that girl is."

Johannes found it hard to breathe. He was still nauseous and it felt like his head was about to explode.

Göran saw the horror in his son's eyes and hugged him tight.

"You'll be okay," he whispered into the boy's ear at the same time as he looked into Torsten Venngren's anxious eyes.

The interrogation started once Johannes's mouth and the inside of his cheeks had been swabbed. "DNA test," Venngren had explained, "nothing to worry about."

Torsten let Johannes tell his story while he listened attentively. Johannes told him everything that he had and hadn't done. The defence counsel listened without interrupting and Göran had to focus hard to stay quiet. Torsten managed to ask completely objective questions. He had been an interrogation officer for a long time and knew the importance of conducting the interviews without emotions involved.

Johannes had been at his friend Alex's house. They had been there until almost 2 a.m. Then Johannes had decided to go home, as he needed to go to school the following day. He knew it was late, but still. He had walked along Grönegatan. Then he had crossed Gyllenkroks Allé and walked on top of the old city wall that ran along Lund City Park. He hadn't seen anyone on the street and he hadn't heard anything strange when he crossed the park close to Mejeriet and suddenly spotted the naked foot in the bushes. He couldn't really explain why his clothes had blood on them. He assumed it must have got there when he leaned over the girl.

"I have no idea who she is," he said. "All I saw was the girl and a shadow on the other side of the bushes. Then everything went black."

"What did you see?"

"I saw that she was bleeding from her mouth and that she was breathing slowly."

"What hair colour did she have?"

"I don't know. I don't remember. Or I couldn't see. Or both."

"What did you do when you saw her?"

"Called 112. Then someone punched me. I promise."

The interrogation ended after about an hour. The boy needed to rest.

Torsten left the boy's room and picked up his phone. He called the on-call prosecutor.

"So?" the prosecutor said, urging Torsten to give him the boy's story.

"I don't think this kid did it. He has sustained injuries from an assault. He has a concussion and a broken rib," Venngren replied, absolutely sure that Johannes was innocent. Even if Johannes *hadn't* suffered any injuries, he was clearly too weak and completely lacked aggressive tendencies. The boy was terrified.

"Okay," the prosecutor said. "But I want to keep him under our protection until we have examined all the DNA tests. The time of his arrest is 6:22 today."

The prosecutor wrapped up the conversation by giving Venngren further instructions. Then he sighed and said he would be going home to sleep very soon. A clear signal that he didn't want to be interrupted.

Torsten Venngren hadn't seen the decision coming, but reluctantly filled in an arrest warrant. He felt uncomfortable, but he knew that there was no point debating it. If the prosecutor had made his mind up, he wouldn't change it. Venngren's experience told him that the on-call prosecutor wasn't a man you questioned. Especially when it came to major crimes like this one, where the prosecutor always tended to play it safe.

He entered the boy's room again and sat down in the chair. He felt tired, and something about the whole situation didn't sit well with him.

He looked at the counsel—a young woman with her hair cut in a short, boyish style. She saw what was coming and put a hand on the boy's shoulder. It almost looked as if she was bracing herself against the boy, rather than supporting him.

"The on-call prosecutor has decided that he wants to arrest you, Johannes," Venngren said, looking at the boy. He really wanted to instil confidence in him but didn't succeed.

The counsel's grip around the boy's shoulder tightened. Göran Vallén looked down at the table. Johannes looked pale.

"But I didn't do anything," he whispered. "I could never do anything like that! Never. Ask my mum. Ask my dad."

Göran Vallén shook his head.

"You're all crazy," he said. "This is completely bizarre. I refuse to accept that Johannes should be arrested. I refuse to let him end up in one of those cells. Never."

He turned to Venngren and then to the defence counsel.

"Make sure he gets out quickly," he said through clenched teeth. Göran Vallén's hair was a mess. He had a desperate expression on his face and, for a second, Venngren almost thought he was going to punch him. Vallén's eyes were full of rage. But he didn't say anything else. He stood up from his chair, lost his balance for a second, and steadied himself again. Johannes Vallén stayed seated in his chair. As if nothing could save him now.

The counsel let go of the boy's shoulder. She turned to Göran Vallén and Torsten Venngren.

"This is insane. Johannes found the girl and called the police. And now he is being arrested. Insane. That's the only word that can explain this situation. I hope you find the guy who did this quickly, and that you don't forget to look for him."

# 11

Concussion, a broken rib, and an intense headache. That was what the doctor had said over the phone. Sara almost thought that she would pass out when she heard the great news about Johannes's condition. It supported his story.

But now it was as if all hope had abandoned her again. She had just got off the phone with Regional Police Chief Beatrice Larsson, and their conversation still echoed in her head.

"Don't worry, Sara. It will be okay. None of us thinks that your boy did this and we're doing our best to speed up the forensic examination. Our top priority is the DNA tests, and the analysis will be done soon. Until we know more, we want you to stay home. I'll call you as soon as I hear anything."

Sara sat there with the phone still in her hand. She had a sip of coffee. It tasted bitter. She felt rage bubble up inside of her.

She hopped down from the windowsill, walked over to the coffee machine, and poured some fresh coffee into her mug. She was scared, terrified. For the first time in years. How would she be able to save Johannes? Both her instinct as a mother and her experience from years on the force told her that her son could never murder anyone. He didn't have it in him. He lacked both the aggressiveness and the ability that it would take. Johannes could never do anything like that to another human being. Never.

She sat down in the kitchen window again and felt a strong urge to call her ex-husband. He had been there when her son was placed under arrest. She knew that she had to talk to him and that they needed to support each other. Who else would she call? She hesitated. Göran was furious with her. When they talked to each other after Johannes's arrest, he had cried and screamed at her in pure frustration.

She held the phone to her ear and, just as she was about to hang up, someone answered.

"Britt Williamsson," a voice said at the other end of the line.

"Mum," was all Sara could bring herself to say.

"My dear child, what has happened?" her mother asked. She sounded worried.

"Johannes has been arrested."

She was crying now and her mother couldn't make out what she was saying.

"What was that?" Britt asked.

Sara pulled herself together and choked back her tears.

"Johannes has been placed under arrest for a horrible crime. The victim is a young girl," she cried.

Sara heard her mother gasp.

"I'll be right there," was all she said. "I'll get on the next train."

"No, Mum. I don't want you to. I need to deal with this." Suddenly, it all felt clear as day. She had to pull herself together and do everything in her power to save Johannes. Her faith in the legal system had gone down the drain the moment she found out that he had been arrested. How the hell could they even suspect anything like that? How could they? Her head was spinning and a wave of anger, anxiety, and fear washed over her.

"But I want to," her mother said.

"Okay, you can come. I'll pick you up at the train station. I actually want you to come."

She surprised herself at her rapid change of mind, but she felt good about it. There was no space for tears, grief, worry, or anger. The only thing there was space for, now, was to clear Johannes's name. She was known for her ability to think rationally, and rational thinking was what would get her through now.

They hung up. Sara dialled another number.

"Rita Anker," a very tired voice said.

"You have to help me," Sara said.

"With what?"

"Johannes has been arrested. He didn't do this, Rita."

"Of course he didn't," Rita said. Sara heard how her colleague shook off her sleepiness in an instant. "What the hell is that about anyway? Why did they arrest Johannes? Didn't the perpetrator knock him out? Don't they know how to read people?"

"It was after the interrogation at the hospital. They took him there. Torsten questioned him and the on-call prosecutor arrested him immediately after."

"On what grounds?" Rita asked. She sounded upset.

"He had blood on his clothes. I guess the prosecutor didn't care about the fact that he had a concussion and a broken rib. The medical examiner will look at it, of course. And the blood will obviously belong to the girl. Which proves nothing."

"And what about the solicitor?" Rita's question was the straw that broke the camel's back. Sara was overwhelmed and surprised by the tears that suddenly started streaming down her face. The word *solicitor* had really stressed the seriousness of the situation.

"I'll be right there," Rita said.

"My mother will be here in about an hour," Sara said once she had calmed down slightly.

"That's good. Have you told the girls yet? They might need their grandmother. Have you called Göran?"

"No, I'm just about to and I hate it. He was there when Johannes was arrested. He blames me and says that he hates me more than anything. I can't stand this, Rita. I can't stand it."

"I know. But we'll figure this out. Don't lose hope, Sara."

"It hurts so bad," Sara said before hanging up. She rolled up into a ball on the floor. The pain was too much to handle and she screamed.

# 12

We need to get him out of there," Göran Vallén said. He sounded bitter, angry, and almost aggressive.

"I'm doing everything in my power," said Anna Lindell, the defence counsel. She forced herself to smile and look at Göran Vallén. She noticed his dark eyes and the grey streaks in his hair. A face with sharp features. The conversation with Johannes had given them nothing new. He stuck to his story about finding the girl in the bushes. And she believed him. Completely. There had been no weapon found at the scene. Nothing that could have been used to injure the girl. Honestly, she didn't even understand why he had been arrested. She hoped that it would be a somewhat capable officer who would handle Johannes's interrogation.

The boy sat on a chair in the cold interrogation room. His head hung from his body as if it wasn't really attached to him. His long legs were tense and trembled nervously.

Göran Vallén kept having to be told to be quiet. The solicitor didn't need a warning. She knew.

The officer who was about to question Johannes said hello to the solicitor and to the father.

"Inspector Otto Karlsson," he said, and sat down on a chair across from Johannes and the counsel. Otto wore his hair in a ponytail. Göran Vallén stared at it bouncing up and down as Otto nodded his head and read through some documents in a file. The tattoos on the officer's neck, the earring in his right ear, and his ponytail; it all distracted Göran, but he couldn't say anything about it. He suddenly felt annoyed.

"What were you doing in the park?" the officer with the ponytail asked.

"I've told you already," Johannes said. He sounded tired.

"Tell me again," the ponytail said.

*This is bloody stupid,* Göran thought, but he bit his tongue.

"I walked through the park to get home after seeing a friend. I've told you that already."

Johannes sounded so exhausted that even the ponytail-man reacted. He looked up and studied the boy. Johannes was still looking down at his hands. His legs twitched. His arms were crossed in front of him. His hands kept opening and closing.

The ponytail continued his interrogation.

"Are you feeling guilty?" he said. It sounded more like a statement than a question.

"For what?" Johannes said wearily. Otto hadn't expected his voice to be as dark as it was. *Seventeen years old,* he thought. *Dark voice for a seventeen-year-old.*

"For hurting that girl," ponytail said, sounding a bit hesitant.

Johannes laughed. A short and stiff laugh. He ran his fingers over the scar on his scalp. It felt strangely comforting.

"You're all fucking idiots," he said. "Do I look like a murderer? A rapist? Do you think I would have called you guys if I had done something so horrible?"

Johannes straightened his back. Although they were all sitting down, he was almost a head taller than the officer with the ponytail.

"It happens," the officer answered, but didn't look or sound very convinced.

Johannes could tell, but he didn't really care. Instead, a wave of anger washed over him. He felt offended and strengthened at the same time. He looked at his father, who nodded his head.

"I think you underestimate me," Johannes said. "I found her. I was attacked, but I managed to call the police before that. Doesn't that sound like a pretty dumb thing to do if I was guilty? And where the hell is the weapon? Her tongue was cut out of her mouth, for God's sake. Do you think I did that with my hands, or what?"

"Hmm," the officer said. His ponytail danced behind him as he turned to the solicitor, and then to Johannes's father. It looked like he was trying to find the right word. But nobody in the room was planning to help him.

"What did you do when you—in your own words—*found* her?" he asked, and turned to Johannes again.

"I was scared. She was lying there with her foot outside the bloody bushes. I leaned over and saw that blood was pouring out of her mouth. Then I saw a shadow, and everything turned black. But I had called the police before that. I called when I saw her foot. That's what happened. I don't give a damn what you think. That's what happened." Johannes scoffed, and one of his eyelids started twitching repeatedly. It made him look arrogant, but anyone who knew him would have seen how scared he was. His long legs had stopped trembling and he put his hands on the table.

# 13

It was 8 p.m. when the new chief inspector, Christer Söderström from Helsingborg, stepped into the conference room in the recently renovated police headquarters in Lund. Maybe the new conference room looked a bit too much like a hospital, but at least it felt fresh and modern and the air conditioning was great. Three white walls, and one painted in a light green hue. Brand-new furniture. Chairs made from birch with green cushions, an oval table in the same wood as the chairs and a modern coffee machine in one corner of the room. For some strange reason, someone had hung a painting of a crying child on one wall. It was the only piece of art in there.

Söderström had reluctantly moved to Lund and left his office, his routines, and his colleagues behind. But he knew that the team that was waiting for him around the table had a lot of experience, just like him.

Söderström scoffed loudly when he saw that the seat at the end of the table was already taken by Jonny Svensson.

He sat down and looked at his new colleagues. They all looked tired and he knew that some of them had worked all night. He started speaking.

"The girl's name is Kajsa Lindahl. She is seventeen years old and attends school here in Lund. She lives with her parents in Klostergården, also in Lund. Her parents both have creative jobs. Her father's name is Gunnar Lindahl and he is an author—if I have understood correctly. Her mother's name is Margareta Lindahl. She is a composer. Of course, we will bring them in for questioning, but then we will have to intensify our hunt for suspects."

"But we already have a suspect," Jonny Svensson said, and sighed. "Shouldn't we focus on that?" He hitched up his trousers. The constant night-shift intake of burgers and pizza was to blame for his size.

Söderström rewarded Inspector Svensson with a smile.

"Kajsa has been subjected to rape and serious assault. The perpetrator cut her tongue out. She would have been dead if she hadn't been found so quickly. We still aren't sure if she will survive. Right now, she is in a stable condition, but the extent of her injuries makes it hard to say what will happen. She is sedated at the Neuro ICU at the moment. Oh, and she was holding a white lilac branch when she was found."

"We know!" Rita Anker said. She sounded annoyed and ran a hand through her blonde hair.

"How was the door-to-door?" Christer Söderström asked, ignoring Rita's comment. He knew that the outcome had been poor, but he followed his routine and ran the meeting in the same way as he always did.

"Well, we're still working on it," Rita said. She was still annoyed.

"Nothing to show yet, then," Söderström said.

Rita Anker shrugged her shoulders.

"Does it look like an assault rape? Stranger meets stranger? Or do they know each other? Does the perpetrator hate women in general, or just this woman? Oh, and does anybody know if white lilacs grow in Lund City Park?" Christer Söderström continued, and gave them all an encouraging look, but nobody seemed to know. "Find out," he said.

"The forensics team will give us all the information this afternoon, and Jörgen will receive a preliminary report from the medical examiner within an hour or so," Torsten Venngren said.

*Torsten has probably never broken a single rule in his career*, Rita thought. Their eyes locked and he smiled. She was impressed by how calm he was, how kind he was, and how well he seemed to understand the human mind. Although his wife had just left him, he didn't let it affect his work.

"That's great," Rita said. "But what do we know about this perpetrator? Who is he? How does he work?"

"It's probably a crazy person from St. Lars asylum," Jörgen Berg said.

Christer Söderström gave him a baffled look. Jörgen was sitting in a corner behind him, leaning against the wall. Rita laughed on the inside.

Jörgen's analytical ability wasn't always switched on, and he could go on and on about something forever. Still, most people liked him a lot. Everyone knew that nobody understood the archives or databases as well as he did. In fact, he knew them like the back of his hand, and he knew everything there was to know about the worst crooks in southern Sweden. Also, he always found a way to connect with the criminals, and he had access to plenty of informers as well as a big network within different criminal circles.

"And why would that be?" Jonny Svensson asked, and raised his eyebrows.

"Because it has to be. Those people are free to walk anywhere they want nowadays," Jörgen said. "Oh, and the Vallén boy is not guilty. Every single person with half a brain can see that," Jörgen Berg said, and stared at his colleague.

"First of all, St. Lars isn't an asylum anymore. Secondly, it's probably a little too early to draw such a conclusion. We haven't even started investigating the case properly yet," Rita said to Jörgen with a friendly smile. "I guess we can assume that the perpetrator isn't mentally well, but that's all we can really say."

Jörgen kept going on about how horrible it was to let all these crazy people walk the streets and how embarrassing it was that the politicians didn't take any responsibility for it. He kept talking until Torsten Venngren raised his voice.

"Stop it, Jörgen! You've been talking about this for at least ten years now. It doesn't change anything. Maybe you should become a politician!"

Jörgen stopped talking and Rita turned to stroke his cheek in a motherly gesture. Jörgen looked down as if he felt ashamed. But Rita knew better. He was pouting. She let out a short laugh. Jörgen instantly decided not to pout anymore. *She knows me so well*, he thought, and couldn't help laughing too. *Rita is so refreshing*, he thought, and started missing Sara.

Jonny Svensson was also thinking about Sara Vallén, but he didn't miss her. He was relatively happy to have her out of the picture, at least for a while. The fact that she had lived in the south of Sweden for fifteen years didn't mean that he accepted her as a southerner. Or as his boss.

"Does anyone else have any ideas?" Christer Söderström did not sound happy.

"I've been thinking," Torsten said, breaking the silence after a couple of seconds. His moustache moved on his upper lip. "The crime was obviously extremely violent, but I'm convinced it was planned, although it might have escalated. I mean, he cut her tongue out. Sure, it could be a man with weak impulse control, but why even bring a knife? And why the tongue? And why take the time to place a lilac branch in her hand?"

Torsten's words fell like heavy raindrops in the room. The type of rain that makes you want to take cover.

"Also, we aren't even sure that the lilac in question comes from the park, which is very relevant," he continued.

"If I understood it correctly, she has no defensive wounds. And the crime scene didn't show many signs of a struggle. If that was the original crime scene, of course," Rita Anker said.

"By the looks of it, that was the crime scene," Söderström said. "But why would you cut someone's tongue out?"

"A sign of some kind of complex, maybe," Jörgen said, deciding to be constructive instead of sulky.

"What do you mean?" Söderström asked.

"Maybe he hated gossipy women?" Jonny Svensson interrupted, clearly pleased with himself.

"Or maybe it was an attempt to get attention?" Rita said.

"No, I think Jörgen might be right. About the complex," Torsten said. "Maybe it has something to do with him not being accepted for who he is."

"And what about the lilac?" Rita said, taking the reins again. "What do you guys think that's all about? I didn't think it looked like the common lilacs that usually grow around here. It definitely looked different. It looked almost cultivated if you ask me."

A discussion broke out about the meaning of the lilac, but they couldn't agree. Jörgen thought it was a symbol of grief. Torsten thought it was about respect. Rita thought it was placed there to taunt the police. Jonny didn't say anything.

"Can someone else have put the lilac there?" Jörgen said suddenly.

"That could be the case," Rita said, "but when? I mean, Johannes Vallén was also assaulted, and he also had a lilac branch in his hand when he woke up. Who would have done it?"

"Maybe this discussion won't get us much further today," Christer Söderström said. He wanted to regain control of the meeting. "I was thinking about something relating both to the lilac and the tongue. What differentiates this crime from other crimes that we have investigated?" he continued.

"A lot of things, not just the lilac and the tongue," Torsten Venngren said. "The perpetrator cut the girl between her legs and all over her body, and he used very blunt force against her head. I for one have never seen such a violent and aggressive, yet sexually charged, crime."

"You might be right," Söderström said.

"We will probably have to widen our search for a crime of this calibre. We might have to look nationwide. Or what do you say, Jörgen?"

Jörgen Berg nodded. Words were not necessary. He knew exactly what to do.

"Should I talk to her family and find out who she really is?" Rita asked. "Who wants to come with me?"

"You will be responsible for the assignments I give you," Christer Söderström said. "I need to contact the prosecutor. And, Rita, I need you to go to the hospital and check on Kajsa's condition. Talk to the doctors. *Then* I want you to question Kajsa Lindahl's parents."

Nobody said anything. They all waited for further instructions.

"Torsten and Jonny, question her classmates."

Jonny let out an unhappy grunt.

"Jörgen, do your thing and ask Ovesson or Karlsson when they're planning to get here."

Jörgen nodded again.

"But . . ." Jonny started. He was happy that Söderström had taken the lead on this case, but not as happy about the assignment that he had been given.

"No buts, just do your job and everything will be fine," Christer Söderström said. Everyone could hear that he was trying to hide how irritated he was. Although he wasn't very fond of Jonny and thought he seemed like a meathead, he saw the value in him as a resource.

Jonny Svensson shrugged his shoulders. He swore quietly to himself, although it could be heard as clearly across the room as if he had spoken out loud. Nobody paid attention to him.

"Let's go," Söderström said, and pointed at the door. A typical police gesture.

"Oh, shit, I forgot about the press contact. Anna Gradin called this morning and wanted something for the media. I promised her that we would hold a press conference at around 2 p.m. instead. She told me that the journalists are all over this. They want to know as much as possible, of course. But I've changed my mind, I won't hold a conference. She'll have to face the press on her own."

Söderström held up the morning newspaper and showed them the front page.

"'The most violent crime in Lund's history,'" he said, reading the headline out loud.

The article didn't say much as they hadn't given anything to the press yet. The investigation was being kept under wraps and the media hadn't got their hands on any information yet, not even the fact that there was a suspect.

"Let's only give the press enough to keep wild speculations at bay," Söderström said. "And let's ask the public to contact us immediately if they saw or heard anything strange around the time of the crime. Let's tell them that a young woman has been the victim of a murder attempt. Something like that. It's important that we don't scare people. Let me think about it for a while."

"The newspapers already wrote more than that yesterday," Jörgen said, "not to mention all the speculations online. It's better to hold a press conference. It makes it so much easier."

Söderström hummed but didn't say anything. He turned his back to them and left.

Jörgen went into his office. He needed to structure himself a little before he got started. While he was arranging his notes, his phone rang. It was Ovesson.

"We won't be in until tomorrow," he said. "There is quite a lot of material. If that's okay, of course? If not, you are more than welcome to come over here and look at it all."

"No, that's not necessary. We have plenty of other things to do. Tomorrow is fine," Jörgen answered. "By the way, did you look into the lilac?"

"Yes, it's a *Syringa pekinensis* from north-eastern China. I doubt that they grow in Lund City Park. You'll have to look into where they grow in Lund, but my guess is the botanic garden."

As soon as the call ended, Jörgen called the botanic garden, but nobody picked up. *It can wait*, he thought. *The lilac won't go anywhere.*

He systematically started going through records and archives while he looked for sexual offenders in the different search databases that he had access to. He had a feeling this was someone they didn't know. He knew that he would probably have to look for quite some time before he found someone who matched the profile of the perpetrator. *There can't be too many of his kind out there*, he thought.

# 14

Lena Johannesson stood in front of the class, behind her desk. She didn't know what to say. The students seemed unsettled and apprehensive. *Restless*, she thought to herself. Lena normally didn't have a problem knowing what to say, but now she was lost for words. She swayed back and forth and didn't know what to do with her hands.

"Put your pens down and listen to me for a second." She stopped talking and observed the students. They looked curious. Or did they look defiant? She felt nervous. What was up with everyone today?

"So, Kajsa isn't well. She won't be here today. We're not completely sure, but things look pretty bad. She is in the hospital, in the ICU. Something happened to her the night before yesterday. We're not quite sure how bad it is. So, I'm not sure what to tell you. But the principal will be here in a bit to talk to you all."

The students stared at her. They looked confused.

A couple of them stared at their feet and one girl started to cry. Lena knew she was Kajsa's best friend, Josefin Elvebrandt. A good girl, just like Kajsa had been until about a year ago. Lena caught herself staring out of the window at the schoolyard outside. It was empty. *Why Kajsa?* she thought.

There was a knock on the door and Ingvar Kleve, the school's principal, stepped in. He looked very serious and the students sat up a little straighter. They were completely silent.

"Kajsa Lindahl was attacked the night before yesterday and she is now in the ICU here in Lund."

Kleve was not known for being very emotional, but his voice trembled and he was noticeably affected by the situation.

"We don't know much more than that. I have spoken to her parents, and this is all they can tell us for now," he said. "It is my understanding that you will all be interviewed by the police."

Lena's eyes filled with tears. She turned her face away from the class and covered her eyes with her hand. *Not now, do not cry*, she thought.

The old and majestic school looked impressive where it stood among the green trees and with the sun shining down on it. It all felt like a contradiction—Kajsa's terrible fate alongside the beautiful summer.

A student kicked the gravel and another leaned against a lamp post with a hockey stick in his hand. *So much sadness*, Lena thought as her eyes wandered across the schoolyard from the window in the teachers' lounge.

Josefin Elvebrandt sat on a bench and cried. Two other girls hugged her.

*That's good*, Lena thought, and returned to her coffee cup. She sat down next to the other teachers, who were talking loudly to one another. But she didn't have the energy to join the conversation. *What if Kajsa doesn't survive?* she thought, but the idea was so horrific that she pushed it away.

She thought about the meeting they were supposed to have on Tuesday after class. Kajsa had wanted to talk to her about something, but she had refused to tell her what it was.

Kajsa had changed during the last year. She had always been a happy, active, and ambitious girl, but lately, she had turned into a quiet, disengaged, and bored young woman. She had also seemed a bit more guarded lately. As a mentor, it was Lena's job to keep an eye out for her students, but she'd had too much personal drama to deal with lately to keep up with it. Now she felt guilty.

She thought about calling the police. Maybe what she knew was relevant after all? She had a look around the room and decided to call when she got home.

The bell rang and all the teachers returned to their classes. All teachers except Lena. She stayed seated and picked up her phone. Olof had promised to text her the moment he knew what time he would be home, but she still hadn't heard from him. She sent an inquisitive text. Maybe he would reply, but probably not.

Was she expecting too much from their life together? Why did he work so much? She thought about all the time that she had spent waiting for him and all the moments when she had told herself that he really cared for her. And she thought about the disappointment she had felt when she realised that he didn't.

Her phone vibrated. She opened her inbox to see if it was something important. She normally only got junk mail, but this time it looked like something different. A strange email from an unknown sender. A bunch of letters that didn't make sense, and an attached file. When she opened it, a man popped up on her screen, accompanied by a terrifying scream. Lena jumped out of her chair.

The man on the screen had blood around his mouth. He may only have been an animation, but he was still scary. Above the man were the words: *"I see you, I hear you, I know where you are."*

Terrified and angry, Lena collected her things and walked to her next class.

# 15

Please, mother, stop talking about food!" Sara stared at her mum, Britt, who was setting the breakfast table. The twins sat silently by the table. They both hung their heads. Gabriella, known affectionately as Bella, was crying.

"We're not hungry. We're scared. I know you're trying, but it is what it is. Scared people aren't hungry. They want to escape," Sara continued. She tried to sound polite. Her body was trembling and her head felt like it was about to explode. All she wanted to do was scream. She was on the edge of insanity. Or maybe hysteria.

"I know," Britt said slowly.

That's why she was cooking. It felt safe and close to home.

Klara looked up.

"Mum, will Johannes be detained?"

"I don't know," Sara heard herself say. She wanted to tell her daughter that he would definitely not be detained, but she didn't want to lie. And that would have been a lie.

Sara's neck was tense and her face stiff. Both her daughters and Britt looked nervously at her, as if they were afraid that she would snap in two. It all made Sara even more tense.

She walked up to the kitchen island and sat down on one of the bar stools. Suddenly, she pulled herself together.

"Everything will be all right. But I will be gone quite a bit. Thanks for looking out for the girls, Mum."

Sara felt her strength return to her.

"I'll figure this out. Do you hear me! I'll figure this out."

The doorbell rang.

"Saved by the bell," Klara said, and smiled at her mum, who made her way towards the door.


Rita hugged Sara and kissed her on the forehead.

"Come with me. I'm going to the hospital and then I'm meeting Kajsa Lindahl's parents. Nobody needs to know. We have to hurry. We only have a couple of days before the prosecutor needs to send in the detention order. We need to do everything in our power to get Johannes out of this," Rita said.

Sara looked at her closest friend. Her big and strong body, light blue eyes, and blonde—almost white—hair was a sharp contrast to the warmth that she radiated. Rita grabbed Sara's hand and held it tightly. She tilted her head.

"I *know* you're off this case, but nobody will know if you come along."

"You don't have to ask twice. I'll definitely come," Sara said, and smiled, but her eyes were empty. Inside, chaos was always lurking around the corner. Normally, she could push it away. Sometimes, she couldn't. But for now, everything was calm. And desolate. She wrapped a lock of hair around her little finger, as if it was the only way that she could find comfort.

Rita waited outside the door while Sara sneaked into the house, put a pair of sneakers on, and left again.

"Aren't you going to say something?" Rita whispered—she felt like a teenager who was on her way out for the night.

"Oh yes, of course." Sara turned around. "I'm just popping out for a while," she shouted. Within a second, her mother appeared in the hallway. She looked worried and her lower lip trembled. She smiled at Rita.

"Hi, Rita. Nice to see you," she said.

Rita nodded and mumbled, "You too."

"Don't worry, Mum," Sara said, "I'll be right back."

They walked next to each other down the stairs. Rita Anker had a large stride. Despite being a head shorter than her colleague, Sara's stride was just as big.

# 16

A girl was sitting on the side of Kajsa's bed. Kajsa was still sedated. There was something serene about the scene—something in the air that felt as uncomfortable as it felt right. Sara Vallén could almost touch it. The girl stroked Kajsa's head gently. It was covered in bandages that were held in place by a mesh hat. She was breathing with the help of a respirator and her breaths were calm and even. Tubes were sticking out of her thin body. The IV stand was right next to her.

Her hair stuck out of the mesh hat in thin strands, and the little you could see of her face was very pale. Her body was completely still, except for her eyes, which moved underneath her eyelids as if she was dreaming.

"You have to wake up, Kajsa."

Sara Vallén and Rita Anker approached the girl carefully, but with steps loud enough not to make her jump.

The girl was crying and it felt wrong to just step right into her grief.

The girl turned around when she heard the footsteps. She flinched and stopped crying. Rita walked up to her and placed a hand on her shoulder.

The girl looked confused when she saw the sturdy woman behind her. Then she noticed Sara, who was dressed in jeans and a red hoodie, and felt a bit more at ease. She made an effort to pull away from Rita's hand. Rita didn't remove it right away but let it linger for a couple of seconds to show the girl that everything was okay. The girl seemed to relax a little.

"My name is Rita Anker and I'm with the police," she said, and then pointed at Sara. "This is Sara Vallén and she is also with the police."

"Josefin Elvebrandt," the girl said, and shook Sara's hand. Then she shook Rita's hand too. *Probably raised too well to do anything else*, Rita thought, and smiled. She knew that a lot of people found her a little intimidating.

"I'm Kajsa's best friend," Josefin continued. "We're in the same class."

"Yes," Sara said, and smiled her warmest smile. "I've been wanting to talk to you. I thought we could have a conversation about Kajsa. You probably know her better than anyone."

Sara hoped that the girl wouldn't think she was trying too hard, but the girl just smiled slightly at her.

"Yes, we've been friends forever. So I know her very well."

"Great. There is so much that we don't know about Kajsa."

Rita nodded to Sara in silent agreement that Rita would go find Kajsa's doctor while Sara took Josefin to the cafeteria.

*Hospitals are always like this*, Sara thought to herself. *Cold and sterile. No effort to make things cosy. And always the same boring food . . .*

The idea was to keep the questioning as informal as possible. She would have to figure out how to solve all the formalities at a later time. She had no authority to interrogate this girl, but neither she nor Rita intended to let that stop her. She got the girl a Coca-Cola. She didn't want anything else. *She is incredibly sweet*, Sara thought. Then she had an idea.

"Maybe you know my son, Johannes Vallén? He is the same age as you, but he isn't in your school."

"Johannes, yes, I know him." The girl blushed and Sara Vallén couldn't stop herself from smiling.

"It's okay. You don't need to be embarrassed. I was just thinking that as this town is pretty small, you probably know quite a lot of people the same age as you, even if you're not close to all of them. He has actually mentioned a Josefin; maybe it's you?"

"Maybe," Josefin said, but it was clear that she wanted to change the subject.

*That didn't work as planned*, Sara thought. *I shouldn't have assumed that what works as an icebreaker in conversations between adults has the same effect with teenagers.* She suddenly became nervous about accidentally revealing too much about Johannes's current situation. Maybe the girl already knew about it? It was probably better not to mention him again. It only made her sad anyway.

Josefin had a lot to tell them about Kajsa—and it was all positive. When Sara started asking about boyfriends, Josefin didn't seem to want to answer. All she said was that Kajsa was liked by everyone, and not very interested in guys. For some reason, Sara felt as if there was something that Josefin wasn't telling her.

"Did Kajsa have any admirers? Maybe someone that she didn't like in return, or the other way round?"

"No," Josefin answered, and her mouth turned into a thin line.

Something wasn't right. Sara wasn't sure how to interpret Josefin's reluctance to answer her questions about boyfriends or girlfriends.

She decided to switch direction.

"Does Kajsa normally walk through Lund City Park after dark?"

"I have no idea, we never walk there together though, that's for sure," Josefin answered, obviously relieved not to have to talk about relationships anymore. She relaxed a little but still seemed nervous and anxious. Sara instinctively felt that the girl was hiding something.

"It's super scary there at night. Why was she even there? Why?"

Sara felt the full force of the girl's sadness.

"I don't know," Sara said. "Maybe she decided to take a shortcut? I really don't know, but we will find out."

Josefin's lower lip trembled. Sara put her hand on top of the girl's skinny wrist.

"We'll do everything we can to find the person who did this to Kajsa, I promise."

"Can I leave now? I want to go back to Kajsa," Josefin said, and stood up.

"Just a little while longer. I understand it's hard, but I need to ask you a couple more questions." Sara braced herself and met the girl's gaze. *I hope I'm not pushing her too far*, she thought.

The girl sat down again. She had barely touched her drink. Now she took a small sip.

"What were you doing on Sunday night?" Sara asked. She heard how tired her voice sounded.

"I went to see a film with Kajsa at twenty past six. I can't even remember the name of the film, but it was sci-fi."

The girl started crying again. She took a deep breath and kept going.

"Then we went to Ariman. We were there until the place closed. Around eleven."

"Ariman, what's that?"

The girl smiled behind her tears.

"It's a café on Kungsgatan."

"Did you say goodbye to her after that?"

"Yes, I told you."

"And why do you think that Kajsa didn't go straight home? Where do you think she went?"

"I don't know. I truly don't know."

The girl looked down at her hands. Once again, Sara had a feeling that there was something left unsaid. But she didn't want to push Josefin any further. *It will all be revealed, sooner or later,* she thought.

"Is Kajsa a good friend?" she asked instead.

"The best," Josefin replied without hesitation.

"And is she a good person? If you know what I mean?"

The girl nodded. "Kind, good, and cool."

Still no hesitation. Sara assumed that Josefin was telling her the truth, or at least that she was telling her what she thought was the truth.

"And how is she in school?" she continued, despite the girl's short answers.

"Good. But sick of it lately," Josefin said while her eyes wandered.

Alarm bells started ringing in Sara's head. *There is no point pushing this any further,* she thought, and decided to accept that certain things had to take time. *Patience, Sara,* her inner voice told her.

"Can I go now?" the girl asked.

Now it was Sara's turn to nod.

"Concluding the interrogation at 12:05," she said before pausing the recording on her phone and turning to Josefin. She was already standing up.

"Normally, I would give you a printed transcript of the interview right away. But as you probably understand, I can't do that now. It will take some time. Once I have it on paper, you'll be able to read it and listen to the recording, if you want. Is that okay?"

"Yeah," the girl said, and walked away.

Sara hadn't achieved a lot with the interview, but at least she had something. For some reason, Kajsa had stayed in the city, or possibly gone to someone else's house. Then she had walked through Lund City Park on her way home. But it didn't make sense. The story didn't make sense. Sara decided to talk to Josefin again, as soon as possible. She didn't have much time.

# 17

He walked with heavy steps across Stortorget. His shoes were soaking wet and covered in mud. The sun had been shining all day but as soon as he set foot outside the door, the sky had opened up. He was cold and picked up his pace.

He turned the corner by restaurant Herkules and continued up onto Kyrkogatan. *It's so weird that they decided to change the street's name here,* he thought. *It's still the same street.* He turned onto Klostergatan and then onto Lilla Gråbrödersgatan, where he entered the entrance code and climbed the stairs in five big steps. The flat was dark and quiet. The air was stale and reeked of cigarettes, alcohol, and rubbish. He closed the door to his bedroom just in case his father was home, even if everything indicated that he was out. He started his computer and turned on the TV. The computer—his father's old one—beeped and whined for a while before it was finally ready to use.

His inbox was empty, except for some junk mail from a travel agency. *One can always dream,* he thought. For a second, he locked eyes with himself in the reflection on the screen.

He took a deep breath and shook his black locks away from his forehead. Then he started to look for horrific figures and animations in the archives of a hidden website. After a while, he chose one and sent it anonymously via the website, together with the message, "Dead people can't rat."

The front door opened with a loud bang.

"Where are you? Fucking kid!"

He ran to his bedroom door and locked it. Just in time. The kicking on the door started the moment he had turned the key.

"You're drunk. I won't open." He backed away from the locked door. You never knew. His father could probably kick the door in if things were really bad.

He heard the familiar sound of his father stumbling around in the flat. Then everything fell silent and he knew that he had passed out on his bed. At least it would be calm for a couple of hours now.

He sat down in front of the computer and opened a chat. Maybe he could find someone to talk to for a while. Or frighten. Or scam. He changed his mind and picked up his phone instead. *Just one call,* he thought.

# 18

The result of the interrogations was unsatisfying so far. There were a couple of guys who seemed interested in Kajsa Lindahl. She was well-liked and a couple of boys at her school had, or used to have, a crush on her. But the interviews hadn't led to anything and they all had alibis. They left Josefin Elvebrandt alone for now. Rita Anker had already talked to her. There were still two boys in Kajsa's class that they hadn't been able to talk to. They had contacted the parents of all the underaged kids and asked them to bring their children in for questioning. All of them had declined. *Typical,* Torsten Venngren thought to himself. *People don't care what their kids are up to.*

"Do you know if Kajsa had a boyfriend, or if she was in love with someone in her class? Girl or boy?" he asked a girl who cried her way through the interview.

"No. Or yes, Martin, I guess. But I don't think they were serious," she said. "I really don't think that Kajsa has been in love with anyone. She doesn't say much. The only one she talks to about these things is Jossan."

"Jossan?" Jonny Svensson asked.

"Josefin Elvebrandt. They are always together, except for handball practice."

"So Kajsa plays handball?" Torsten Venngren asked. He really didn't care for the sport on a personal level.

"Yes. But she isn't playing much nowadays. That's all I really know."

"Okay. Is there anything that makes Kajsa Lindahl special? Something about her personality?"

"I don't know." The girl thought about it for a while and placed a finger on the tip of her nose, stroking it gently back and forth. Torsten smiled. His daughter Veronica had always done the same when she was a kid, still sucking her thumb. It must feel calming and comforting somehow.

Torsten Venngren cleared his throat to get the girl's attention and urged her to go on.

"I mean, Kajsa was the happiest, sweetest, and funniest girl in class last year. Then something happened this year. I'm not sure what, but she became quieter and her attitude changed. She became more . . . What's the word . . . You know, the way she flirted with certain guys. Never mind, I can't find the right word."

"Do you mean provocative?" Torsten Venngren suggested.

"Yes, that's right. Provocative. Harder and tougher, and more provocative. The boys didn't like it. Maybe Martin did, but nobody else. And she stopped caring about school. She was doing so well last year, but that all changed this year. She started acting as if she didn't care."

"Do you know what happened?" Venngren gave the girl an encouraging look.

"No, no idea. Maybe Jossan knows."

"Thank you so much for the information," Torsten Venngren said, and smiled.

"Are we done? Can I leave?"

Venngren nodded and she hurried out of the room that the school had let them use for their interviews.

"Bring that guy Martin in here." Venngren pointed at the door and Svensson got up to open it.

Martin stepped into the room. He looked miserable. And angry. He was fit, but not very tall. *On the contrary,* Torsten Venngren thought as he studied the young man who sat down across from him.

"Do you know why I'm here?" he asked once he had shaken hands with the boy.

The boy stared at Venngren's bleached jeans, and his eyes seemed to linger for a while on the officer's moustache. He was obviously in no rush.

"Because Kajsa almost died," the boy said pragmatically. "Because some arsehole almost beat her to death," he continued, not as pragmatically.

"Yes, in a way you are right," Venngren said. "But we're also here to get to know more about Kajsa. You were friends, right?"

"I see," the boy said. "We weren't really friends in that way."

"In what way do you mean?" Torsten Venngren smiled at the young man.

Martin squirmed in his chair.

"Well, I mean . . . I guess we weren't really friends. I liked her for a while, as a girl you know. But she was annoying. So I stopped liking her—as a girl, you know. And we were never really friends, so . . ."

"I see," Torsten Venngren said. "But what made you not like her anymore?"

"I don't know," Martin said, and Torsten could see that he was upset. Something was bothering the boy, but Torsten didn't insist. It had been a couple of intense days at work and he was tired.

"What were you doing Sunday night?" he asked.

"I was with some mates at a friend's house, and then I went home."

To Venngren's surprise, the boy looked right into his eyes as he spoke.

"What friends?"

"A couple of guys from class, Rickard and Andreas."

"When did you leave the house?"

"Around midnight, I think."

"What did you do after that?"

"I stopped by Ariman, but it was closed, of course. I guess I didn't realise what time it was."

"Why did you go there?" Venngren looked at the boy with a neutral expression on his face.

"I thought some of my friends might be there," he said, and hesitated for a moment. He looked down at his shoes. "I thought Kajsa might be there."

"Oh, okay," Torsten Venngren said. "And was she there?"

"I told you, it was closed."

"Right. And did you go to find Kajsa?"

"No way. I went home. Why do you ask?"

"I'm the one asking the questions here," Venngren said sternly.

"Sure."

"And where did you go after that?"

"Home, but first I went to the cashpoint on Stora Södergatan. Then I walked through Kattesund up to Mediterranean and out on Stora Fiskaregatan. Then I crossed Bantorget to get home."

The boy answered all the questions at once, and Venngren couldn't stop himself from smiling a little while the boy talked.

"Why didn't you go to the cashpoint on Lilla Fiskaregatan? That would have been easier."

"I don't know," Martin said, and shot the interrogation officer a sour look. "I guess I forgot that there was one there," he added.

"Okay," Torsten Venngren said. "Were your parents in when you got home?"

"Yes, they were asleep."

Torsten Venngren found no reason to doubt the boy. And he liked him. He seemed like an honest and open young man.

"Do you know if Kajsa had a boyfriend or girlfriend? Or maybe she had friends that she could have been with between the time when Ariman closed and just after 2 a.m.?"

"No idea, but I have suspected for a while now that she is seeing someone in secret. She has been acting funny for a long time. Cold. She didn't want us to see each other and stuff."

"Were you in love with her?"

"Maybe. I'm not sure. As I told you earlier, I didn't really like her new attitude."

"And still, you went looking for her at Ariman?"

"It's complicated."

"Yeah, I get it," Venngren said, ending the interrogation.

Torsten Venngren and Jonny Svensson left the school building without a word. Neither of them felt like commenting on the interrogations. Adolescence—the best and worst time of one's life—why would you ever want to go back?

Suddenly, Torsten felt sad. Maybe it was because of how beautiful the summer was. The pain of being left felt a lot more tangible when he was surrounded by all this beauty. The fact that he was accompanied by Jonny Svensson, the saddest figure of them all, didn't help. He pitied the man next to him. At least Torsten had Veronica, even if she lived in

London. She loved him, almost as much as he loved her. That was good. Jonny, on the other hand, was completely alone.

Jonny broke the silence.

"Do you really think it's a young guy? I mean, considering the degree of violence and the aggressive nature of the crime?"

"I don't know," Torsten said. "However, I'm willing to bet my salary that Martin did not do it."

"Yeah, maybe it takes a truly aggressive person to do something like this," Svensson said. "I'm not sure if I think we're looking for an adult or someone younger here, but I'm convinced it was planned."

Jonny fell silent. Torsten knew what was coming next.

"I'm just glad that I never crossed the line—or got caught—at that age. Then I never would have been able to join the force," Jonny said, almost whispering.

Torsten placed a hand on his colleague's shoulder and squeezed it. He felt a connection with him that he had never experienced before. Their eyes met and Torsten removed his hand. He felt slightly embarrassed by the whole situation, especially as he didn't really like Svensson.

"At least we got something out of this," Torsten said.

"What?"

"That this girl had changed. Two of her classmates said the same thing. It makes you wonder why."

"Yeah, I guess it does," Jonny Svensson said, and shrugged his shoulders. "Maybe it's just a teenage thing. What do we really know about teenagers anyway? And what do they even know about themselves?"

"Not much," Torsten answered laconically.

When they got back to their car, they got a phone call from Jörgen Berg. He told them that he had received two interesting tips from the public and wondered if they could interview the callers before they headed back to Malmö.

"Sure," Torsten Venngren said, "we've already done twenty-two interviews, so what difference will two more make?"

Jörgen pretended not to hear the sarcasm in Torsten's voice. Instead, he thanked him and hung up.

# 19

Sara Vallén and Rita Anker rang the doorbell on Sunnanväg. Kajsa and her older sister, Magda, lived there with their parents. It was always so hard to have to interrogate people who were in this much pain. But it was necessary. So you did it.

The apartment complex was depressing. Sara lived with her three children in a small house with a big garden in the southern part of Lund. Rita, on the other hand, lived on her own, and her front door opened right onto Grönegatan. Neither of them would want to switch places with each other, but most of all they wouldn't want to live on the second floor on Sunnanväg. The concrete was grey, the railings were grey, and the building itself was grey. And then there was the family's nightmarish situation on top of all the greyness.

Torsten had already held the customary initial interrogation, so Rita and Sara had not met the parents before. Rita made a plan for the interrogation, although this was normally Sara's job. This was the second interrogation that Sara would hold without being authorised to do so. But the two women were on the same page. Sara's presence was as necessary as it was unavoidable. Her experience was worth a lot and Sara would never have accepted not being there. Rita asked Sara to question Margareta, the mother, while she would talk to Gunnar, the father. The plan was to focus on Kajsa's social life, her hobbies, if she was doing okay in school, and if there had been any sudden changes in her life recently. Sara had told Rita about her interrogation with Josefin and mentioned a couple of things that had made her suspicious during the interview. So far, all they had to go on was a feeling of not being told the whole story. It was time to find something more concrete. Magda would also be questioned. They agreed to leave that task to Rita as she came across as a bit cooler than Sara. Hopefully, she would be able to approach the young woman as an equal, instead of being placed in the motherly box. Sometimes this strategy worked, sometimes it didn't. The parents had promised that Magda would be home around 3 p.m.

Gunnar Lindahl let them in, and as the two women stepped into the hallway, they could see that the flat was elegantly decorated and very tasteful. A huge grand piano stood in the living room. Rita felt a strong urge to ask them how they had managed to get the piano up all the stairs but stopped herself. The family had no TV. There was, however, an old CD player and a couple of expensive speakers in the living room.

"What about secrets?" Rita asked.

"Well," Gunnar Lindahl answered, "don't all teenagers have secrets?"

Rita nodded.

"How is Kajsa doing in school?"

"Great, but slightly worse lately," Kajsa's father said. "We haven't seen the final grades for this semester yet. I think she's a bit bored of school. I remember feeling the same way when I was her age. It normally gets better with time."

He wiped his right eye with the back of his hand and snorted.

"Have you noticed any signs of Kajsa being depressed, scared, sad, or angry? Has she behaved differently somehow?" Rita asked, looking at Gunnar Lindahl with a calm smile.

"I'm not sure," he said, and frowned. His eyebrows were thick and impressive.

"I see," Rita said, nodding. "Was there, maybe, something that just felt a bit different somehow?"

"It's hard to say. We haven't spoken very much lately. She is closer to her mother. Magda and I are more different, so we get along better. Me and Kajsa are too much alike. Sometimes, this leads to arguments. She slams the door to her room quite often. But I thought it was just normal. It's tough being a teenager. I think Kajsa got along better with

Margareta. But I'm not sure she told her anything either. As I said, it's hard being a teenager and I assume that the urge to break free from your parents is strong. We are quite sensitive, me and Kajsa. So I'm not sure. If it was something more than just being young and wanting to break free, I mean."

Kajsa's father spoke so freely that Rita didn't know how to respond. She tried to sort it all in her head but realised quickly that she would have to listen to the recording later to really make out what he had said. As always, information had to land before you could start connecting dots and reading between lines. Once the information had been processed, you could formulate new questions and hold new interrogations. There was always something more to find out.

"Do you think that Kajsa was keeping anything or anyone from you? Someone that she was seeing for example?" Sara asked Margareta Lindahl while they sat in the kitchen.

"Maybe from Gunnar, but not from me . . . At least nothing serious," she continued after a short pause and smiled at Sara Vallén.

"What do you mean?"

"Sure, Kajsa had crushes here and there. Her classmate Martin was probably one of them. But I don't think it was serious. I think she is still waiting for the one, or at least a proper love story. Or maybe she is just too busy to have time for boyfriends."

"How has Kajsa been doing in school?" Sara asked.

Margareta Lindahl massaged the bridge of her nose while playing nervously with her black curls with her other hand.

"Very good last year. But then this year her performance has been a bit less impressive. When we talked to her about it, she just said that she found school boring. We thought it was just her being a teenager."

"Has she been acting differently lately?"

"What do you mean?"

Kajsa's mother sounded defensive now. Sara braced herself.

"I mean, has she seemed bothered by something? Or maybe happier than normal?"

"No, not that I have noticed."

Something in the mother's eyes and body language suddenly seemed more guarded.

"Are you sure?" Sara asked again.

"How dare you come into my house and insinuate that my daughter has been keeping things from me?" Margareta said—her rage was tangible.

Sara forced herself to stay calm and did her best not to let her feelings show on the outside.

"I have to ask, it's part of my job. If I don't ask, there is no way for me to find out," she said.

Rita and Sara asked if they could have a look at Kajsa's room while they waited for Magda. Gunnar pointed out that it had already been done, and that a couple of forensics had looked through the room once.

"We know," Sara said. "We just want to have a look. Someone's room always says a lot about a person and we promise not to touch anything. Just a quick look."

Rita and Sara glanced at each other. They both knew this was a sensitive matter.

"That's fine," Gunnar Lindahl said, and nodded to his wife. She didn't say anything, and she wasn't showing any signs of agreeing with her husband.

"It's fine," he said again.

Kajsa's room was surprisingly big with beautiful oak floors. Its walls were painted lilac purple and it was as elegantly decorated as the living room. A couple of photos hung on the wall—one of Josefin and a couple of Kajsa herself. They spotted a bulletin board with a little calendar hanging from a string. Except for some notes about upcoming handball matches, the calendar was empty. The room had already been emptied of things that might be relevant for the investigation.

They were on their way out when Sara turned and walked back to the bulletin board.

"I knew it," she said.

"What? What did you find?"

"Here," Sara said, and pointed. "On one Sunday a month, she has written the letter *E* with a circle around it. What do you think it means? And how come the forensics team hasn't seen this already?"

"They probably have, but they obviously didn't think it seemed important. We'll take the calendar with us so that we can examine it in peace and quiet," Rita said. "I'll tell the parents."

Rita put the calendar in her pocket and they went back into the kitchen, where the parents were waiting for them.

"Magda will be here any second. When you're done with your questioning, we're going to see Kajsa. One of us always sleeps there, so that she doesn't have to feel alone or scared if she wakes up," Gunnar Lindahl said.

Margareta Lindahl slouched down in her chair and looked like a punctured balloon.

A feeling of hopelessness spread through the room. Rita was overcome by an uneasy sensation. *This won't end well*, she thought to herself. Gunnar Lindahl put his big hand on his wife's shoulder.

"There, there," he said in an attempt to calm her down. "Everything will be okay."

*Somewhat awkward*, Sara thought, *but sweet*.


Magda, a long-legged nineteen-year-old, came home. She wasn't very interested in talking about Kajsa's love life. After a while, Rita lost her temper and her patience. It made the girl clam up even more. Sara stepped in and before they knew it, they had fallen into the good cop/ bad cop routine. Either Magda didn't realise it, or she agreed to play along, because suddenly she opened up a little. Something serious came over her face and she looked older.

Magda told them that Kajsa had been in love with Martin, but that it had never developed into something serious. It became more and more clear that Kajsa and Magda were close.

"Does the letter *E* mean anything to you?" Sara asked.

Magda Lindahl shook her head and Rita showed her the calendar.

"I'm not sure," Magda said. "But it might be connected with the rest."

Once again, Sara felt like she wasn't being told the whole story. The young woman lifted her eyes and glanced past Sara.

"In what way?"

"Maybe she hasn't told me, although I thought she would have. She might have been seeing someone that I didn't know about. I can ask Josefin, maybe she'll know."

"Thanks, I really think that would help," Sara said, although she doubted it very much. An arrogant smirk played on Magda Lindahl's lips. Sara didn't like it.

"I'll check," Magda said, and smiled for the first time.

Her smile told Sara that she would have nothing to tell her.


The lilacs smelled amazing. The air was warm and the sun was shining. Rita paused on her way to the car.

"You're right, there is something strange about this girl," she said, and looked up at the sky. "She is nice, good, popular, beautiful, happy, you name it. It makes me suspicious. Can anybody really be that perfect? I wouldn't think so, right?"

Sara laughed for a moment before realising that she was late.

*This is crazy, I should go home to the girls and my mum*, she thought. But it was too late to cancel her shift as an emergency buddy. Once a week, she volunteered at a chat centre where her role was to give anonymous, confused, and sad youths advice online.

"What's up?" Rita called out after Sara.

"I'm in a bit of a hurry. I need to be somewhere in a couple of minutes. I'll drop you off on my way there."

"Have fun."

# 20

Maria Lind lived on the first floor at the corner of Stora Söder-gatan and Gyllenkroks Allé. She told the officers that she had gone to bed around 10 p.m., even though she had planned to watch a thriller on TV, just like she always did on Sundays. But this Sunday she had simply been too tired. She shared the elaborate and detailed story about her sleeping difficulties and her restless leg syndrome with Torsten Venngren.

"So, when I had finally managed to fall asleep at 2 a.m., of course I was woken up by someone talking loudly right outside my window!"

Torsten Venngren straightened his back. Finally.

"Did you recognise the voices?"

"No, why would I? It was a man and a woman. I have no idea how old they could have been. Young, I think," Mrs. Lind said, "but everyone is young compared to me. I would probably recognise the voices if I heard them again."

Mrs. Lind proudly told them that she had been very good at imitating voices when she was younger, but she found it more difficult now that she was old. But at least there was nothing wrong with her memory.

"Did you happen to hear what the couple were talking so loudly about?" Torsten Venngren asked without too much hope.

"No, young man," Mrs. Lind said, "I didn't. But their discussion was definitely lively. And I think they both had a southern accent, otherwise

I probably would have noticed it," Maria Lind said, and stroked Torsten Venngren's cheek.

Jonny finished up a separate interrogation at another location and picked up Torsten outside Maria Lind's flat when he was done. They decided that it was time to go grab a beer and a bite to eat, so they parked their patrol car in the garage under the police station and drove their private cars back to Malmö. The walk to the restaurant made them even more hungry—and thirsty. The first sip of beer tasted like heaven. Torsten normally didn't drink during the week; it was against his principles. But today his patience was running out and it felt like a great idea to have a beer to relax.

"How was your interview?" Torsten asked.

"Horrible. Gave me nothing. Apparently, he is Sara's neighbour. He had been to a late dinner and saw a young guy walking on top of the old city wall in Lund City Park on his way home. He said it looked like Johannes. So yeah, nothing new. How about yours?"

"What do you think?" Torsten said. "Who is he, the guy who did this?"

"Sara's kid, of course," Jonny said laconically. "I don't understand why we're still looking when we already have a suspect," he said, and chuckled so hard that Torsten almost thought that his big stomach would flip the table over.

Torsten glanced at Jonny to determine if he was joking or not.

"Hmm," Torsten said. "I don't think it was Johannes Vallén."

Jonny stared into his beer glass.

"Look, there's a fly in my glass."

Their discussion about who the possible perpetrator could be was over. Jonny started poking around in his beer to get the fly out. He failed.

Once again, Torsten Venngren was reminded of how much he disliked his colleague. They had worked together as patrol officers for years. Jonny had always been the arsehole who ignored rules and regulations. He was the type of police officer who felt that he had the right to cross any line simply because he was on the force. This also meant that he had no problem beating the bad guy up that little bit extra in the holding cell or in the back of a patrol car, as he felt that crooks never got fair penalties anyway, even if they were brought in front of a judge. He was the type of police officer who would make a note about a suspect resisting arrest, when he was, in fact, the one who had started the fight. Torsten had hated working with Jonny back then, but nowadays he didn't have to care too much. Jonny wasn't a patrol officer anymore and Torsten was pretty sure that he wasn't beating anyone up nowadays. *Especially now that he is so fat he can barely move*, Torsten thought, noting the irony. But Jonny was still rude and a bit of a bully, which often led to shitty interrogation results.

Even if Torsten was known to be one of the best interrogation officers on the force, he knew he wasn't perfect. One time he had put a colleague in danger, just because he had hesitated to use his gun. His colleague had been badly wounded and almost died. Luckily, it all led to him becoming chief inspector, and then police chief. He had forgiven Torsten ages ago, and Torsten was now using his competence where it was better suited. Torsten had decided that he would never again put a colleague in danger again like that, no matter what. But somewhere in the back of his mind, he worried that his principle might not apply to Jonny Svensson if it came to it. He ignored the thought and remembered how they had connected earlier that day. That was a good sign, after all.

Torsten looked at the little square outside the window. A lot of people were moving about. The Swedes had obviously missed the sun. This time of year, the streets were always full of people. Women walked around with their pale legs peeking out of short skirts. Torsten smiled and felt happy for them. He thought about his daughter in London.

Jonny Svensson was also watching the square in silence. *Half-naked women, girls, that's what I'm talking about*, he thought to himself. But he knew that none of them would ever look his way.

Torsten Venngren had finished his dinner and waved to the waiter. He was ready to pay. Jonny didn't even notice. He was busy staring at the girls. Or, more accurately, he was staring at their legs. *Jonny Svensson sure isn't very discreet*, Torsten thought before saying goodbye.

Jonny nodded but didn't even bother to look up when his colleague walked across the square and turned right towards Gustav Adolfs Torg.

Torsten Venngren slowly made his way home to get some rest.

# 21

The chatline had been bursting with anxious youths and it felt tougher than normal to be there for them all. Sara found it hard to gather her thoughts and give each teenager the attention, advice, and support they needed. The abused boy who didn't trust grown-ups. The girl who had been sexually abused by her stepbrother. Bullied children, teenagers who hated school. Divorces, crime, and addiction. It took all Sara's energy to let these young people know that there were adults out there who wouldn't let them down.

When her shift was over, she felt dizzy and exhausted. As soon as she came home, she turned on some Chet Baker and sat down on her sofa. She listened to Chet's soft voice, leaned back, and enjoyed the calm. Most people probably preferred silence when they rested, but Sara found it easier to relax to the sound of music. It was the only way she could disconnect her mind and truly connect to her emotions. The music gifted her relief and a much-needed mental break. It also helped her when she needed to focus. She found it difficult to shut out her surroundings, and music helped her do that. And she liked to sing. Nowadays, she mostly sang to herself. The vocal range of her voice had been impressive when she was younger, but not anymore.

She sat on the sofa listening to *My Funny Valentine* on low volume. Chet Baker's voice rocked her to stillness.

The rest of the household was asleep.

# 22

Morning and another meeting. Söderström, who was already weary of covering for Sara Vallén, felt as if he had just left the previous meeting with his new colleagues. Everyone around the table looked tired after two intense days.

"So, anything new?" he said with a sour look on his face.

"Well," Torsten said, "we found a couple of things that might be interesting. I guess that's a good outcome for the situation so far. The girl's classmates are clueless. Except for two of them, Malin Sonesson and Martin Lingryd. They didn't really know anything either, but they told us that Kajsa had changed lately and become colder somehow. Martin is in good shape, but way too short and small to have done this. Everyone basically has an alibi. We have talked to everyone except for Josefin Elvebrandt and Rodney . . ." Torsten glanced at his notes. "What was his name again?"

"Ritger," Jonny filled in. "Rodney Ritger. As I understand it, he is a bit of a social disaster. His grades are terrible and he barely attends school. And then there is another boy, Karl Johan Ivarsson, who is always sick. We haven't got hold of either of these kids. But you talked to Josefin, right?" Jonny said, and turned to Rita.

"Of course, and her story might not be completely objective. We . . ." She corrected herself. *Damn it*, she thought. "I've talked to Kajsa's family. And I found a calendar in her room. On one Sunday per month, there was a hand-drawn circle with the letter *E* written inside it. The forensics team hadn't taken it. I assume they didn't find it interesting as it contained nothing except for this *E*. The mother got defensive as soon as I asked her if Kajsa might have been unhappy. The father didn't seem to know much about her or her recent change. He did mention that the two of them hadn't been getting along. But that's about as far as I got. Her sister, Magda, mentioned a Martin. It's probably the same Martin that Torsten interrogated. She promised to let us know if anything else came to mind."

"Tricky," Söderström said. "And what do you think the letter *E* means? One Sunday a month . . . Maybe it's someone she meets? And were these Sundays circled?"

Rita nodded.

"Also, I want to mention that both Josefin Elvebrandt and Magda Lindahl made me suspicious. They were keeping something from me, I just know it. Could *E* possibly be a person who she met on the night of the attack? And is it possible that everyone is hiding something?"

"Okay, if the letter *E* refers to a name, I guess it's fair to assume it's a man . . ." Söderström said. "I looked through the transcript of Josefin Elvebrandt's interrogation and it says that she and Kajsa went to see a sci-fi movie. Then they went to Ariman, a café on Kungsgatan. They stayed there until it closed at 11 p.m. They said goodbye, and that's the last time Josefin saw her. At least according to her."

"And Martin Lingryd told us that he had gone to Ariman around midnight, only to realise that it was closed. He says that he never saw Kajsa, or anybody else for that matter," Jonny filled in.

"Interesting," Söderström said. "So, we have a window between 11 p.m. and 2 a.m., approximately. That's when the old lady told us she heard a man and a woman outside her window, right?"

Torsten Venngren nodded. He looked down at his notes and his hair fell in front of his eyes. He brought it back behind his ears again. When he was young, he had shaved his hair and always wore it short. As he got older, he let it grow out. He felt less and less tempted to look like a typical police officer. His wife had loved it. At night, when they were in bed together, she used to run her fingers through it and play with the long curls. He knew that she had always found his hair beautiful. She had found all of him beautiful. She also found him quite boring. She had told him this plenty of times, but always with kind and loving eyes. And with her mouth shaped like a kiss. He loved her hands, her eyes, her mouth. He missed her. *You never know what you've got till it's gone*, he thought, and tried to focus on his papers again.

"I'm pretty sure this is someone she knows," Torsten said suddenly. He held a hand up to silence the others. "We have a three-hour window. If she talked to a man outside the old lady's place, it must have been someone she knew. Someone she probably trusted. The only question now is who? I know it wasn't Johannes Vallén."

Everyone nodded except Jonny, who stuck with his theory that Johannes did this—mostly because he wanted it to be true, and not so much because he really believed it was.

Venngren's theory gave them an opening. If it was someone she knew, it would be easier to find him. Everyone knew that. The reality was that most violent crimes were committed by someone close to the victim.

"It's not good that we have no idea what she was doing between 11 p.m. and 2 a.m.," Söderström said.

"No," Jörgen and Torsten said at the same time.

"We have to find out. It might give us all the answers," Torsten continued. "Where was she before the attack?"

"We don't know," Söderström said, and smiled for a second before his face turned serious again. "Speaking of men, did anyone look into that man who was going out for a jog?"

"Shit, I forgot about him," Jörgen said, and bowed his head in shame. "I was supposed to look him up. What was his name again?" He looked at Rita, who shook her head.

"Berg, how the fuck could you forget him? It's your job. What the hell are you doing?" Rita was obviously frustrated.

"Okay, I'll take care of it right after the meeting," Jörgen said without looking at Rita. "But Ove Ovesson will be here in a moment. And by the way, the lilac is a *Syringa pekinensis* from north-eastern China. I looked it up and it's growing in the botanic garden here in Lund. Apparently, it blooms for a much longer period than your average lilac."

"Great, Jörgen," Söderström said. He wanted to turn the focus away from Rita's angry outburst. "Then we can assume that our perpetrator walked past the botanic garden before he met the girl, or maybe they even walked through it together. We'll have to knock on some doors around there to see if anyone saw or heard anything between 11 p.m. and 2 a.m. I've been to the hospital. Kajsa is stabile but they can't say if she's going to make it. The doctors have confirmed serious trauma to the girl's head as well as aggravated sexual violence. However, there was no sperm inside the girl, which probably means that he never penetrated her with his genitalia. Instead, the perpetrator has used some kind of an object. He also cut her vagina. Only superficially, but still. Her tongue is cut out and she has been stabbed in her stomach. Multiple doctors have been involved. Anaesthesiologists, brain surgeons, general practitioners, ear-nose-throat doctors, orthopaedists, and gynaecologists. I can't even count all the people who have been digging around in this poor girl, fixing her and stitching her up. It's bloody awful. They can't do anything more now. How much will her parents be able to take? Can you even imagine how horrible this is for them? And here we are, with no answers."

The room was silent.

After a couple of seconds, Ove "The Shadow" Ovesson slipped in through the door.

"Take it away, Ove," Söderström said, and smiled awkwardly but warmly.

"Well, we've found some really interesting stuff. Partly from the girl's clothes that we found in rags in the bushes, and partly from the sperm that was spread out on and around her head for some reason. We found some skin under her fingernails and some lint, probably from a grey shirt. We also found a shoe print and a cigarette butt. The girl had a couple of smaller defensive wounds as well. Maybe she never really had the chance to put up a fight."

"It's interesting that she had sperm in her hair," Rita said. "We should be able to get DNA from it straight away and compare it to Johannes's."

*There might be hope, after all,* Rita thought to herself.

"What did you find on her clothes?" Jonny asked, seemingly uninterested in the sperm.

"Hair from someone's head and genitalia. And then there was the lint that definitely wasn't from her own clothes. We have sent it all off to the National Forensic Centre for analysis." Ove Ovesson paused for a moment and looked through his papers. He hummed a melody to himself as he read.

"Jörgen is on top of that," Ove said, and nodded to Jörgen Berg, who nodded back. "We haven't heard anything from the NFC yet but my guess, although it might not be the most qualified one," he added modestly, "is that we won't find a match in our archives when it comes to the DNA from the sperm, pubic hair, skin scrapings, or cigarette butt. It all probably comes from the same person. And I'm confident that this person is not Johannes Vallén."

"I think you're right, Ove," Rita said. "I have a feeling that this isn't someone we've heard from before."

Jörgen nodded.

"It's just horrendous," Ove said. "A young girl with her whole life ahead of her. What will happen to her now?"

It was a rhetorical question, but Jonny Svensson answered it.

"She'll probably not even survive. She doesn't have her whole life ahead of her. So there is no point thinking about it."

His belly bounced a little. Jonny chuckled. They all looked at him with raised eyebrows, collectively disliking his comment. Torsten couldn't hold it in.

"You are an idiot, always have been," he said. Then he got up and shook his fist in front of Jonny's face. "Show some compassion for once."

Everyone looked at Torsten. Jonny scoffed at his colleague's clenched fist.

"You don't scare me," he said, and stared at Torsten with cold eyes.

"We've also had a look at her computer," Ove Ovesson said in an attempt to steer the conversation away from the argument. "There were a couple of emails in there that could probably be seen as threats. But they were quite childish. It's a monster appearing on the screen together with a text that says, I quote: 'Dead people can't rat.' It doesn't make much sense, especially as it was sent after Kajsa was attacked, but it could still be relevant. Unfortunately, the email is untraceable. It was sent from a public server and there is no sender address. It's hard to explain, but there are pages on the dark net that allow you to hide behind a bunch of doors, if you know what I mean. There is no way of knowing how serious this threat is."

"Bloody hell," Rita said. "She was threatened via an email?!"

"It could definitely be relevant, but let's not get stuck on it. Was there anything else on the computer?"

"Well, we still have some material to go through. Chat conversations and things like that. We have only gone through her email for now."

"Have we received any relevant information from the public?" Torsten asked after recovering from Jonny's inappropriate comment.

"Nothing special so far. Torsten and Jonny conducted two interviews. If we assume that it was actually Kajsa Lindahl and a man who walked past Mrs. Lind's window just past 2 a.m., it would certainly fit into the timeline," Jörgen Berg said.

"And then we have the letter *E* in her calendar," Rita said. "What does it mean? Did the calendar give us something else?" She turned to Ovesson and then to the others. She avoided even looking at Jonny. She really didn't like him.

Ovesson shook his head.

"Should we talk to Josefin Elvebrandt about it, considering that her surname actually starts with an *E*?" Torsten asked.

Söderström nodded.

"I need to know more about this jogger," he said, and turned to Jörgen Berg, who shrugged his shoulders and put his hands out in front of him.

It looked like he was about to say something, but then he changed his mind. His professional confidence was in the gutter. How could he have forgotten?

"Also, it might be relevant that his first name is Evert," Rita Anker said.

"Oh, right," Torsten said, and looked at Rita. They both couldn't believe that they hadn't thought about that until now. They nodded at each other to confirm that they were thinking the exact same thing.

"But then again, it might not mean anything at all," Rita said.

For some reason, the fact that there was clearly some kind of a power struggle going on between Söderström and Anker seemed to lighten the mood in the group. She was probably twenty years younger than he was, but she didn't care. This was her territory. When Sara wasn't around, she was the self-proclaimed leader. And nobody, except for Jonny and Söderström, seemed to mind it.

To ensure she had the last word, Rita stood up, ending the meeting.

# 23

She choked back her tears. Every cell in her body blamed herself. And her head was full of anxiety and worry. She hadn't been able to visit her son yet. Instead, Göran had taken on the task without asking any questions. He was angry, and she didn't blame him. She had failed. She hadn't been able to protect Johannes. Every time they spoke to each other, Göran made sure she knew that. She knew he was trying not to rub it in, but he just couldn't help it.

"How the hell could you have let this happen?" he had screamed into the phone when they last spoke. Then he started crying before gathering himself and firing a new round of anger her way. And his words always hit her hard. He broke down her wall and she couldn't even convince herself with her own arguments.

She was sitting on the stairs outside her house. She got up and opened the door, leaving the beautiful summer evening outside. The girls were sitting in the kitchen as their grandmother was clearing up after dinner. She was crying quietly. Klara and Bella stared down at their phones. The silence in the kitchen spoke for itself.

"I'm going out for a moment," Sara said quietly. She stroked her mother's back and left the kitchen.

The floor in the hallway was full of shoes. She kicked a couple of them to the side to see if she could find her sneakers underneath the pile. It took her a while to find them. *Clean—we'll do that once I'm out of here,* she thought, and chuckled to herself. Sara's mother's aunt said that once. Shortly thereafter, she had started putting her cheese on the hat shelf and her dirty laundry in the fridge when the dementia began to eat into her brain. She was an exceptionally intelligent woman once though. And Sara thought that the expression still worked. She chuckled again, but her laughter sounded empty.

Her mind was filled with an unbearable feeling of anxiety and restlessness, but it would be nice to get some fresh air. She couldn't separate her work from her worry over Johannes, and she definitely couldn't stop thinking about what a horrible mother she was. Also, she felt stressed by the fact that she probably wouldn't have time to arrange the girls' graduation party. To host a graduation party now felt just as impossible as not hosting one.

The conversation she'd had with Göran about the party a couple of weeks ago felt distant, but she still remembered every word of it. He had refused to help and told her that he would throw his own party in his house, with his family. Sara had tried to convince him to throw a joint party.

"Please, Göran. At one point, we have to accept that we will be tied to each other forever through the kids. Sooner or later, there will be weddings, grandchildren, housewarming parties, dinners with new in-laws, Christmases, and God knows what."

"So what," Göran Vallén answered her without showing any emotion. "It doesn't matter. I don't want to spend time with you, so it doesn't change anything."

"But it's not for me. It's for the kids," Sara tried. "Don't they have the right to see both their parents? Do you really want them to carry the shame of their father not showing up to their graduation party?"

"I'm not ashamed," her ex-husband said, "and if I'm not ashamed, they shouldn't feel ashamed either."

"Be a stubborn arsehole then," Sara exclaimed. "I just wish you could think about someone besides yourself for once!"

At that point in the conversation, Göran had fallen silent and Sara hung up, realising there was nothing more to say.

Now everything had changed.


Her phone rang.

Rita was calling with exciting news. Judging by all the evidence found on and around the girl, this case would be solved fairly soon. If nothing else, it would prove that Johannes was innocent. In the middle of all the misery, Sara felt slightly hopeful. The case was moving forwards. She wanted to get back to work as soon as possible and asked Rita if they had done anything to rush the NFC.

"Of course," Rita said. "You'll be back as chief inspector in no time."

Sara allowed herself to feel happy for a second. She walked with an assured and confident stride. As she passed Mejeriet, she felt a sudden urge to walk past the crime scene. But first, she decided to have a look at the programme outside Mejeriet. Maybe she could attend a jazz lunch on Saturday if there was a good band playing. She was glad to see that a group she really liked would be performing that coming Saturday. *If I can find somebody to join me, I'll go,* she thought to herself. Everything would be okay. She would be able to go back to work any day now.

She walked down the footpath and stopped a few hundred metres from the crime scene. She thought about it for a moment, hesitated, then decided to keep walking past the rhododendron bushes. She picked up her pace. A feeling of maleficence hung over the place. And what was she even doing there? All the evidence was gone, there was nothing more to get here. She continued towards the pond and sat down on a bench. A group of children was standing by the water, feeding the ducks. An older lady did the same. They were all so innocent and completely unaware of what had happened a few metres away, just days ago. The old lady chatted with the ducks, who happily devoured the bread they were given. The children laughed with their parents as they watched the ducks hunt the little crumbs in the water. The adults kept a watching eye over their kids. *You better enjoy it while the children are young,* Sara thought, and was overcome by a sense of nostalgia that was almost pleasant. But she was happy that her children were all grown up now. They didn't need her as much anymore and their future and life as adults waited for them around the corner. Once Johannes had been removed from the nightmarish situation he found himself in now, she wouldn't have to be there for them constantly. Sara felt certain that it would happen any day now. As a mother, she knew that she would always worry about her kids. But she had accepted that a long time ago.

She suddenly started thinking about how to move forwards in the investigation. Maybe the man who had been going for a jog around 4 a.m. had some kind of connection to Kajsa Lindahl? Would the girl even survive? And would she ever be herself again? Life could seem so long and so incredibly short at the same time. Why did something like this have to happen to a young woman like that? What was the meaning of it all? She didn't know. A sadness bigger than herself washed over her and her eyes teared up.

She realised that what she felt was fear, fear that something would happen to her own children. Fear combined with relief that it wasn't one of her children who was the victim this time. Selfish and obvious. There were things about this case that she couldn't find a logical explanation for—yet. She knew that she would figure it out though, sooner or later. There had to be meaning behind the tongue and the lilac. There was no such thing as coincidence. She had learnt that a long time ago. Things that seemed meaningless at first glance always pointed in some kind of direction in the end. But which direction?

"What are you thinking about?"

Sara flinched and looked up. She ran a hand over her face and wiped her tears away. The man who had just approached her gave her a suspicious look that signalled distance, although she recognised his voice.

"Oh," the man in front of her said, and took a step back. "Don't you recognise me?"

Sara shook her head and tried to place him.

"Vaguely," she said.

"And yet we worked a case together only a couple of days ago."

*Oh,* she thought. *He must be a fellow officer from Lund. Probably a patrol officer.*

An image suddenly appeared in the back of her head and she instantly felt reluctant to give him what he wanted—her attention.

"Well, if we worked a murder case together, I highly doubt that I noticed you," she said. "I never pay attention to colleagues who come and go in those cases," she added to clarify.

The man didn't seem to care about her rudeness. He nodded and reached his hand out to her.

"It wasn't a murder case, not yet at least," he said. "Deputy Sergeant Peter Matsson. Me and my partner were the first ones on the scene when Kajsa was found by that kid Johannes."

"Sara Vallén."

Matsson took a seat on the bench next to her. Not too close, and not too far away from her.

For a brief moment, she wondered what he was doing walking around in Lund City Park at the same exact moment as she was. But then she realised it wasn't all that strange. The park was basically the only recreational area in town. At least on this side of town.

The man next to her kept talking. Sara didn't say much. She found it hard to focus on what he was saying as she constantly caught herself looking at him instead of listening to him. Matsson was attractive. He was tall and athletic and he had a nice smile and green-blue eyes. But there was something arrogant about him. Although she couldn't specify exactly what it was, she didn't like it.

"Do you live around here?"

His question felt a bit misplaced and interrupted her thoughts. She immediately felt defensive. Slightly bothered by his straightforwardness, her tone sharpened.

"Why do you want to know?"

"Oops," Peter Matsson said, "I didn't realise I'd stumbled into a sensitive area." He grinned sarcastically.

*There it is again*, she thought.

"Not exactly sensitive," she said. "I just like to keep my private life private."

"That's fine with me. I'm just trying to have a conversation. You obviously don't have to share any information that you don't feel comfortable sharing," he said, and smiled.

"It's fine. I live around here, in the southern part of Lund."

To lighten the mood a bit she told him that she lived with her two cats and three kids and threw in a comment about them being Siamese. She threw a glance at him and met his gaze. She made sure not to look at him for too long as she didn't want to give him any ideas. Didn't want him to think that she was interested, maybe. He, however, kept his steady gaze focused on her face.

"The children are Siamese?" asked Peter Matsson, sounding interested.

"No," Sara Vallén said, laughing, "but the girls are actually identical twins. Not quite the same. The cats are Siamese. I have Siamese cats."

"That makes more sense." Peter Matsson laughed. "It would have been pretty sensational to have Siamese twins. But then again, they exist."

"Yes, but not in my house."

Sara pictured the twins Klara and Bella as Siamese twins and giggled. Like most identical twins, they were figuratively joined at the hip. They could always read each other's minds and often finished each other's sentences.

"It sounds exciting with identical twins too though."

"Yes, it has its pros and cons. Oh well, otherwise I've got nothing interesting to tell you. I spend most of my time working and when I finally have time off, I take care of my kids, feed them, and deal with mountains of laundry. That's basically my life."

*I'm acting nervous*, she thought, and tried to take it back a notch. She didn't mention Johannes.

"I see," Peter Matsson said next to her. His hand was resting on the back of the bench, dangerously close to her shoulder. She instinctively moved away from him.

"Boring, huh?" she said, and smiled as widely as she could to try to cover up her scepticism.

"No, why? I live alone these days in a big flat on Klostergatan. That's boring if anything. I got divorced two years ago after a short but intense marriage with a woman who almost killed me. Not literally, but close enough."

To her enormous surprise, Sara realised that she was attracted to Peter Matsson—physically attracted. *What's wrong with me?* she thought. Their eyes suddenly locked. His gaze pierced her and she was too afraid to hold it. She looked at her hands instead. For once, they were lying still in her lap. Normally, she moved her hands frantically in front of her as the words poured out. Motormouth. She was different from her colleagues in that way.

"Do you want to go and grab a beer?" Matsson asked, as if he could tell that she needed a helping hand in the situation. And although she wasn't sure if she was going to be able to handle it, something urged her to accept his invitation. She wanted to take her mind off things for a while.

Peter Matsson's efforts were almost comical and although Sara didn't want to admit it to herself, they made her feel relaxed—and flattered.

She sat on one of the dirty-white plastic chairs under the white canvas outside the restaurant while Peter went to the bar to order their drinks. She wanted to pay for her own beer, but he had insisted on buying her a drink. When she saw him returning from the bar with two beers in his hands, she felt butterflies flutter in her stomach. He smiled at her and the arrogant vibe wasn't there anymore. *Maybe I was imagining it,* she thought.

They finished their first beers quickly. The more interested he seemed in her, the more scared and nervous she felt. Her nerves made words pour out of her mouth and the more she talked, the more scared she felt. *Catch-22*, she thought. *I want out but I don't want to leave.* She didn't really have the energy to be on what started to look like a date, but for some reason, she couldn't stop herself from sharing endless stories about herself. She wasn't sure if it was to impress him or to save herself. But she kept talking as if she was unable to stop. Her emotional state changed rapidly from harmony to fear—and then back to harmony and calm again. It all depended on where her mind wandered.

She told him about how she beat her colleague in a judo contest at the Christmas party. He laughed so hard that he almost fell off his chair. It was probably because the chair couldn't handle his weight. Its back was simply too soft and flexible. He managed to regain his balance and leaned across the table to relieve the chair. They both started laughing out loud. The other guests turned towards them with stern faces, which only made the couple laugh even harder.

They took their time with their second beer. Her exhausted mind moved more slowly now and she felt a sense of calm. She hoped that she would be able to cling on to it for a while. Her defensive strategy stood no chance when it went up against Peter Matsson's charm. She knew that he was dangerous—dangerous for her confidence, self-esteem, and general well-being. But she couldn't help being tempted by him, his scent, his masculinity, and the possibility of experiencing pleasure for the first time in ages. She didn't dare to think any further than that.

She looked down at her hands and saw that they were resting dangerously close to his. An alarm went off in Sara's mind. She felt her heart skip a beat and pulled her hands away, placing them back in her lap in a nervous and jerky movement. He just smiled. *Does he have to be so confident and calm?* she thought. *Why can't he be as dull as me?* It almost made her feel angry.

"Oops," he said for the second time that day. "Another sensitive area, I guess." It sounded more like a statement than a question.

"Don't be so full of yourself," she said, and stared at the table. "I think I have to leave."

She stood up a little too suddenly, accidentally overturning her chair. He smiled again, a genuine smile. Her hair fell in front of her eyes and she brushed it away.

"It's okay, Sara. I get it. It's been a while, huh?"

He was teasing her. She realised that she had made a fool of herself and tried to make up for it.

"I'm not scared," she said, "I just don't have time for these things. It's been fun doing something other than staring at the TV all night though," she said as she stood there in front of him. He studied her. She wondered what he was thinking. He had a contented smile on his lips and she straightened her back.

"Well, thanks for tonight," he said politely, although she still thought he sounded interested.

"Yes, right. Thanks for tonight." She was overwhelmed by a sudden urge to kiss him and quickly took a step back. *What's wrong with me?* she thought again. *I'm ridiculous.* She grabbed her coat but it was far too warm to wear it, so she threw it over her shoulders and started walking away. She refused to turn around. For some strange reason, she didn't want to give him the satisfaction. Suddenly, she heard footsteps in the gravel behind her. Then she felt a hand on her shoulder. She turned around. It was Matsson and he was holding out her sunglasses. *Pathetic*, she thought before thanking him and turning to go. He touched her shoulder again.

"Hey," he said, "Do you want to meet up again someday?"

She decided quickly—too quickly, and not at all in accordance with what she thought she would do. She didn't want to give herself a chance to change her mind, so she blurted out her answer: "Sure."

Her response went against all rational thinking and completely ignored her intuition, which told her that this was wrong—very wrong. Her eyes sparkled and her lips were wet, involuntarily moistened by her tongue.

"Great," he said.

He ran a finger along the ridge of her nose. Nothing else. Then they left Lund City Park together. In silence. It was as if neither of them had anything more to say. Things were way too charged between the two of them.

They said goodbye and Chief Inspector Sara Vallén—the professional, capable, calculating, logical, and unshakeable—had lost herself in her desire for a man that she didn't know. That was the feeling that lingered with her all the way home. She was determined not to see Peter Matsson again. And she was just as determined that she had to see him again. An impossible equation. She had lost her ability to think logically. She decided to let it go for now.

# 24

Rita sat in one of Lund's more exclusive restaurants, dressed in an open-back dress. Her chair was clearly cooler than it was comfortable. The patina table was sturdy, like something straight out of an Italian farm kitchen. Andreas von Bahr sat next to her.

He was just one of the many men she had been seeing since her relationship with William had ended abruptly. His motorcycle had crashed into a car and the accident left him paralysed. He lost the will to live. She had refused to give up, but after a couple of months, he refused to even look at her when she came to visit. That was the moment when she gave up. She never returned. That day was a painful memory. To survive, she knew that she had to get out of the house. She worked hard and more than she had to. Desperately, she had started seeing other men—many men. She went through them one after the other and skilfully ducked every attempt from their side to take the relationships to the next level.

She and William had been together since they were teenagers. They had done everything together. They practiced karate, travelled around Europe on his motorcycle, climbed mountains, and dived in the Red Sea. She never thought she would survive without him, but after a while, she realised that she would have to. And she didn't just have to survive, she had to live. She was a positive woman, after all, and she finally managed to find joy in her life again. But she still hadn't found a man who could replace William's place in her heart.

A man of about Rita's age sat across from her. She had no idea what his name was. A woman—whose name she couldn't remember either—sat next to the man, and two other couples were seated on the other side of the table from them. One of the women was a redheaded bombshell. She laughed without inhibitions and Rita liked it. The others were stiffer and much quieter. *What am I doing here?* Rita thought. She didn't fit into the crowd. They were all so stiff that it wouldn't surprise Rita if it turned out that they had left the hangers in their blazers. But the redheaded woman didn't seem to care about the fact that you weren't supposed to laugh loudly like that in their company. Andreas scoffed and whispered to Rita:

"She isn't from here, she's from Eslöv. I have no idea how Robert managed to find her."

Apparently, Robert was the man across from them and he was staring at his date with hungry eyes.

"Is there anything wrong with Eslöv?" Rita whispered to him.

"The countryside. No manners, no culture," he said with a disgusted smirk on his face. "They are all idiots."

He stared at the redheaded woman. Rita felt more and more bored by the situation, and by Andreas especially. So far, the conversation had been focused on tax issues. They all seemed very upset about the subject in general. At least those who opened their mouths. *If you don't speak up, you don't disagree*, Rita thought, but stayed quiet. The next thing she knew, Robert had started a discussion about immigration. He was upset about how many immigrants were committing crimes. Rita listened but couldn't muster up the energy to jump into the discussion.

"They probably only come here to commit crime," one of the men said. He sounded upset.

"But that's simply not true," the redhead said.

"What do you know about it?" one of the other women said with a smug smile.

"Quite a lot actually," the redhead said. "I work as a criminologist."

The discussion ended abruptly and Rita felt warm and happy inside. She turned to the redhead.

"Where are you from?"

"I'm from Eslöv," she said. Her southern accent was thick.

"Nice," Rita said. "And you seem to know how to have a good time," she continued loud enough for the others to hear her.

"Sure, I always have as good a time as I can manage," the woman said, and laughed. She threw her head back so that her red hair brushed against a passing waiter. He muttered something and shot the woman an irritated glance. She didn't seem to care at all.

"That's great. I wish I could have as much fun. This place is so stiff and boring that nobody in their right mind could stand it for very long. I'm probably going to leave soon."

"No, don't be silly," the woman said. "You just have to keep being yourself—otherwise, it's unbearable." She laughed again.

The others didn't seem to be listening to them. Just as Rita was about to get up and leave, one of the women turned to Andreas. She didn't want to be rude or interrupt, so she stayed seated.

"I read in the paper that the feminists are back at it again," the woman said.

Rita was desperately trying to remember her name but couldn't. She was a cool, blonde woman with long arms and pale hands. Rita's hands were covered in calluses. Practicing karate and building a summer house back in her hometown wasn't exactly a spa treatment for her hands. She saw it as a sign that she was actually living her life. *Unlike certain other people*, she thought, and glanced at the blonde woman.

"Feminists," Andreas said, and pulled another disgusted face. "They are nothing but power-hungry communists."

"Exactly," the woman answered, "What is feminism good for, really? Women aren't better than men. I like the differences. I don't exactly want to become a man, if you know what I mean?"

The woman spoke with an accent that radiated upper class, even if it sounded like it was rehearsed, rather than genuine. *Maybe she's also from the countryside*, Rita thought. She was getting angry at this point. When she finally opened her mouth, she spoke much louder than usual.

"It's thanks to the feminists that you can have sex with whoever you want and that you can decide for yourself if you want to have children or not. And if you do get pregnant, you don't have to marry the father if you don't want to. Thanks to the feminists, nobody will treat you like an outcast for your choice. If it wasn't for feminism, you wouldn't have been able to pick your own education, you wouldn't have had a say in politics, and you wouldn't have been able to become a boss. Your only choice would have been to be a housewife, or maybe a nurse or teacher. Did they not teach you history in school?"

The woman and Andreas both stared at Rita.

"Yes, but," the woman said quietly, "that's easy for you to say, you obviously know about history."

The woman didn't seem to hear how stupid she sounded, but the others looked uncomfortable. Rita's face had turned white and she clenched her fists. She'd had enough.

"And now you know about history too. But keep looking the other way, for all I care," she said, and her voice was sharp as a knife.

The redheaded woman started laughing even louder than before and clapped her hands. Rita stood up, grabbed her purse, and turned to Andreas. Then she whispered aggressively: "You think that you're such a smart man, superior to everyone else. You chose to go out with me, a woman from the countryside. And I mean, countryside. I'm basically from the woods. And I'm a feminist. What did you expect? Do you really think that I'm impressed? Just so you know, I appreciate real people. But I assume you don't even know what that is? Don't call me again."

All Andreas could do was let out a nervous laugh. The other people around the table were quiet. The blonde woman across from them scoffed before exposing her sharp little teeth in a smug grin.

"And what are you smiling about?" the redheaded woman said to her before standing up too. They both left the restaurant with their heads held high. One of them tall and blonde, flexing her muscular back in her open-back dress. The other one shorter and rounder, swaying her hips from side to side. Although Rita was wearing high heels, she managed to walk confidently all the way out the door. The women didn't turn around once, even if it was tempting. The others probably had no idea why they had left, or why they were even upset. Outside the restaurant, the women started laughing. It felt liberating.

"I don't like Robert anyway," the woman laughed.

"And I despise Andreas," Rita said.

"Yeah, I could see that pretty clearly," said the redhead. She reached her hand out to Rita, and Rita took it.

"Linda Andersson," she said.

"Rita Anker," said Rita. "Nice to meet you. We probably left those people in there quite offended and confused. 'Against stupidity the gods themselves struggle in vain,' right?"

"It's very nice to meet you too. And, of course, there is no point going to war against stupidity. I have to hurry to make my train, but I hope I'll see you again," Linda Andersson said.

"I'm sure you will. I hope so at least. Now I'm going home to get this dress off and change into something more comfortable. I am a vulgar woman after all," Rita said sarcastically.

Rita took her shoes off and started walking home—barefoot. It was liberating. She turned around and waved. Linda Andersson had followed her lead and held up her own shoes as she waved back.

Rita stopped outside her building, paused for a moment, and turned around. She walked a bit further up the street and stopped by the entrance door to the jogger's building. She stood outside his door, listening. It was completely silent. There were no lights in the windows. She walked away, lost in her own thoughts.

She changed into her pyjamas and lay down on her sofa. She picked up her phone and called her mother. The conversation lasted for thirty minutes and they took turns talking. Her mother laughed at her daughter's antics on her date with Andreas von Bahr. Then she told her about the new piglets on the farm and about the calf that had to be bottle-fed as his mother was sick.

Rita's parents' life was so genuine and homely and couldn't have been more different from Rita's violent life. Her mother was Swedish and her father Finnish. They had lived together in Sweden for thirty years and then moved to Finland. It wasn't true that Rita had grown up in the countryside. That was only something she had said to spice up her life story. Her parents were hobby-farmers now, but before that, they had both worked as teachers. Her father had been a woodworking teacher and her mother a teacher in maths and physics. So they weren't exactly farmers. That's also why her mother was laughing so hard at Rita's story.

"I can't believe you told him we've been working hard as farmers all our lives! You're crazy, Rita." She caught her breath and forced herself to stop laughing before she continued: "I don't work all that hard and I sure don't feel like a real farmer, but I understand why you said it. People like that can drive you insane. I can see why you felt out of place."

When they had said goodbye to each other, Rita stretched her legs out and sighed. Then she bent her knees again so that she could reach her feet. They were sore after wearing high heels all night. She massaged her right foot and then her left one. It felt great. She felt disappointed that the date hadn't led to anything, but she wanted to meet an intelligent and kind partner, not a quasi-intellectual and pretentious arsehole. In the end, it was better to be alone than to be with someone who would probably end up making you feel lonelier than ever. Without showering or brushing her teeth, she nodded off on the sofa with a smile on her face. She fell asleep just as she was, a police inspector with sore feet.

# 25

Jörgen focused hard as he went through all the material he had collected and all the information that he had received. It was late. He was tired but kept working.

Söderström entered his office. There were stacks of papers scattered around the place and Söderström gave them a quick but serious glance. Jörgen turned to him and pointed at his computer screen.

"Johannes Vallén is out of the game, it wasn't his DNA. We did find DNA, but just as we expected, it didn't show up in our database. The pubic hair and the sperm come from the same person. The DNA on the cigarette is from someone else, but not Johannes Vallén. Do you think it's possible that we're looking for two suspects?"

"I don't know, but we can't rule it out. It wouldn't be the first time that two men cooperate in a case like this, but I don't know how likely it is. If that's the case, we have another issue on our hands."

Söderström glanced at the computer over Jörgen's shoulder.

"I'll call the prosecutor," Söderström said. He picked up his phone and realised that it was late and that he would have to call the on-call prosecutor.

"Zetterlund," a voice said at the end of the other line.

Söderström sighed to himself. Another prosecutor from the Economic Crime Authority unit with little or no experience in major crime. He took a deep breath, recited the case number, and shared the results from the NFC.

"Okay," the prosecutor said, "I guess Vallén is free to go. Time is 21:55."

"Thanks," Söderström said. He immediately called the station where Johannes was being held. Then he called Sara, who didn't pick up. Finally, he decided to call Johannes's father.

"Vallén," a male voice said over the phone.

"Hi, this is Christer Söderström from the police. Johannes is cleared of all suspicion and free to go. You can pick him up at the Lund Police Station."

"He's free to go? Did you call Sara?"

Göran's voice was unsteady.

"Yes, she's not picking up her phone."

"I'll get him," Göran said, and hung up. Söderström kept the phone up to his ear for a moment. He smiled.

"Great, this means that Sara can come back and I won't have to commute anymore."

Jörgen looked at him as if he was insane. Söderström shrugged his shoulders.

"Of course, I'm glad that her son is free to go too, I just meant that it's *all* good. But as Sara isn't picking up her phone, I'll stay for the night. From tomorrow, she'll take the lead again," he said, and tried to curb his enthusiasm.

# 26

Johannes's eyes were red from crying. His ordeal was over. He had been sure that he would have to spend the rest of his life in prison—serving time for something that he hadn't done. And now, now he was utterly confused. The world of grown-ups was even stranger than he could have imagined. His father was waiting outside the door. An officer shook his hand and thanked him. Johannes wondered why he was being thanked.

"Where is Mum?" he said. Göran shook his head.

"I don't know. She's not picking up her phone. You can call her tomorrow. I was thinking that you and I could go out for a bite to eat. If you want?"

"I want to go home," Johannes said. "I'm not hungry. I want to go home."

"Sure, then I'll take you home instead," Göran said, and put his arm around his son's shoulders. He walked him towards the car. "Are you sure you're not hungry?"

"No. I want to go home and sleep. At Mum's house."

"You can't. Tomorrow, but not tonight. Your mother isn't home."

"I don't care. I want to go home anyway."

Göran nodded.

He tried to hide the fact that he was hurt by the fact that his son didn't want to go to his place. But he understood why and buried his jealousy deep within. They got into the car in silence. They were both used to silence by now. Göran decided to at least try.

"How are you feeling?" he said.

"I don't know, Dad. Everything feels empty. Meaningless, somehow," Johannes answered honestly.

"I understand," Göran said, and realised that he would never understand. How could he?

"No, Dad. You don't."

"No, I guess I don't. Sorry," Göran said.

They both fell silent again.

# 27

Sara woke up in the middle of the night. Someone was shaking her. She reached out and turned on the light.

"Hi, Mum!"

Sara smiled when she saw Johannes kneeling next to her. She took his hand, kissed it, and cried. She didn't know what to say.

"It'll be okay, Mum. It'll be okay."

Johannes lay down next to her in the warm double bed. Sara felt calm and filled with infinite love. A feeling of joy covered her like an extra cosy blanket. She put her arm around him and lay there for a long time, looking at him while he slept.

"Yes, it will be okay," she whispered as she stroked his young face.

The girls were still asleep, even though it was past 8 a.m. They should have been on their way to school by now, but Sara had turned their alarms off. She had also called their teacher to tell her that they wouldn't come to school until later.

Sara stood in the bathroom, brushing her hair. The door was open and Britt popped her head in.

"Johannes is out, he is no longer a suspect, and he is finally back home," Sara informed her mother.

Britt threw her arms out, hugged her daughter, and started dancing around. Then she started crying. Sara started crying too. The two women held each other's hands while they sobbed and sobbed.

After a while, they wiped their tears, laughed, and walked into the kitchen.

Sara made breakfast. She had probably never felt as happy as she did at that moment.

When breakfast was done, she sat down on a stool in the hallway and put on her shoes. She couldn't wait to get back on the case. For real. And now she was free to do so.

"I'll probably be late tonight," she called out. "Take care of them, Mum. Johannes needs to talk, I know that. But I'll have to take care of that when this is over."

Britt shook her head. It was obvious that Johannes needed his mother. But he would have to settle for his grandmother, at least for now. And his father.

"You have to talk to Göran as well," she said to her daughter. Sara nodded and shrugged her shoulders.

"Later," she said.


Sara rushed into the police station, took the lift to the right floor, and dumped her bag in her office. Everyone was waiting for her in the kitchen. They all stood up to greet her, except Jonny Svensson. Rita ran up to Sara and picked her up.

"Finally! Finally, you're back," she said, spinning Sara around as if she weighed nothing at all.

People started coming out of their offices and the kitchen turned into a hug-party that was really something out of the ordinary for this kind of environment. A moment later, Rita was telling Sara about what the team had been doing over the last couple of days, and that they had completely ignored the fact that Johannes had been a suspect.

Sara felt like the whole world was smiling at her. She stepped into her office and started her computer. She read her emails and then walked into Jörgen's office. He was reading some documents while he tapped his keyboard, proving he was by no means unable to multitask, despite his phlegmatic personality.

"Did you look into the jogger?" Sara asked, and pointed at the screen.

"Yes, Evert Karlesson. It's pretty creepy. He served four years for sexually assaulting his daughter. It was quite a while ago, but still. He has been out for years and as far as we know, he hasn't done anything illegal since. He recently got a job with a construction company and he was telling the truth when he said his shift started at 6 a.m. I've gathered some material about him. He has only been convicted for the abuse of his daughter, but there is some background history about the abuse of children in general as well. I'm not sure if those stories hold up though. I've snooped around a bit and he seems to be a bit of a loner. His neighbours and colleagues—everyone we talk to—say he has no friends. I actually sent a couple of inspectors to check with the neighbours. I hope that's okay?"

"Hmm, interesting. Very interesting. And of course it's okay. Great initiative, Jörgen," Sara said. "Our dog picked up a trace that led us to Grönegatan. Maybe it's something worth looking into?"

"Yes, I guess," Jörgen said, "but on the other hand, the trace didn't lead to Karlesson's door. Also, Kajsa Lindahl isn't really a child, right?"

"No, that's true. But you never know with people like him. Keep looking into him. I hope Kajsa Lindahl survives this . . ." Sara paused for a second. She had spoken to the doctors and knew that Kajsa's chances of surviving were minimal. The girl was still sedated.

"Isn't it possible that the letter *E* in her calendar stands for Evert?" Jörgen said as a reminder.

"Yes, you're right. That's definitely a possibility!" Sara's heart skipped a beat and she clenched her jaw. The whole situation felt so strange. Jörgen didn't know that she was aware of this information, but he acted like she knew what he was talking about. And she actually did.

"But what could possibly attract a girl her age to a man like him?"

Jörgen's question remained unanswered as Torsten Venngren and Jonny Svensson showed up in the doorway.

"We're going to pay a visit to one of the guys who wasn't in school for the interrogations. His name is Rodney Ritger. We might as well get it over with. The other kid hasn't been sick at all. He is in Africa with his parents. He should be home in a week or so."

"Good," Sara said. "Also, Karlesson is very interesting." She smiled triumphantly, but her smile quickly faded. Perhaps the lead wasn't *that* much of a triumph after all. Torsten and Jonny looked at her. They didn't look convinced.

"So, what are we talking here? Reasonable suspicion?" It was obvious that Torsten was sceptical.

"Well, not really, but at least we have something to work with. But you're right, I'm not going to assume anything."

Jörgen's phone rang and he stepped out into the corridor, only to return a couple of seconds later.

"Kajsa Lindahl has passed away," he said, and turned to his colleagues with a sad look on his face. "This means that we are looking at *murder* instead of rape and *attempted* murder."

"No, no," was all Sara could say. She was overcome by confusion for a second, but quickly gathered herself and started giving orders.

"I'll drive over to the hospital to see if the doctors can tell me anything more. This wasn't completely unexpected. But still very tragic, of course," she said, and left the office. "And don't forget to talk to forensics!" she shouted as she made her way along the corridor.

# 28

Sara walked quickly through the intensive care unit and into Kajsa's room. There she was. She looked just like she had done the last time Sara paid her a visit. The room was as tranquil now as it had been then. A nurse stepped into the room and told Sara that the girl was being transferred to the coroner shortly.

"We have called her parents; they will be here soon," the nurse said.

"Poor people," Sara said, and the nurse nodded. The night staff were sitting silently around the lunch table. A therapist and the hospital chaplain were on their way, mostly to take care of the parents. The staff would have to wait.

Sara left the hospital before Kajsa's family arrived. She wasn't even sure why she had decided to go to the hospital in the first place. Maybe to make sure that it was true—make sure the girl was actually dead. Either way, she had decided to leave the task of facing the parents to the hospital staff. *They are better at that than me anyway*, she thought.

It was warm and humid outside. She wanted to go to the beach. She wanted to swim in the cool water. But it would have to wait. She had to get back to work.

She drove back to the police station, walked into her office, and opened up the database where all the interrogation's relevant documents were collected. She started at the beginning and read every note, interrogation transcript, and memo. She tried to find loose strings that she could pull. There were many of those. She was satisfied with how her colleagues had handled the case so far, but the evidence didn't point them in any clear direction—yet.

It was late once she packed up her stuff, turned off her computer, and headed home to her kids. She had a lot on her mind. And in the midst of it all, she found herself thinking about Peter Matsson. Before she opened the door to her home, she pushed the thoughts of him away and placed them in a box that she wouldn't open until later. She also pushed away the disappointment she felt over not being able to face the girl's parents. She hadn't avoided them out of consideration. It was fear of facing their darkness that had made her leave. It didn't feel good. Not at all.

Johannes met her in the hallway. They walked into the kitchen together and sat down at the table. Johannes could tell something was wrong and gave her an inquiring look.

"Kajsa Lindahl has passed away," she said, and looked at her son. She knew that this might be the last straw for him. He had *almost* managed to save her, but only almost.

Johannes looked at his mother with blank eyes, then he shrugged his shoulders. *He is almost an adult*, she thought. *But not quite yet*. Then the look in his eyes suddenly changed, as if he had finally understood the severity of the situation. A dark shadow rested over his face and he immediately looked much older. He lowered his gaze and pressed his lips together. He walked away, towards his room. Sara heard him start his computer and turn up the music. Rock music, or maybe punk. Normally, she would knock on his door and asked him to turn it down, but now was not the right time for that. She left him alone.

Johannes didn't come out of his room. He had been in there for two hours. Sara heard his fingers against the keyboard. Except for the music, it was the only sign of life coming from his room. She was worried. Johannes was pulling away. It suddenly sounded like he had stopped typing.

Sara decided that it was time to step in. She knocked on the door and walked in. Her son was lying on his bed, staring at the ceiling.

"How are you?" she said gently.

Johannes didn't answer her. She walked over to his bed. Stroked his forehead.

"How are you?" she asked again, and felt helpless. He kept staring up at the ceiling. Not a word.

Sara ran her fingers over his mouth, forehead, and shoulders. She knew that she couldn't help her son. She knew that he would have to get through this on his own, or ask for help. She knew that being there was all she could do for him. *All people have their limits, even if everyone's limits are different,* she thought. She had a look around his room. The air in there was full of anxiety.

She sat down by the kitchen table, picked up her phone, and hesitantly dialled a number. She checked the time and decided to call even if it was late.

"Louise Malmberg," said a familiar voice.

"Hi, Louise. It's Sara Vallén. Sorry for calling this late."

Her voice was unsteady and Sara looked straight into the black hole as she was falling into it. Malmberg had been in Sara's life for a long time, ever since the betrayal that had left her restless and empty. Sara thought that the therapist was one of the most beautiful women she had ever seen. She reminded her of a grown-up version of a kind, sweet, and beautiful little girl from an old movie she had watched as a child. Louise Malmberg had taught her how to deal with the feeling of letting yourself down and not being able to protect yourself. She had turned Sara's experiences into teachable lessons that had taught her who she was and what she was carrying with her. Louise Malmberg had helped her out of the darkness. She had helped Sara to slowly find her way back to herself and realise that she wasn't crazy just because she couldn't muster up the energy to fight her anxiety. Louise had pointed out that her asking for help was proof that she wasn't crazy.

"Hi, I haven't talked to you in ages," Louise said. "How are you?"

"I'm good, thanks. But my son is going through something lately and I'm worried that he won't be able to handle it on his own," Sara told her.

"What happened to him?" the therapist asked.

"He found a girl who had been brutally raped and beaten. He was arrested and detained as a suspect, but they let him go. He thought that he had saved her by interrupting the assault, but the girl passed away yesterday. Johannes is taking it very hard. Of course, that's understandable, but I'm worried that he will bury himself in guilt, you know, that bloody guilt."

"Do you think that he would be willing to come here?" Louise asked after a while.

"I haven't asked him, but I don't think so. Do you have any advice for me? How should I approach him?"

"What helped you?" Louise turned the question on Sara, as always. She had always told her that she held all the answers within herself. And she had been right. To realise that she already had all the answers and all the wisdom had been the biggest victory of her life.

"That you were here for me. That you guided me into my inner self and my darkest thoughts, and then out again, without really showing me the way. That you helped me find the right way and made me realise that it wasn't my guilt to carry. That the shame wasn't mine. That I should forgive myself."

Sara remembered it all so clearly. The trip she had taken into herself. The most important trip that a person can ever take. She felt nothing but love for Louise. In fact, the affection she felt for her was so strong that she could almost touch it. Louise Malmberg had given her new life and freed her from guilt, shame, and darkness. She would be forever grateful for it.

"That's right. All you have to do now is be there. If he wants to talk to a professional, I'm here. Let him come to you. He probably needs some time to figure out how to deal with all this."

"It sounds so simple when you say it," Sara said.

"You know it's not simple, but it might be simpler than you think. You're a strong woman, a good person, and a great mother. You love your child, that's all you need to do. That's pretty simple, isn't it?"

That last bit was more of a statement than a question, and Sara understood what she meant.

"Yes, pretty simple. Thanks, Louise. I guess I just needed to hear it from you."

"No problem. And as I said, I'm here if he needs me. But I think that you and your son will get through this on your own. And remember that Göran is there too." It sounded like a piece of friendly advice, but Sara knew that the woman she was talking to meant it as a stern instruction.

After the call, Sara's mind felt more at ease. She decided to call Göran. Better late than never, she thought as she dialled his number.

"Hi, Göran. It's Sara."

"Hi, is everything okay with Johannes?" he asked. Sara could hear that he was irritated.

"I would like you to come here, for Johannes's sake. He needs our support. First of all, we need to help him deal with the fact that he was arrested. Also, the girl he found in Lund City Park has died. And somehow, I think that hit him harder than his arrest. He needs support from both of us. Okay?"

"You have never needed me for anything before," Göran said accusingly. "I can talk to Johannes when he is here with us."

"Would you stop it?" she said, and felt how her patience was running out. "This isn't for me, it's not about you and me. It's about our son. And his well-being."

She heard her ex-husband take a deep breath and knew that he was clenching his jaw. She knew that he was tempted to let rage take over, but he managed to hold it back.

"Fine, when? I'm still working. The budget needs to be done by tomorrow."

"I understand that, but I want you to come over right away. Johannes needs our help now."

"I'll be there in thirty minutes," Göran said, and hung up.

*End of discussion*, Sara thought, happy that he had agreed to come. They had been divorced for many years, and their divorce had been an ugly one. Too much anger and too much fighting about nothing. So, in a way, the phone call had ended in a manner that was a win for both of them.

# 29

Thirty minutes later, the doorbell rang and Sara opened the door. Göran looked sceptical, as if he didn't really trust her.

He walked around her hallway as if he was inspecting it.

"Fancy," he said after a while. She felt angry but kept it in, determined not to get into a fight with her ex.

"Yes, they pay me better nowadays. And I've saved a lot," she said, and pinched herself, angry for even apologising for her success. *It's none of his business*, she thought.

"Yes, I can tell."

"I'll let Johannes know you're here. He's expecting you." Göran sat down by the kitchen table without a word. He pulled at the chequered tablecloth. A vase full of flowers from the garden stood at the centre of the table.

When Johannes came into the kitchen, he studied his parents carefully as if he was trying to find out if they were annoyed with each other or not. Göran got up and gave him a big hug. Johannes relaxed. He was half a head taller than his father.

"It's my fault. If I had got there earlier, she wouldn't have died. I know it," Johannes said. "If I had just walked a bit faster. Do you understand? Five minutes would have meant so much. I could have stopped it all from happening. Do you understand? Five minutes. That's nothing."

Johannes looked at Sara, and Sara met his gaze. Her hands were on the table, still—for once. She looked into his big dark eyes and marvelled at how fast he had grown up. The two of them were alike in many ways, there was no doubt about that. Sometimes she grieved that he had turned out to be so sensitive. She wished that he was tougher, she really did. But at the same time she realised that he couldn't possibly have turned out differently than he did. He was her son, after all. She had only become tough because life had demanded it from her. But underneath the surface she was still sensitive and vulnerable. What she had managed to create for herself was an iron heart. He wasn't there yet.

Johannes didn't even mention being arrested or his time in the cell, which was strange. Sara suddenly felt unsure how to handle it all. She tried to catch Göran's attention but he wasn't looking at her and seemed impossible to reach. She decided to meet Johannes where he was right now.

"You carry no blame in this," she said. "You carry no blame for the evil that exists in our world."

Sara felt as if that was something she had needed to hear, back when she was hurting. Each and every person has their own suffering to carry and nobody else can ever understand what someone else is going through. Sara knew that he had to suffer through his challenges, just as she had suffered through hers.

"No, maybe I'm not to blame, but things would have turned out differently if I had arrived there five minutes earlier. Right?" he said, looking for answers. "And I wouldn't have had to sit in that damn cell. None of this would have happened."

He was angry.

"Maybe you could have saved her, maybe not," Sara said. "Maybe things could have turned out differently, but this is what happened. And there is no going back. There is so much in this life we can't control, honey."

Göran stayed quiet, nodding discreetly as Sara spoke. Now and again, his hands reached out for the boy. It was enough, and Sara was happy that he was there. And she was happy that he could ignore his dislike for her for a minute.

Johannes stretched his long legs out under the table and slumped down in his chair. He put his feet on top of Sara's much smaller ones. She remembered when the children had been young and she had let them stand on her feet while they danced with her. It was so long ago, although it felt like yesterday. She looked at his hands. They had been tiny and chubby once and now they were big and long. But when she took them in her hands, they felt just like they had felt when he was a child. It was a physical memory, stuck in her forever.

"I know, Mum. I know you're right. We can't control what happens, but I still wish I had got there sooner. That I could have saved her. I know I can't change that. But I just wish that I could turn back time and do everything right. Don't you guys wish the same sometimes?"

Now he turned to his father. Göran flinched. It was as if his son had touched a sore spot. Göran looked down at the table and clenched his jaw.

"Yes, of course," Sara said to help her ex. She saw how the question had affected him and realised that there were a lot of things that he wished he could change—do right.

"I'm sure we all feel like that every time we do something wrong, or when things don't turn out the way we want them to," she continued. "I don't mean to take away your feelings or wishes. I just want . . . I just want you to see that you're not the one responsible for Kajsa's death."

"I know, Mum, but still. If I could turn back time, I would be happy."

The boy looked at his mother and moved his hands nervously in front of himself to underline the importance of what he was saying—or maybe because he simply couldn't keep them still. After all, he was just like her. Sometimes she loved this about him and sometimes it filled her with sorrow. Just like it filled Göran with frustration. Still, Johannes was Göran's favourite. *Or maybe that's exactly why he loves him so much*, she thought.

Johannes squirmed in his chair.

"I need to finish an assignment for school."

*The young ones heal quickly*, she thought, and glanced at her ex-husband, looking for support. But he turned his head and looked out the window. His chin was tense and his lower lip trembled slightly as if he was struggling not to cry. He turned to his son and placed his big hands on his cheeks. Then he leaned over and kissed his forehead.

"I love you," he whispered.

His son smiled at him. A smile full of love.

"And I love you too, both of you." He stood up. "Thanks," he said quietly.

"What are parents for if not for support?" Sara said. Johannes leaned over and kissed her on the cheek. She kissed him back. His cheek wasn't as smooth as it normally was and his stubble felt scratchy against her lips.

# 30

It was 8 a.m. and they were all gathered again, like the Knights of the Round Table. Zandor Mårtensson, who was an expert when it came to psychopaths and sex offenders, would arrive shortly. Torsten and Rita talked about the interrogations while Sara listened and asked a question here and there. Jonny cleaned his nails and Jörgen read the morning paper, sometimes out loud to share news he found particularly interesting. Sara knocked on the table to attract the others' attention. She turned to Torsten and gave him an encouraging look. He cleared his throat.

"If the perp is someone she knew, she has probably seen him many times in the past. Without realising he's a maniac," Torsten Venngren said, sounding as convinced now as he had done throughout this whole process. Now he even made it sound as if he spoke the absolute truth.

"Probably," Sara agreed. "Let's hope that looking into Karlesson gives us something to go on. Jörgen is still working on that. The issue is that we don't have his DNA. But we are allowed to collect DNA from someone even if she or he isn't an official suspect. So maybe that's what we should do."

"I agree," Torsten said. "Let's collect a sample from him. What do the girl's parents have to say about Karlesson?" he said, and turned to Rita.

"Neither her parents nor her sister has heard the name before. I called them the moment we started discussing the name. They all say that she hasn't told them anything about him. But, who knows? Maybe they prefer not to share the information with us."

Rita held up a bunch of interrogation transcripts. Jörgen, who was the one in charge of all the documents related to the case, snatched the transcripts from her to make sure that they were all in order. Rita muttered something to him.

"What was that?" Jörgen said. He sounded annoyed.

"These are copies, I said." She threw her hands out in front of her.

"Sorry," Jörgen replied, and nudged her gently on the shoulder, "I thought you had taken them from my archive."

"Nope, definitely not." She pushed him back, a lot harder than his gentle nudge.

"Don't stress," said Jonny Svensson as he grabbed a cinnamon bun and shoved it into his mouth. They were having breakfast together during the meeting and there was an assortment of fruit, bread, and pastry on the table.

"I'm not stressed. By the way, when will Zandor Mårtensson be here?" Jörgen scratched his head. "I think I might have lice. The kids brought some home with them from school a while back, so who knows? My scalp itches like crazy," he continued.

His colleagues gave him a surprised look. Even Jonny looked baffled. Nobody said anything more about it though.

Sara cut in. "He will be here at nine—in twenty minutes. So maybe we don't have to overwork our brains before he arrives?"

"Great, as soon as we get a psychiatrist in here, things will be sorted out," Rita muttered sarcastically to herself.

"What will be sorted out?" Jörgen asked.

"Everything, or nothing," replied Rita.

"Oh, okay," Jörgen said, "so you're not a fan of us bringing in a psychiatrist? Is that what you mean?"

"Well, I'm sceptical. But I'm all for bringing in experts."

Sara raised her hands to get attention.

"Think about what you want to ask Zandor Mårtensson when he gets here. I would appreciate it if you did it silently."

Sara leaned back in her chair and studied her team. They were all very different, but there was something that had kept the group together for many years. Now that they had all worked separately and in different locations for a while, their differences seemed more obvious. Her mind wandered from one thing to another. That's how she found patterns in all the chaos.

She thought about the fact that there had been multiple DNA traces at the crime scene. The cigarette butt belonged to someone else.

"Where are we when it comes to the cigarette?" she said, breaking the silence.

"It didn't give us much. No DNA match in the database," said Torsten Venngren.

"That cigarette butt confuses me," she said, and looked at her colleagues.

"Couldn't someone else have thrown it there earlier?" Rita asked.

"Sure," Sara said, "but it could also belong to a second perpetrator."

*Saved by the bell*, Jonny thought when Sara's phone rang and she left the room to get Zandor Mårtensson.

Sara had never met Mårtensson before, but she quickly realised that he had a very attractive aura. An aura of confidence and calm. It was a pleasant encounter.

"We have spoken quite a few times now, so it's about time we meet," he said.

"Yes, absolutely," she said, and looked at him. "Let's go."

He nodded and walked behind her into the station and up to the second floor.

"Don't get intimidated if some of my colleagues come across as a bit rude. Most of them are great people with a lot of experience. They are really ambitious and eager to find out who did this."

Mårtensson laughed, but didn't say anything. Sara had provided him with quite a lot of information that he had been trying to sort into different boxes in his brain. One box for the chain of events and one for the modus operandi—the perpetrator's methods and profile. He was hoping that his profiling of the man who did this would at least point them in the right direction.

Mårtensson looked at the team. *A strange mix of people*, he thought. Sara caught a glimpse of the amused expression on his face.

Mårtensson started presenting his conclusions. He underlined that it was all speculation, but that he was convinced the crime had something to do with power. He told them they were probably looking for someone age sixteen or older, and that it was likely someone who wasn't yet middle-age, judging by the aggressive nature of the attack. He suspected that the perpetrator was someone who hated girls or women. The fact that he had cut her genitalia pointed to that. He interpreted the severed tongue as a symbol that could represent a couple of different things. It could be a symbolic action saying that the person who did this had been offended or humiliated by someone in front of others, maybe.

"The lilac might be his signature. Or maybe it's a reconciling gesture. It's hard to tell. Maybe it's his version of a funeral. You know, when you say goodbye to someone by leaving flowers at their coffin. The flower was white, which could be a symbol of innocence. Or maybe a symbol of the complete opposite. Maybe he was trying to show us that the girl wasn't innocent at all."

Mårtensson agreed with the theory that the perpetrator and the girl probably knew each other. It was a fair conclusion to come to as there were almost no signs of resistance or struggle.

"Girls tend to be careful about walking alone in areas that are dark and empty," Zandor Mårtensson said. "But we don't know for sure, of course."

Sara thought about how easy it was to turn to truths created from clichés as they were easy to understand.

"Could there be more than one perpetrator?" Rita asked.

Zandor Mårtensson looked at her with a surprised expression on his face.

"Why do you ask?"

"There were multiple DNA traces at the crime scene," she said.

"Well, it's hard to say. Probably not very likely. But I guess we can't rule it out. It's just that these types of men normally work alone. It would be difficult for them to find each other, and would take considerable effort for them to work together to stage such a violent attack. To do so, they would have to synchronise their violent behaviour, which doesn't seem very likely. But sure, it's a possibility. For example, two men could have planned a rape together and then one of them might have escalated in the middle of it, leaving the other one too scared to come clean. The problem is that parts of the attack seem planned, like the tongue. But it's not very logical or rational to leave sperm behind."

Mårtensson's hands moved calmly as he spoke and his eyes rested on the person he talked to for a second. Then he looked at the rest of the people around the table, one after the other, to make sure that he still had their attention. *This guy is an experienced lecturer*, Sara Vallén thought. *He obviously knows exactly for how long he can look at someone before making them uncomfortable.*

"At least we have a person of interest," Sara said. She hadn't told Mårtensson about Karlesson as she didn't want to steer his mind in any set direction.

"Yeah? Give me some details."

"He is about to turn fifty. He is athletic and likes going for jogs in the mornings. Works in construction. Did four years for sexually assaulting his daughter a while back. He is known for being a tough guy. Hard to reach, according to the prison staff," Jörgen said.

"Okay, how old was his daughter?"

"She was about six when the sexual assault started. At least the assault that they were able to prove at the time of the trial. He used her until she was twelve. That's when it all came out. Mostly oral sex. A couple of times vaginal. The assault wasn't very violent in terms of physical injury, even if it was obviously brutal in other ways."

"Well, you never know," Mårtensson said. "It doesn't really sound like he would be behind a crime like this, but as I said, you never know. A lot of sexual offenders become more brutal over time; they simply need more and more to get their kicks. And obviously, there is a difference between his daughter and a girl he is not related to. The question is what his sexual preference has been up until now. Has he had sexual relationships with women? Is he interested in teenage girls too? I'll need to think about this for a while. To count him out because of the nature of his earlier crimes would be stupid. Definitely. Has he shown any signs of this type of aggression before? Does he have a history of using symbols in other ways? I would look into that if I were you. And if there is another perpetrator involved, who might he be? How much of your resources are you willing to use to look for a perpetrator who might not exist? Are there any other options for now?"

"No, not really. But there are some things that make it impossible to take Karlesson out of the picture. For example, the dog led us to an entrance door close to his flat. And while all of his neighbours were still in their pyjamas when we knocked on their doors, he was already up and dressed. He said he was going for a jog. He didn't have any blood on his clothes, but it's possible that he had already changed by the time we got there. There are circumstances that could make him a suspect, and circumstances that point to his innocence."

"Okay. And I would keep looking at her closest circle. In cases like this, it's normally someone you have a relationship with," Mårtensson said. "And as I said, the aggressive nature of the violence tells me it's probably a younger man. Testosterone levels decrease with age and usually make people less and less aggressive. Aggressiveness is strongly linked to sexuality, which in itself can be a trigger. If you follow my reasoning?"

"Yes, we see what you're saying. Karlesson isn't our only priority, but we are trying to figure out who he is, what kind of life he lives, what he is up to, and so on," Sara added.

Mårtensson stood up. He had given them what he came for.

"Well, I need to leave. I'm going to the prison in Kristianstad to mediate a conversation between staff and inmates."

# 31

The group ended the meeting. Jörgen went into his office to keep working on Evert Karlesson's profile. Sara walked into her office to call Prosecutor Baum and to sum up the evidence they had gathered so far.

Her phone rang before she had time to make the call.

"I have something to say," a man's voice whispered. Sara didn't recognise it.

The man on the phone sounded drunk, which made her suspicious.

She started tapping her pen against the notebook on her desk.

"Sure," she said reluctantly.

"I know someone. His name is Evert Karlesson. I know that you know about him." The man paused as if he had asked her a question.

"What is it that you want to tell me?" Sara said.

"He worked at her primary school. The girl who was attacked, I mean. The name of the primary school was the Ladybird. It was a long time ago. And you know what he has been up to, right? He was suspected of sexually assaulting the kids there. But they could never get him for it, the creep."

"Who are you?" Sara's question was left unanswered. The person at the other end of the line had ended the call.

Sara went into Jörgen's office and asked him if he knew anything about Karlesson working at a primary school in Lund. Jörgen didn't but promised to look into it right away. Then, out of curiosity, he asked her why she wanted to know. Sara told him about the anonymous caller.

"That would definitely strengthen our suspicions regarding Karlesson," he said.

A while later, he returned to Sara to confirm that Evert Karlesson had indeed worked at the Ladybird Primary School about twelve years earlier. He also confirmed that Karlesson was suspected of sexually assaulting the children at the primary school at one point.

"Okay, let's put Karlesson under surveillance," Sara said. "I'll talk to Prosecutor Baum to see what he has to say about it first. I think we could argue for reasonable suspicion here, but not more. And I assume Baum will agree to it. It's the lower level of suspicion, after all," she continued, as if to convince herself.

Prosecutor Baum agreed with her.

"I think we should keep an eye on him. Maybe it's dumb to let him know that we're on to him. Maybe it's better to keep him under surveillance and see what he's up to, especially if there is a risk that he is not the only perpetrator here. And hey, I'm glad your son is no longer a suspect."

"You should have been able to see that straight away if you ask me," Sara replied. "And yes, I'll put Karlesson under surveillance. Anything else?" she said, quickly changing the subject. She was still upset about the situation with Johannes, but didn't want it to show.

"Talk to someone at the primary school about his time there. There must be someone who still works there. It's not that long ago." Baum ignored Chief Inspector Vallén's comment about his involvement in arresting her son.

"Of course," Sara said. We're on it."

She had obviously already thought about that. And if it turned out that their daughter attended the Ladybird Primary School twelve years ago, Kajsa's parents would need to be interviewed again.

"Stay in touch," Åke Baum said.

"Of course, sir," she said, bowing to the phone.

"Did you just bow to the phone?" Prosecutor Baum asked.

Sara's jaw dropped.

"How did you know?" she said. She turned towards the door and screamed when she saw Åke Baum standing in the doorway.

He waved his phone at her.

"Your call has been forwarded," he said, and laughed so hard that he had to put his hands on his knees. Sara was still in shock. She hated surprises.

Once she had gathered herself, she felt a wave of anger wash over her.

"What are you thinking, surprising me like that?" she shouted, and pretended to give him a slap in the face.

"Sorry," Baum said, and let his arms fall to his sides. "I was in the building and thought I would pop in. I'm on call. Didn't mean to scare you."

Sara quickly gathered herself together.

"No, I know, sorry. But you really did."

Baum sat down on the edge of Sara's desk.

"Karlesson is definitely interesting," Baum said. "I wonder if a paedophile can even be attracted to a teenager? It doesn't make sense."

"According to Zandor Mårtensson, it's possible," Sara said.

Suddenly, Jörgen appeared in the doorway.

"I just heard that Kajsa Lindahl *did* attend the primary school where Karlesson worked," he said. "So, they do have a connection."

"Very interesting," said Baum. "I still think we should keep him under surveillance. Wasn't the nature of this crime extremely aggressive?"

"Yes, Mårtensson said that it's hard to know how aggressive tendencies develop over time. He didn't seem convinced that Karlesson had done this though, as there is a connection between testosterone and aggression, and testosterone levels decline with age," Jörgen said. "But he seems to be quite an adventurous man, this Karlesson. He owns a motorcycle, for example."

"So what?" asked Sara. "Why would that matter? There isn't a clear connection between being adventurous and being aggressive."

"No, maybe not." Jörgen looked defeated.

"Well, keep me in the loop," Baum said.

"Of course," said Sara, gesturing for Baum to have a seat in her office chair instead of on her desk. The gangly prosecutor looked sceptically at the chair. It looked like a rocking chair and, somehow, you were supposed to place your legs on pillows that were held up by a strange contraption. The idea was to put all the pressure on your thighs and knees and relieve your back. He did his best to sit down in the strange chair but couldn't really get his legs into the right position. Sara Vallén started laughing and Jörgen Berg giggled. The prosecutor looked embarrassed and tried to stand up again, but he was stuck. Jörgen Berg helped him out of the chair and Sara pulled out a normal chair instead. Nobody said anything, and Sara and Jörgen couldn't stop giggling.

Baum looked very pleased with the option of sitting down on a normal chair and started writing down the instructions he had just given them. He wanted to be in full control of the decision he had just taken.

"I want to hear from you the moment you make progress. Depending on the situation, I'll promptly give you my decision regarding arrest or whatever it is you need," he said. "I want you to call me whatever the time is—night or day."

Both Baum and Jörgen left Sara's office. She leaned back in her chair and thought for a moment. Then she made a few notes in the notebook on the desk.

They would collect a DNA sample from Karlesson as soon as possible. Hopefully, very soon. But first, they had a couple of other things to do. Next on the list was a visit to the botanic garden. She pulled out a folder and put it in her backpack.


Rita was waiting for her outside the gates. She looked confused and threw her hands out in front of her.

"You'll see," Sara told her colleague, and guided her into the garden.

She pointed at a lilac bush in full bloom.

"Do you see it?"

Rita's eyes opened wide and she nodded.

The two officers walked up to the information desk and were introduced to the curator, Susanne Nilsson, who told them about *Syringa pekinensis* as they walked through the garden. She told them it was a very rare species and guaranteed that it didn't grow in too many places in Lund.

"Very beautiful, isn't it?" she said proudly, and stroked one of the flowers.

Rita and Sara nodded. To them, the bush was connected to the death of a young girl, which made it difficult to appreciate its beauty.

"Do you have visitors who come here often enough for you to recognise them?" Sara asked.

"Oh yes, definitely. Many of our visitors are very interested in flowers," the curator said. "But maybe you mean someone who shows a specific interest in the *pekinensis*?"

"Something like that."

"Lilacs are quite popular," Susanne Nilsson said. "Many of our visitors come here only to see the lilacs, but most of them are probably interested in flowers in general. Are you looking for someone in particular?" the curator asked, giving the two officers a curious look.

Now it was Sara's turn to be curious.

"Yes, we are. Do you think you would recognise which of your visitors come specifically for the lilacs?"

"Definitely," the curator said without hesitation.

Sara pulled out the folder from her bag. The folder contained a bunch of photos that the forensic team had given her—twelve photos of men in their mid-thirties and forties. Susanne Nilsson looked at the photos, one after the other. Sara started recording. Susanne Nilsson shook her head as Sara discreetly reported the curator's body language into the microphone. When the curator looked at photo number nine, she flinched. She put her finger on the photograph and turned to Sara Vallén and Rita Anker.

"Him, that guy, I'm positive. He comes here all the time and he is very interested in the lilacs. I talk to him quite often. He tells me that he loves lilacs. And he knows quite a lot about them. He's a bit of a lilac nerd."

Sara and Rita couldn't help smiling at each other before quickly forcing themselves to look neutral again. They both knew the importance of what had just happened. The man that Susanne Nilsson had recognised was Evert Karlesson.

"He hasn't been here for a while though," Susanne said. "At least not since the last time I spoke to him."

"Can I ask you to keep looking at the rest of the photos?" Sara asked, and the woman did as she was told. She shook her head. She didn't recognise any of the other men.

"Do you think that man could've been here without you noticing?" Sara asked, and knew she was dangerously close to overstepping a line. But as Susanne Nilsson had seemed so sure, she decided to give it a go. A defence counsel could argue that Chief Inspector Vallén had revealed that he was the one they were looking for, and that this might have encouraged the curator to share things that weren't necessarily true, only to make the officers happy.

But Susanne Nilsson turned out to be quite smart.

"Are you asking me these questions for any particular reason?" she asked, and looked at the two police officers.

"Well, all we want to know is whether a certain person has a specific interest in lilacs," Sara Vallén said with an innocent smile. "That's all I can tell you for now. I hope you understand, and I have to ask you to keep this conversation between the three of us. It's important."

"Well, in that case," the woman said, "I can tell you that it's *possible* that this man, who is definitely the same man as the one who regularly comes here to talk to me, came here without me knowing about it. But I'm here almost every day, and he always seems to make sure to come by when I'm here." She emphasised the last words of the sentence. "And he only speaks to me."

Sara and Rita looked at each other.

"Are you trying to tell us that he might be interested in you?" Sara asked.

The woman nodded.

"He might be. If you ask me, he comes across as a bit tense and strange. A big fan of his own muscles, if you know what I mean? But still, he seems to love his *Syringa pekinensis* most of all. Isn't it ironic?"

"Yes, maybe. When was the last time he was here?" Sara asked.

"He hasn't been here this week. Not during the daytime, at least. I'll check with my colleagues. Wait here, I'll be right back."

Sara and Rita looked at each other again.

"This is bloody marvellous," Rita said.

Sara felt both happy and hopeful. "It's definitely something."

The curator came back and told them that the man in the picture hadn't visited the garden that week.

The two officers thanked Susanne Nilsson for her help and left, each with a satisfied smile on her face.

Sara knew that ordinary people would never understand that smile. A young woman was dead, and still, they felt excited about finally seeing a possible solution to the case. There was no contradiction there, even if an outsider might see it that way. Every step in the right direction led to an adrenaline rush that was intoxicating. It was even possible this rush was what had made her stay on the force for so many years, even if she had often felt frustrated with how slowly things moved in the organisation. The satisfaction it gave her to capture a bad guy after weeks of tedious police work was the reward that made it all worthwhile.

# 32

It was time for gym class and he knew that it would play out just like it always did. His teacher would yell at him for not bringing the right kind of clothes and shoes, and after class, his classmates would make fun of him for not bringing a towel. But, how could he? There were no clean towels at home and he didn't want to bring a dirty one to school. That would have been much worse. Instead, his plan was to move as little as possible during class so that he wouldn't even need a shower afterwards. His only friend was super athletic and didn't care about him at all once gym class had started.

After making it through the class without being criticised by his teacher or bullied by his classmates, he hurried into the changing room so that he could wash his face and get out of there before the others showed up. It was the last class of the day, and he would be off the school premises before the other kids stepped out of the showers. He ran across the school playground.

His father had given him money to buy some essentials on his way home from school. The cheapest store around was located in Kattesund and owned by immigrants. He rushed through the store and picked up some apples, a couple of bags of crisps, and a litre of milk. A bag of pasta also ended up in his shopping bag. It would at least last them for a couple of days. He stopped by the coffee shop in the same building as *Sydsvenskan* and bought himself a coffee and a cinnamon bun. He decided to sit down for a while.

He hoped that his father wouldn't come home at all that day. He hoped that he would end up in a drunk tank somewhere. It was easier to relax when his father wasn't home. He was way too unpredictable. Every time he stepped in through the door he knew that there was a risk that his father would attack him and start a full-blown fight, or he could be passed out on the toilet with sick all over the floor. Sick that reeked of wine, liquor, beer, sausage, and maybe some chips. He hated it. And he was the one who would have to clean it all up. If he didn't, he wouldn't be able to use the toilet.

Maybe he should do some laundry when he got home too, but he wasn't sure where his father had put the keys to the laundry room.

He finished his coffee, devoured his bun, and left the coffee shop to go home. Maybe he would have a quick shower and then head out again. There wasn't much to do at home except to sit in front of the computer. For a second, he thought about calling his older brother to ask him if he wanted to meet up, but he decided not to. He rarely heard from his brother since he had left home.

His father had pretended that it was all so bloody lovely when social services had paid them a visit. Now he was nothing but a wreck, an arse-hole, and a bully. *I hate them all*, he thought, and pulled a face that turned his soft mouth into a wolf-like grin. He hadn't eaten a decent meal since his mother left. The laundry never got done. No clean clothes, no clean sheets. His mother had taken care of all that—at least before she really fell off the wagon. Even if he hated her, at least it had all been better when she was still around. It was a miracle that his father managed to keep his job at the local newspaper. He should have been fired a long time ago. But for now, they let him stay, which was the only reason they still had a roof over their heads. Hate filled his head and burned like a fire. His father was a pig. But then again, it would be over for him one day. The thought made the boy feel better. He knew he would get his revenge one of these days.

# 33

Around woman with red cheeks sat across the table from Rita.

"I remember him very well. They could never prove anything, but something was definitely off about him. Everyone who worked with him felt suspicious about the way he handled the children. There was something disrespectful about him."

"How do you mean?" Rita asked.

"Well, it's hard to explain. But he looked odd. He wore strange clothes and was terrified of getting dirty. He never played with the children, at least not outdoors. He liked going with them to the bathroom and he always loved laying down with them during nap time. Other than that, he wasn't really involved. I remember him saying some very strange things. He had ideas about raising children that felt very outdated. It was all about obedience and things like that. He really wasn't suited for working at a primary school."

"And what was it that was disrespectful about him?"

"I never thought he respected the children's personal space, and he was far too stern. But I grew more suspicious once the children started to avoid him and when they didn't want to sleep in the same room as him. They were so young. He worked with boys and girls that were all under five years old, most of them two or three."

"Did you ever suspect any kind of criminal activity?" Rita asked seriously.

"Well, not at first. But many of us found him strange and a bit inappropriate, if you know what I mean? His behaviour could be pretty unsuitable towards his younger colleagues and I heard that he could be a bit touchy-feely; yet at the same time, he was always very stern with them."

Rita gave the woman a surprised look.

"He was stern with adults too? Was that what you just said?"

"Yes, many of his younger colleagues hated him. I know one of them called him *extremely disrespectful*."

"And stern at the same time?"

"Yes, isn't it strange? As if he wanted to force people into obeying him and then smooth it over with what I assume was his idea of affection. I'm not sure."

The woman frowned. When Rita saw her dark and expressive eyebrows, she couldn't help thinking about her own eyebrows. They were almost white. The woman nervously wrapped a piece of tissue paper around her fingers. Rita sat at a respectable distance from the woman, but now she cursorily leaned forwards. The woman also leaned forwards, as if she couldn't help herself.

"What made people suspect him of sexually assaulting the children?" Rita asked carefully.

"One of the children told his parents that Evert Karlesson had touched his penis and pulled it. Or something like that. That's all that was really said. The children couldn't tell us much more. I guess you weren't that good at interrogating children back then."

"Yes, maybe that's just it," Rita said. "It's hard to interrogate young children. They lack words and references. Nowadays, we have specialised interrogation officers for that."

"Well, he was fired. And we were all very relieved. It was so sad when we found out that he had assaulted his daughter like that. Horrible. And back then we never requested a background check before we hired someone. It was such a shame."

"There was no way you could've known," Rita said. "And today it's different. Still, there are no guarantees, of course . . . I have one more question. Do you remember the name of the child who told his parents?"

The woman shook her head.

"No, but I've just remembered that there was a little girl who was also molested—allegedly. But her parents refused to let her go through with the examination and the interrogation. They thought it would be too traumatic for her. She was a bright girl, very sweet."

"What was her name?"

"Kajsa, as far as I remember."

Rita Anker couldn't believe what she was hearing. *A real stroke of luck,* she thought, and triumphantly clenched her fist under the table for a moment before opening it again once she realised that there was nothing to celebrate about the situation.

"Thank you, I'm so grateful that you could come in on such short notice. I only have two more questions now. Do you remember if Evert expressed any interest in a specific type of flower?"

"How funny you would ask that," the woman answered. She looked genuinely surprised.

Rita couldn't wait to hear what she had to say next.

"He was very fond of cherry blossoms and lilacs. He always brought them into the primary school. And he knew quite a bit about lilacs, especially. It was almost a bit strange. At least, I thought so, along with the other women at the school. He was such a *man*, you know. He was into diving, drove a motorcycle, and went to the gym. He was very athletic. I think he was a very complex person."

Rita was shocked. Karlesson's interest in lilacs seemed to have been there for years. She tried her best to look professional and friendly, and to not give anything away.

"What do you mean when you say he was complex?" Rita asked.

"Well, I'm not sure. He was always so strong, physically. He was very masculine and loved stuff that is traditionally seen as very manly. That thing about the lilacs always felt a bit off, as if it didn't match the rest of his personality. And as I said, he was strange in general. Inappropriate and insecure somehow. It was as if he didn't get along with all sides of himself, as if he was socially awkward at the same time as he was physically over-confident. I don't know how to explain it in a better way."

"I understand," Rita said, and smiled.

"Also, he found it very hard to express himself concisely. Unless he was being stern, of course, then he used very few words."

Once again, Rita felt surprised by the fact that everything seemed so connected. *The tongue,* she thought to herself.

"And the last question: Did he ever show any violent tendencies?"

"No, he didn't. His mind was scarier than his body, even if he was a big guy."

"I want to thank you, once again, for your time and all the valuable information," Rita said. "I think we will end the interview here."

The woman let out a sigh of relief and stood up.

"We will get back to you if there is anything else that we need," Rita said, and shook the woman's hand.

# 34

It was already 4 p.m. Jörgen was still sitting in his office searching his computer for information about Evert Karlesson's life. He had contacted most of the other regions within the Swedish police. So far, nobody had anything interesting to tell him. He looked up when he realised that Sara was standing in the doorway.

"Hey," he said. "It looks like Karlesson has stayed out of our databases since his last time behind bars. I'm assuming he isn't very active in the criminal world. But then again, sexual offenders normally aren't. He hasn't even been given a speeding ticket."

"That's a shame, I guess. Did you get the ball rolling with the surveillance?" Sara asked.

"Jonny and Torsten are stationed at Grönegatan. In a flat across from Karlesson's flat. It's perfect. It lets us see everyone who comes and goes. Otherwise, I don't have much to tell you. I'll keep looking, of course."

He pulled up his sleeves, ready to go back to work." His strong arms were covered in tattoos. Sara knew that he had a big dragon tattooed across his back. He had showed it to her many years ago, before she became a chief inspector.

"Rita and I will take over from Torsten and Jonny tonight," Sara said.

"His motorcycle is a Yamaha XJ900, by the way. A pretty boring machine, but fast. Black."

"Okay, anything else?"

"No, nothing else. *Zero, zip, zilch, nada*."

"Does he have any friends?" Sara asked. "Have you checked if he is connected to other criminals, specifically other sexual offenders?"

"Of course, but as far as I can see he isn't connected to anyone interesting. Totally clean. There isn't much in the databases about him, just some pornographic images that were found in connection to the case involving his daughter. Cartoons. The material wasn't even considered pornographic as it didn't contain images of real children. Otherwise, we might have been able to find something interesting there."

"That's the worst thing about dealing with these guys," Sara said. "They normally don't have any friends at all. Maybe he wasn't into child pornography back then?"

"Maybe not, although I must say it feels strange. I mean, paedophiles are normally quite active in that area," Jörgen said. Sara could tell that he felt disappointed with how little information he had managed to gather about Evert Karlesson.

"But we do know that he is interested in lilacs," Sara said, and sounded both excited and proud.

"What?! How do you know?"

"We went to the botanic garden," Sara said with a mischievous smile on her face. "And we did a photo line-up."

"Did you put that together by yourself?" Jörgen scoffed.

"Of course not. I asked forensics for help," Sara answered from the corridor. She had already left Jörgen's office but popped her head back in through the door again to ask him something.

"Hey, by the way, has anyone interrogated Kajsa's mentor?"

"No, that hasn't even been on the table," Jörgen said.

"Then I want you to do that. Right away!"


Rita waved Sara into her office just as she was about to sneak out to get something to eat.

"Come in here," Rita said, and told Sara about her interview with the primary school teacher.

"The Ladybird lady told me that one of the children who might have been molested by Evert Karlesson was Kajsa Lindahl."

"Jesus," was all Sara could say.

"Isn't it strange that her parents didn't even mention this when we talked to them?"

"Very strange, they would definitely remember a thing like that. Okay, so he seems to be our guy, right?"

"Sure," Rita said. "It's really starting to look like Karlesson is the perpetrator here."

"Torsten and Jonny are keeping him under surveillance as we speak. You and I are taking over from them tonight at ten o'clock, so you should go home and get some rest. We're keeping an eye on him from now on."

"Well, I'm not really tired. But I'm hungry," Rita said. "Do you want to grab a bite?"

"No," Sara said. She had already forgotten that she had been on her way to grab a baguette and something to drink. Hunger was a feeling that she found herself ignoring quite often.

"I need to go home for a bit," she said, turning to Rita. "And hey, Jörgen checked with our colleagues in the rest of the country. Nobody has ever seen a signature or a modus operandi that reminds them remotely of our murderer. And according to the prison staff, Karlesson was a model inmate."

"Hmm, I'm not one hundred per cent convinced about Karlesson, now when I think about it. Isn't it a bit strange that he has moved his focus from children to a girl who is almost an adult, and from sexual crimes with close to no physical violence to the extreme nature of this crime, which seems to be about so much more than sex?"

"Yes, I agree. But who knows what goes on in people's brains?" Rita's uncertainty was contagious, but Sara wasn't ready to give into it yet. They had been so sure they were on to the right guy, just seconds ago.

"We'll take over from Jonny and Torsten tonight. They've found a good flat for a stakeout."

Rita looked up only to see that Sara was staring out the window.

"I know. You already told me," Rita said. "See you there at ten."

"Can you make sure that Jörgen tells the press that we want the public to get in touch with us if they have seen anything interesting in or around the botanic garden in the days leading up to Kajsa's murder?" Sara asked.

"Of course," Rita said. "You go. I'll take care of it."

"Okay, then I'll head home now. I need to relax for a moment, while I still can," Sara said, and walked towards the door.

* * *

Sara liked her old, ugly Saab. It worked pretty well, except for when it was really cold outside. She ran her hand over the dashboard, prayed that the car would start, and turned the key. She heard a slight buzzing sound, and then it started. She gave the dashboard another pat. On her way home, she had an impulse to drive east, through the beautiful summer landscape. She rolled down her window. The fields flew by outside and the air smelled like the bright yellow rapeseed flowers that grew everywhere.

When she got to Lake Vombsjön, she parked her car on the side of the road, stepped out, and threw her clothes in a pile on the little beach. Nobody else normally swam here, and there wasn't a lot of traffic. She had a quick look around and stepped into the water. It was lovely and the temperature was perfect. The water was slightly red, probably because of the high iron concentration in the lake. She swam out and rolled over on her back. She stayed like that until the lake had cooled her off, all the way into her core. She got up and let the sun and the wind—it was always windy down here in southern Sweden—dry her skin. Not a single car drove by.

# 35

Jonny Svensson had seen him walk up to the entrance door, open it, and sneak inside. Then nothing. And more nothing. Jonny watched the man as he moved around in his flat. He sat down by a computer and, even though it was light outside, the blue light from the screen lit up the flat. Karlesson didn't turn any of his lights on.

"Come here," Jonny said, waving at Torsten Venngren, who was sitting on the sofa, talking to the woman who owned the flat they were using. "What the hell is he doing?"

Torsten grabbed the binoculars and had a look. It was hard to distinguish what Karlesson was doing as he sat in a dark corner of the room.

Torsten Venngren looked at the lady on the sofa. He nodded in her direction to make Jonny understand that what he was about to say wasn't for her ears. Jonny walked up to Venngren and leaned closer to him.

"He is masturbating," Torsten whispered.

Jonny looked confused for a second.

"Ah, I see," Jonny said. "He is jerking off, you mean?"

Torsten pushed his colleague. Jonny didn't say anything but made a promise to himself to never tolerate being treated like that again.

The woman on the sofa hadn't heard what the two of them were talking about, but she stood up and left the living room.

"Why the hell did you do that?"

"If you don't get that, you're even more stupid than I thought," Torsten answered.

A moment later, Karlesson appeared in the window. Jonny and Torsten turned their focus back towards him. He was on his phone and then, suddenly, he disappeared into the flat. A couple of minutes later, they saw him walk out of the entrance door dressed in a leather suit, carrying a helmet. He crossed the street and walked into a courtyard next to the house where Torsten Venngren and Jonny Svensson were. The next thing they heard was the sound of his Yamaha. They stopped staring at each other, very aware that they had just missed something important. Karlesson drove towards Svanegatan and then he was gone.

Torsten Venngren reached for the radio and contacted the permanent surveillance unit in Lund. They were stationed in an unmarked car at the corner of Stora Fiskaregatan. He told them that Karlesson had taken off on his motorcycle—a Yamaha—and that they must have seen him drive by. Venngren and Svensson heard the investigators start their car and head off. But they both knew that they had lost Karlesson. Venngren was annoyed with himself and Svensson was annoyed with Venngren.

"If you hadn't been messing around, we wouldn't have missed him," Svensson said. He sounded angry.

"Yeah, yeah," Venngren answered.

# 36

The man stood there with his trousers pulled down. His erection was big and hard. The boy leaned over the table with his trousers pulled down too. The man put his hands on the boy's buttocks. The strong scent from the lilacs on the table made the boy feel sick.

He was quiet. He clenched his jaw. He knew that he had to stay silent and suffer. He knew that there was no other way out. Not now. Maybe never.

"You're a smart boy, obeying. You know I love you, right?" the man said. "You make it feel so good for me." As he spoke, he grabbed the boy's hair and pulled it back. It hurt the boy's neck. But he stayed silent.

The man started moaning as he moved faster. The boy bit his lip so hard that he could taste blood in his mouth. He endured. When the man was done, he slapped the boy's behind and asked him to leave the flat. The boy gritted his teeth, dressed, and gathered his things. Then he sneaked out. He was in so much pain that it was hard to walk. His scalp stung and his neck felt stiff and sore. As soon as he stepped out onto the street, his submission transformed into hate.

# 37

He was lying in bed, waiting for the door to be kicked in. His head hurt. His neck hurt. *What am I supposed to do?* he thought. *What am I supposed to do?* He stared into one of the corners of the room. That thing he didn't want to get rid of was hidden underneath a pile of clothes.

"Stop it, Dad," he tried to scream, but his voice broke.

After spitting out a bunch of swear words, the father gave up.

The boy cried and travelled into the burning darkness again. The darkness that never left his side.

"I hate you," he whispered as all the men in his life morphed into one monstrous figure in his mind. He twisted and turned in his bed.

He sat up. He scratched his face until a pimple started bleeding. He studied the blood under his nails. *You'll never get me, you don't know who I am*, he thought, and licked the blood from his finger.

The phone rang on the table in the hallway. He heard his father pick it up.

"Fuck off," the old man screamed before hanging up. The boy didn't dare ask who it was.

He heard a loud sound and assumed that his father had collapsed in a drunken pile on the floor again. Everything was back to normal. Thankfully, it didn't seem as if he had thrown up—at least it didn't smell like it. The boy gathered a couple of his things and snuck out the door as silently as only someone who has had a lot of practice can sneak.

He walked through the warm summer night. He had a look around and crossed Kyrkogatan. He didn't want to stay at home. He walked into Lund Cathedral instead. He sat down on a bench in the back. He looked at the ceiling and at the walls. It was nice in the cool and quiet church. Nobody could get him there. He had read that churches could serve as sanctuaries and that nobody from the government could touch him in there.

He looked down at his dirty shoes. His sharp toenails had ripped holes in the front. *Maybe God can hear me*, he thought.

He woke up with a jerk when someone put a hand on his shoulder.

"Dear child, you can't sleep in here. We are locking up now."

The man's face was round and soft and lit up by all the candles in the church. He looked friendly.

The boy suddenly felt unsure. The church wasn't for him. He didn't belong there.

"It's okay. I'm sure you're tired. It's nice in here. The candles and the silence," the friendly man said, and ran his old hand over the boy's curly hair.

"But as I said, you can't stay here. If you do, I might end up locking you in here overnight," he said, and laughed. Maybe he was slightly embarrassed by the way he had stroked the boy's head.

The boy grabbed his things and ran out. The man waved at him, but he didn't wave back. *Fucking dickhead*, he thought, but felt bad about it just a second later.

He carefully put his key in the lock and sneaked back into the flat. He closed the door behind him and walked towards his room through the darkness.

When the lights were suddenly switched on, it stung the boy's eyes. His father stood in front of him. He was much smaller than the boy. It didn't matter. He lifted his belt. It hit the boy right across the chest. He fell backwards and landed on the floor. The boy lifted his hands in front of him. The father hit him again, this time aiming at his face. The boy rolled to the side and the belt missed him by a hair's breadth. The father lifted his belt again and hit his son across the back. The boy managed to get up. He ran into his room, slammed the door shut behind him, and turned the key.

No banging on the door. Everything was silent. Like in the grave. The boy stood in his room, trembling.

"Mummy," he whimpered. "Mummy, come home."

The boy sat in his bed all night, rocking back and forth. Back and forth. Back and forth. When the sun came up, he left the flat again and headed down into the basement.

# 38

Jonny Svensson and Rita Anker sat silently in the car. Rita was tired after spending an uneventful night in the flat across from Karlesson's. He had come home, gone to bed, and then nothing had happened. Another patrol had come to relieve them around 6 a.m., and Rita had snatched a few hours of sleep before it was time for work again. Jonny was just as tired as Rita. He hadn't been able to sleep.

Rita took a deep breath. She couldn't help feeling annoyed with Jonny. His fat arms, his washed-out T-shirt, the way his stomach made him look pregnant, and his short hair, which was still a bit too long and stood straight up in a stupid hairstyle—or rather a non-hairstyle. She cleared her throat without looking at him. He stared at the road. She knew that he wasn't a fan of her either. Also, she wasn't very happy about the fact that she had been dragged into an interrogation that Jonny and Torsten had failed to complete.

"Okay," she said. "We don't like each other. But let's get this done. This interrogation has to happen. We can at least pretend to be professional and respectful. Also, it's Saturday. If we do this correctly, we get to go home. If we don't, we'll have to keep working. Either way, I would appreciate it if we could do this without drama."

Nobody would be less surprised than her if it all went horribly wrong.

Jonny Svensson didn't say a word. He didn't even nod. She felt his cold eyes staring at her. *Fisheyes*, she thought.

Out of the blue, he said, "I'll take care of the interrogation."

She nodded. *It will be a disaster, but I'll have to accept it*, she thought.

Jonny Svensson parked in a car park next to Stora Gråbrödersgatan. They stepped out of the car and walked towards Rodney Ritger's address. The entrance door was open. They entered the building and looked at the names on the mailboxes. Rita spotted the name "Ritger" on a mailbox belonging to a flat on the second floor.

Jonny started banging on the door, but Rita grabbed his arm and rang the doorbell instead. Not a sound was heard from the flat. She peeked through the letter box and saw a pair of sneakers. No post, only the shoes.

"At least they have been home today," Rita said, and turned to Jonny, who was leaning against the wall, waiting for something to happen.

"Oh, yeah?" Jonny said. If he had acted indifferent before, it was nothing compared to how he acted now.

"I'm not sure, but maybe we should wait for a while?" Rita looked at her colleague.

He didn't seem to have an opinion about her suggestion. She rang the doorbell again.

Rita picked up her phone and called Sara, who was the one who had asked them to get this interrogation done.

"Nobody home," she said when Sara picked up.

"Are you sure? They might be asleep. It's Saturday, after all. This interrogation has to happen now; it's crucial to get the whole picture at this point. And then I need you to go to Klostergården."

Sara couldn't see it, but Rita looked slightly insulted as she rolled her eyes.

Rita suddenly heard a noise from inside the flat.

"Quiet," she said, even though neither Jonny nor Sara had said a word.

"Did you hear that?" she asked without expecting an answer. She heard the sound again.

"Someone is home," she told Sara over the phone. "I'll hang up now."

Rita started banging on the door and cursed herself for acting like Jonny Svensson. The sound she had heard before was gone now. Rita peeked in through the letter box again.

"This is the police. We would like to talk to Rodney."

Everything was silent and she wondered if she had only imagined the sound from before.

"Hello? Nothing to be scared of here, we just want to have a word with Rodney, and then we'll leave."

Rita sounded almost pleading. She heard the sound again and saw a pair of feet. A man opened the door without unlocking the security chain. It was hard to determine the man's age. His hair was a mess and it looked like he hadn't brushed it in weeks. It reeked of alcohol in the flat.

"He's sick," the man said. His voice sounded coarse and damaged by years of smoking. "Really fucking sick. Leave us alone. Rodney is so sick he can't even talk."

The man repeated the word *sick* as if it was a mantra, but Rita refused to give in.

"We just need to have a quick chat with him. He doesn't even need to get out of bed," she tried, and discreetly held her breath. The smell of his drunkenness was unbearable.

"No, I said."

"Are you Rodney's father?" Rita asked, and looked at Jonny, who seemed frustrated now. *This isn't the way he normally goes about things*, she thought, just as Jonny Svensson grabbed the door and pulled it so hard that he broke the security chain.

"Move over, old man," Jonny Svensson said, and pushed him out of the way. The man instantly started aiming punches in their direction, but Jonny grabbed his arm and twisted it up and back. The man screamed. He was obviously in such a state that he didn't stand a chance against Jonny. He was skinny, his skin was dry, and he looked dirty and sick.

"Let me go. I'll let you in. Jesus."

Rita sighed. She knew they had a very different starting position now than they would have had if she had just been allowed to talk to the man for a bit longer. Her colleague's impulsive attack against the man had compromised the situation.

"I'm just going to have a chat with Rodney, then we'll be out of your hair," she said briefly.

Rita walked into the flat and was met by the pungent odour of rubbish, old vomit, and a mix of other, very intense smells. She discreetly placed a hand in front of her mouth and kept walking. *Poor child, having to grow up in this environment*, she thought. *Where are social services when you need them?* A wave of frustration washed over her and she felt a knot in her stomach. She would report this to social services the moment she got back to the station.

The first door to the left was closed. She opened it carefully and looked inside. There was a bed by the window. The bed was made but the rest of the room was a mess. It was clear that a teenage boy was living there. But where was he?

Rita turned to Jonny Svensson and the man, who was obviously the boy's father. Jonny was still pushing him up against the wall. Rita had no problem using violence when it was necessary. But in this case, it felt completely pointless as the man could barely stand up straight in Svensson's grip. Ritger had stopped trying to break free and Rita felt bad for him. He looked like a sack of potatoes—a tragic sack of potatoes, just like the drunks hanging out on the city's park benches. She couldn't believe that he owned a flat.

"Where is Rodney?" she asked, placing a hand on the man's upper arm, the T-shirt acting like a protective layer between her palm and the man. But then Ritger moved his arm and his T-shirt disappeared from underneath Rita's hand. She did her best not to show how disgusted she was by touching his naked skin.

"I don't know," the father said.

"But you told us that he was sick."

"I thought so, I guess I haven't checked lately," the man whispered.

He looked ashamed. It was all very embarrassing. He lifted the arm that Rita's hand was placed on and scratched his nose. His nails were dirty. Once again, she felt disgusted, but she made sure that her face kept a neutral expression. She knew how important it was to stay professional, and she respected people far too much to ever do anything to make them feel inferior. Rita believed the man. Judging by the way he acted and his obvious alcohol addiction, she doubted that he was even able to determine whether or not he was telling the truth. She also realised that it simply wasn't possible for a man who had so little of his brain capacity left to lie without showing any signs of doing so.

"Where is Rodney's mother?"

"She is in rehab," the man said.

He slurred when he spoke. He struggled to keep his balance and looked more fragile than anyone Rita had ever seen. She also sensed he was quite aggressive and suspected that the lost son got to experience this whenever the man had enough energy. He was too submissive for it to feel genuine. Was he a liar? No. Was he erratic? Yes. She reminded herself again to hand this family over to social services. *Why haven't we already checked if social services are aware of this boy and his family's situation?* she thought.

Rita glanced at Jonny, whose face looked just as disgusted as it looked arrogant. She was suddenly overcome by anger. Why was he standing there, feeling so superior? What did he know about life? What had life taught him, really?

"Do you mind if I have a look around? Maybe he is in another room, scared to come out?"

The man nodded and Rita had a walk around the disgusting flat.

She shook her head when she returned to the hallway, where Jonny still hadn't let go of Ritger. She gave Jonny a stern look. "Let's go."

Jonny let go of the man and walked towards the door. Then he turned around and gave the confused father a superior look.

*He just can't stop himself from displaying his authority*, Rita thought.

"From now on, you open the door for us. Do you understand? We are police officers and you are nothing but a pathetic old drunk," he said calmly, yet aggressively. "And clean up this pigsty. It's disgusting."

They started the car and drove down to Grönegatan. Jonny Svensson parked the car a few doors down from Karlesson's address. Rita stepped out of the car, walked closer to the flat, and tried to look through the window. The flat looked empty. She crossed the street, entered the building, found the door to Karlesson's flat, and peeked in through the letter box. There was a pile of letters on the doormat, but the flat was empty. No shoes. She came to the conclusion there was nobody home. But the question was how the hell he had managed to sneak out. They had interrogators keeping an eye on him from a flat right across from his. She crossed the street, climbed the stairs to the flat, and walked right in.

"Karlesson isn't in his flat," she said, and raised her eyebrows. The men in the flat looked at her. They looked embarrassed.

"No, we know. We heard his motorcycle and then he was gone. We didn't have a surveillance car close by. They were in the middle of a shift change but didn't make it in time."

"Is it too much to ask that you do your job?" Rita scoffed. She rushed down the stairs and stopped to take a couple of deep breaths before she opened the entrance door and stepped out onto the street again. She wasn't sure if she would be able to get a warrant to search Karlesson's home or not, but decided that there was no immediate rush. The most important thing right now was to get hold of him. They could search his home later. Assuming, of course, the surveillance unit that was looking for him didn't find him. Then it would have to be done anyway. It was just so resource-intensive. She shook her head and walked back to the car. But she didn't say anything to Jonny. She didn't feel like talking to him. She felt furious.

"So?" he said, looking for answers.

"So," she said, "he wasn't home."

# 39

They drove towards Klostergården in silence.

Jonny parked the car and stepped outside. Rita followed his example. She looked at his profile and hated him. She hated his personality, his expression—everything that made him Jonny Svensson. And she wanted to punch him. She would never give in to her impulse, of course, but she couldn't control her thoughts and feelings. She turned away from him to hide her anger. Normally, she was a very empathetic person, but however hard she tried, she couldn't seem to empathise with her colleague.

"This time, let me do the interview," she told Jonny. "I don't accept your methods and even if I won't report you this time, I'll keep my eyes on you. Just so you know. I'll interview the parents, understood?"

Jonny looked annoyed but nodded. The silence between them was ominous and they both knew that one of them would have to leave the major investigation team at one point.

Rita rang the doorbell. Margareta Lindahl opened the door. She looked so miserable that Rita had to take a step back. The woman who had once been so full of life was nothing but a shell and her eyes lacked expression. She held the door handle tightly and it was hard to determine whether it was because she needed the support, or she didn't want to let them in. Rita smiled and asked her if they could come inside even though they had showed up unannounced.

The woman nodded.

They walked into the kitchen, where Gunnar Lindahl sat. He was just as pale as his wife. But unlike his wife, there was something resolute about him and his jaw was clenched. He turned towards them.

"What do you want?" he said. "Why can't you just leave us alone?"

Although the words that came out of his mouth were quite aggressive, there was nothing aggressive about this man. He looked empty—empty and exhausted.

Gunnar Lindahl looked away.

"We have a couple of questions," Rita said in a friendly tone.

"I see," he said, and didn't seem to care.

"Maybe I could speak to you first?" Rita asked Gunnar Lindahl. "You can go into the living room, and I'll be with you shortly," she said, turning to Margareta Lindahl, who nodded and left the room, closing the door carefully behind her.

Jonny was leaning against the fridge with his arms crossed in front of him.

"I'm terribly sorry about disturbing you like this, but as you know, we are still looking for Kajsa's murderer, so we have no choice. I hope I can make this as easy and painless as possible for you, even if I'm aware that nothing about Kajsa's death is either of those things."

"I understand," Gunnar Lindahl said, and blinked. He looked tired. Rita also noticed that he was slurring. He didn't smell of alcohol, so she assumed that he had turned to psychotropic drugs. *How would I react if it were me?* she thought.

She truly didn't know. Would she have reacted with anger, frustration, and vindictiveness? Or with sadness, fear, anxiety, and emptiness? She had no idea but hoped that she would handle a situation like this with rage. *I'd rather be angry than empty*, she thought.

"There are a couple of things that I hope you can help me clear up," she said, and felt hopelessly rude. She hated stepping into a home full of grief like this, with no consideration for what the residents were going through. The man in front of her nodded but looked very confused—as if he couldn't fully understand anything that was going on.

"How come you never told us that Kajsa was molested as a child?" she asked, and braced herself. "It has come to our knowledge that a primary school teacher named Evert Karlesson was suspected of molesting Kajsa when she attended Ladybird Primary School. Are you certain that you don't recognise the name?"

Gunnar Lindahl's eyes filled with hatred for a second. He turned to Rita, clenched his fist until his knuckles turned white, and slammed it onto the table.

"Why are you bringing this up?" he asked. "We never want to mention that man again. It was so long ago, and we just want to leave it behind us. What does that have to do with Kajsa's death? Why are you poking around in it?"

Rita took one of the man's clenched fists in her hand.

"I can't stand this. I can't stand it. Leave me alone!"

His voice was breaking. Rita didn't say anything for a while. She just sat there, holding the man's hand. She stroked his shoulder with the other hand to try to comfort him. It seemed to have some effect because, suddenly, he started crying. He cried like only a man who has lost a loved one can cry. Rita struggled to keep his emotions at a safe distance. They wanted to eat their way into Rita's soul, but she closed the door to her inner self and kept holding the man's hand. He shrank in front of her and his pain was hard to watch.

Rita waited. She let his sobbing die out before she spoke again. What could she possibly say to comfort him? *Nothing, absolutely nothing*, she thought.

"I apologise," he said once he had calmed down.

"You have nothing to apologise for," she assured him, and couldn't stop herself from stroking the man's cheek with her big hand. It was wet and he snorted.

Jonny had been staring at them the whole time. Then he grabbed a roll of paper towels and handed it to Gunnar Lindahl, who tore off a sheet and blew his nose on it.

Rita smiled at Jonny. *At least he is doing something*, she thought. She turned to Gunnar Lindahl again.

"The reason I'm mentioning this is that we think Kajsa might have met up with Evert Karlesson again," she said.

Gunnar Lindahl stared at her. Her calm demeanour seemed to have a stabilising effect on him. Somehow, he managed to process the information.

"Why do you think that?"

"Some of our evidence points in that direction. I can't go into detail," Rita said.

"We never pressed charges," Gunnar Lindahl said. "But did you know that his name was Wilkinsson back then?"

"No, I didn't know that," Rita said, surprised, "but thank you for telling us. Can I ask you why you didn't report a man who was suspected of molesting your daughter?"

"Kajsa was only five years old and we didn't want to put her through all that pressure. It wouldn't have led to anything anyway. The police couldn't prove a thing. And Rodney was never himself after the whole thing."

"Rodney?" Now Rita was the one who looked surprised. "Rodney Ritger?"

"Yes, that's right. They are, or were, in the same class. In school, I mean. Rodney was the boy who first accused Karlesson of molesting him. They opened an investigation, but there was no way of proving anything."

"Okay, this information is very valuable." Rita thought about it for a while. "Did Rodney and Kajsa go to school together for all these years?" she asked.

"Yes, basically," Gunnar Lindahl said. "They have always attended the same school, but they didn't end up in the same class until high school. They had the same mentor."

Rita made a mental note. Why had nobody interrogated the mentor? It upset her, but she forced herself to ignore it.

"Have they had a lot of contact over the years?"

"No, none whatsoever. I know Kajsa felt bad for him, but she didn't spend time with him. Not at all."

"How do you know?"

"Kajsa told me."

Gunnar Lindahl looked irritated, but Rita wasn't going to give up.

"But you talked about him," she said calmly. "Why is that?"

"Kajsa told us about him. About how hard things were for him."

"Do you know Rodney's parents?"

"Not really. His mum was already a drunk back then. Rodney's father looked after him. I'm not sure what kind of man he is. I think he works for the local newspaper. I know he was working a lot. He never attended parent-teacher conferences or anything like that. His mother was the one who came to those. I felt bad for the mother. But I guess Rodney was the real victim in it all. We always thought that his mother seemed nice."

"So Kajsa didn't care about Rodney Ritger once they were older?"

"No, they weren't the same kind," Gunnar Lindahl said.

"What do you mean?"

"They belong to different social classes, if you need me to point out the obvious."

"Oh," Rita said, not impressed by Lindahl's superior attitude. "I'll contact you if I have any more questions."

She shook Lindahl's hand, nodded to Jonny, and walked towards the door.

Jonny said goodbye and followed her. Once Rita stepped out of the flat, she picked up her phone and called Sara Vallén.

# 40

Sara Vallén was very focused. The team sat silently and none of the usual small talk could be heard. They were all tired and pale.

"Is there any risk that Rodney Ritger is in trouble?" she asked. "Or that he has been murdered?" she added.

"I think," Jörgen said, "that Evert Karlesson, also known as Evert Wilkinsson, is capable of anything. We still haven't been able to find this kid Ritger. I've looked into the investigation from back then. I asked the prosecutor in Lund to get me up to speed with the case and give me what we have in the archives. I've sent for the physical file as there isn't much to find in our databases. The investigation was dropped, as we know."

Everyone in the room listened to Jörgen Berg.

"Go on," Sara said.

"The thing is that Rodney Ritger's mother, who was already suffering from alcohol abuse at that time, pressed charges along with the primary school and the social welfare office. But the boy couldn't really say anything more than what he had already told his parents to begin with. Also, he didn't show any signs of physical injury or assault. Apparently, the boy developed problems typical for children who have been molested—peeing himself for example—but it wasn't enough. The charges were dropped because of insufficient evidence. Kajsa Lindahl's parents refused to let their daughter go through the same thing. After that, Rodney completely clammed up."

"And what happened to Karlesson?"

"Nothing really, except that he lost his job. He started working in construction. He was a big and strong man. According to what Rita Anker has been told, most people found him strange, disrespectful, and quite inappropriate."

"So far, Karlesson hasn't really done anything suspicious. He managed to get away from us when he took off on his motorcycle, but that was probably unintended. He isn't a rich man. He has some assets, but not enough to get him very far if he has figured out that we are on to him and decides to do a runner. Jörgen has looked into that," Sara clarified. "My intuition tells me that he will stay calm for a while," she continued, brushing a couple of stubborn locks away from her forehead.

"Does he have any friends?" Rita asked.

"Not really," Jörgen said. "According to the prison staff, he spent a lot of time by himself while he was doing time. Nobody ever came to see him. It seems to be the same now, although he has been out for years. His neighbours have barely seen him, even if they know who he is. He never says hello, he never has any visitors, and his flat is always silent. At least that's what his neighbours tell us. And as far as we can tell from our surveillance, this is all accurate."

"Maybe it's time we try something new?" Torsten interjected.

"What do you mean?"

"Well, knock on his door. Talk to him. Pay him a visit. Grab something that will give us his DNA."

"And put the whole investigation at risk, you mean?" Sara said.

Torsten knew that Sara was right, but he didn't want to give up the idea completely.

"Don't forget about the principle of free sifting of evidence," he said.

"Yes, good point," Sara said. "But if we mess up by conducting an illegal house search, the whole investigation is ruined. And I don't feel like being reprimanded just because I couldn't wait for another day or two."

"Okay, I get it," Torsten said, although he thought it was time to do something drastic.

"And Rodney Ritger?" Jonny asked. "What are we going to do about him?"

"Let's put surveillance on him too, or at least place a car outside his flat. If we find him, we'll have a unit following him around to make sure he is safe. And we have to try to get hold of him so that we can interview him."

"And what about the botanic garden?" Sara said. "Anything new on that?"

"Yes. A witness called," Jörgen Berg said.

"And did it give us anything?" Sara felt irritated and wanted to move forwards. They were treading water.

"Of course," Jörgen said. "The witness is a student who was on his way home from campus on Sunday night. He did say that he was drunk, but he is convinced that he saw a man and a young woman walk along the fence of the botanic garden, on the outside. It was around midnight, 1:30 a.m. He'll be in later today. I'll question him. If nobody else can do it, of course?"

Sara looked excited.

"Could he see if the man was young? Or if he was older?"

"No, I don't think so, unfortunately."

"But how does he know that it was a young woman then?"

"He couldn't tell for sure, but he did say that she dressed like a young woman," Jörgen answered.

"Okay, try to get as much as possible from him. I'll give you the photo line-up that we showed to the curator at the botanic garden so that you can show it to him. I mean, it's worth a try."

Jörgen nodded.

"Show him a picture of Kajsa as well. Did he see their faces?"

"No, he only saw them from the side and from behind. He said there was something about one of them that made him react. He couldn't tell me what, but it was enough to make him turn around and look at them once they had passed. I'll show him some photos. Don't worry, Sara," Jörgen said. He leaned back in his chair with one leg crossed over the other. He looked very relaxed and comfortable.

"No, Jörgen, I'm not worried," Sara said, still annoyed.

# 41

He sat in the basement of the apartment building. He didn't want—or dare—to go back to the flat. He didn't know what mood his father was in. He could be drunk and mean. Or sober and mean. He couldn't go to school. That would require him to get his stuff in the flat first. He was tired and hungry. All he had managed to grab on his way out were a couple of bottles of Coca-Cola and some bread. *Just like in prison,* he thought. *But Coke instead of water, of course.*

He studied his own reflection in the mirror outside a toilet next to the basement storage. He thought his big body looked smaller than usual. His hair was one huge mess. His beard had grown long, although it was thin and fuzzy. He ran a hand across his face. It was sore and bruised. He could barely move his left arm and his left foot was probably sprained. He couldn't put any weight on it and when he tried to walk, it just hung there. His right arm hurt as soon as he tried to lift it, forcing him to use the left one instead. *I don't think it's broken,* he thought. *Probably just sprained.*

The summer heat hadn't found its way into the basement. He had found an old blanket and wrapped it around his shoulders. He had tried to clean himself up in the laundry room, but the result wasn't great as he didn't have soap or deodorant. He waited. Waited to be discovered. He tried to think clearly, but his mind kept playing tricks on him. For a while, he thought that he was in a real dungeon. His perception of time was skewed and he felt as if he had been sitting in the basement for a week, even if he knew that it had probably just been a day.

He worried about how the people at his school would react when he finally decided to go back there, given the way he looked. What if they started asking questions? Or what if his father called the police? He probably wouldn't though—if he had even noticed that Rodney was gone.

He curled up into a ball on the cold concrete floor and started rocking himself back and forth. The rocking motion soon sent him to sleep.

He had a dream about his mother, a dream that he had dreamt a lot as a child. His mother came towards him, floating across a beautiful meadow. With open arms. She was wearing a dreamy white dress that looked like a gown. His mother was so beautiful. She smiled at him with big, white teeth. He laughed and ran towards her. He had missed her so much. Her hair looked like a halo around her head and he couldn't wait to smell it. He approached her, but as he stretched his arms out towards her, she pulled away from him. He caught up with her again, desperate to reach her. But every time he got close to her, she pulled away. After a while, she evaporated before his eyes.

And then he woke up, holding his breath. He started crying, just as he had done as a child. He wiped his snotty nose with the back of his hand and stopped crying. "She's a fucking bitch," he mumbled quietly.

It was lunchtime. He was pretty sure that it was in the middle of the day. His father should be at work by now. He snuck out of the basement, towards the light. He stood outside the building for a while, trying to decide if he wanted to keep walking, or if he should go back into the basement again. He finally decided that it was time to leave his hiding place for a while. He took a step down the street and gasped when he saw his father come walking—or, stumbling—towards the entrance door of their building. Rodney quickly limped back into the basement.

# 42

*typical student, slightly awkward and distracted*, Jörgen thought to himself. The young man was taking film studies and seemed keen to share his life story. With his young eyes fixed on the older and much less enthusiastic police officer, he told Jörgen about his future plans—he wanted to direct, or maybe produce.

"Can you tell me what you saw that night?"

"Yes, of course," the youth said, and gave Jörgen an intense—slightly cocky—look. "That's why I'm here, right?"

Jörgen cleared his throat and took a deep breath. *He's one of them*, he thought. *A posh kid from Lund's upper class*. Jörgen came from Kirseberg, a suburb north of Malmö, and was allergic to the academic upper class of Lund. There had always been some conflict between Lund and Malmö and he had learnt early on that Malmö was all about the harbour, segregation, and the working class, while Lund was about the university, academia, and the upper class. He had carried this attitude with him ever since.

"Yes, we usually ask our witnesses that question," he said, trying to hide his scepticism.

"Well," the youth said, "I was on my way home from campus. I walked past the botanic garden and saw a girl and a boy—or maybe I should say, man. They looked like an odd couple. She was pretty. Long, curly hair with highlights. She looked like she took care of herself. He was wearing a hoodie and I couldn't see his face. But he was huge. I'm pretty short," the young man said, and locked eyes with Jörgen Berg. Jörgen nodded. The student in front of him *was* quite short. Probably no more than 5 feet 7 inches.

"So, compared to you, he was huge. And what about in comparison to the girl?"

"As huge. She was probably the same height as me. Just over five feet seven inches," he said.

"And compared to the rest of the world?" Berg asked, and couldn't stop himself from smiling.

"Still huge," the student said, and smiled back.

"Did you notice anything else?"

"Yes, the girl was holding a lilac branch in her hand. I assumed she must have picked it in the botanic garden. I know they grow in there. I'm sure of it. It wasn't a normal lilac. It was a special kind."

Jörgen Berg realised that this was an important witness. A witness who had his eyes opened and his head screwed on.

"Did you say she was holding it in her hand?"

The boy nodded.

"Did you see what colour the lilac was?"

"White," the boy said without hesitation. He didn't even have to think twice about it.

"Great," Jörgen said.

"Is it? Why?" He looked curious. Happy and curious.

"It's just great that you have such good memory," Jörgen said. "Anyway, can you explain why you found them to be an odd couple?"

"Well, odd might not be a great word for it. I just didn't think they seemed to be friends. I'm not sure why. Maybe something about their body language. I'm used to studying people *in action*, so to speak. How they act in each other's company and all. It's part of the industry."

"Right," Jörgen Berg said. "In what direction were they walking?"

"Downwards. I mean, along the fence. When I turned around to look at them, they turned onto Östra Mårtensgatan, towards Mårtenstorget."

"Okay," Berg said. "I'll let you look at a photo of a girl first. Then I'll let you look at a couple of other photos. I want to see if you might recognise this man, or boy."

The young man nodded.

He started by looking at the picture of Kajsa Lindahl. Hummed.

"It could be her. Cute. Bright girl. Great hair. I think it looks like her. But I'm not one hundred per cent sure. It was night-time and I was drunk, but I think it looks like her. But she looked tougher in reality than in this picture."

Jörgen Berg put the photo line-up that Sara and Rita had presented to the curator on the table.

The student looked through the pictures but couldn't really recognise any of the men.

"It could be any of these guys," he said sullenly. "I never really saw him. All these guys look huge. I could be wrong, but I think the guy I saw was younger than these people."

"Why do you think that?"

The young man shook his head. He suddenly looked very serious and turned to Jörgen Berg.

"I'm not sure. Maybe I assumed that, as she was so young—younger than myself, I think. But honestly, I can't really say anything about age or looks, except that he was enormous. That's it. I'm sorry that I can't help you more than that."

"Oh, you've helped us plenty," Jörgen said, and placed a hand on his shoulder. "We really appreciate that you got in touch with us!"

He suddenly felt embarrassed about his preconceptions concerning Lund. This was a good bloke, and so polite.

# 43

Sara wished that she hadn't agreed to cover Carina's shift as an emergency buddy tonight—on a Saturday of all days. She was late, as always. She felt tired and overworked after an intense couple of weeks, and she had stayed in the bath for far too long. She had barely slept or eaten lately. She cursed herself.

"Sorry I'm late," she whispered to a colleague, who was already in the middle of a call.

She sat down by the desk and put her headphones on. Then she pushed a couple of buttons and her phone was live.

It rang straight away.

"Emergency buddy, this is Sara," she said. "What can I help you with?"

"I don't know what to do," someone whispered at the other end of the line. "I'll kill him. I'll kill them all. I hate them."

Sara recognised the voice immediately. She normally only came in on Mondays. This must mean he called several days per week.

"Hi there," she said, and tried to sound as calm and friendly as possible. "You're not feeling so good today?" It was a rhetorical question and she wasn't expecting an answer.

"I hate him."

The boy was whispering, but his voice sounded powerful anyway. Sara could hear how close he was to his limit.

"Did he beat you again? . . . And that other thing?"

She knew that it was unspeakable—what the boy had to suffer. He was always talking in riddles and nothing he said was explicit. But she was convinced that she got it right most of the time.

"Always, he always does—the pig. And he says that he loves me." It sounded as if the boy was struggling to breathe. And he was scared, Sara could tell. Really scared. And full of hate. He couldn't keep the two feelings separate.

"I think you should go to the police," Sara said. She wasn't usually this direct with the boy, but now she felt that there was a risk he would hurt himself, or someone else.

"Never."

"Okay. But what do you want to do then?"

"Kill him. And her and all the other idiots. And him, the worst of them all, the monster. I might kill him too. Maybe I already did."

*He is provoking me*, Sara thought, and decided to ignore it. She had to try to get some more information from him.

"Who are these people that you want to kill?"

"All of them. They're all idiots. I hate them."

"I don't think you do, but I understand that you're angry. What your father is doing is not only wrong and illegal, but it's horrible and bad in every way imaginable. And I want you to call the police, or go to them. Or maybe you can at least talk to the school therapist? Or your teacher? You have to tell someone about this."

Sara knew she had pushed too hard. If she said too much, or if she suggested going to the police, the boy usually hung up the phone. But this time she was lucky. The boy stayed on the line.

"Never, she won't get it. And she knows too much anyway."

"Your teacher? What do you mean when you say she knows too much?"

"She asks questions. Snoops around. Disgusts me."

"But maybe you can talk to the school nurse? Or let me help you?"

"I won't talk to anyone."

"But you're talking to me," Sara said carefully.

"Yes, but you have no idea who I am."

He hung up.

Sara sat there with the phone in her hand, staring straight ahead. She had a feeling that this guy could be dangerous. Sure, she was used to kids calling this number being upset, angry, and sad. Some of them seemed to hate everything about their lives. But there was something about this boy. He went from being cold and full of hate to being very upset and almost childish in his outbursts. Maybe she was only imagining it. Maybe it was good enough for him to vent his anger with her from time to time.

*As long as he doesn't hurt himself*, she thought, and took the next call.

# 44

Sara stood on the stairs with the key in her hand when she heard something behind her. She turned around and scanned the street for threats. It was still light out, the air was warm, and the scent of the lilacs in the garden almost made her feel dizzy. She felt a shiver down her spine when she saw a shadow emerge from the greenery. At first, she felt scared, almost frightened. She was ready to run. Then she realised who the shadow belonged to—a realisation that didn't make her feel any less uncomfortable. It made her put her guard up.

"Hey there, I thought I would swing by and see how things were going," Peter Matsson said, and smiled. "Just a quick visit," he added. His eyes told her that he had picked up on her urge to run. He widened his smile, probably to make her relax. Sara thought he looked like a wolf, grinning at his next prey. *It's just my imagination*, she thought.

"What are you doing here? You can't just show up like this."

She winked to free her stubborn eyelid—once again, it had started twitching uncontrollably.

"Are you angry?" he asked.

"Angry? No. Well, yes. I don't like it when people I don't really know show up on my doorstep unannounced. And I'm tired. It's been a long week. I need to be ready; we're looking for a murderer, as you might have heard?"

"Can I come in for a while?" he asked, and took a step closer to her. She would never let him into her house like this. Absolutely not.

What was he even doing here? Suddenly, she felt a vibration of desire run through her body. She couldn't believe it. From feeling like a cornered animal, she had turned into a woman full of lust. As soon as she realised this, her head filled with confusion and she became defensive. He wasn't extraordinarily attractive, but manly—very manly. His face was powerful and his blue-green eyes were intense. He was standing in front of her with his legs wide apart. His jeans were worn, his T-shirt white, and his sneakers spotless. He kept looking at her face.

"For a little while, then," she answered, and wanted to pinch herself as her emotions refused to listen to her intuition. She took a step back, scared of her own feelings and frightened by the attraction she felt towards him.

"How did you find my address? Sara asked once they had entered the hallway. She still felt uncomfortable with the situation, but the desire she felt was even stronger. The kids were at their dad's house. It all felt dangerous, but interesting.

"Well, I have my sources," he said, and smiled again.

She showed him around the house. He clearly liked it.

"Wow, this is nice," he said, and ran his fingers over the kitchen tiles before taking her in his arms. His embrace was hard and passionate. She thought she would pass out for a second. From happiness. From lust and passion. And from horror.

She pulled away from him. He followed her when she walked towards the bedroom. They only made it to the bedroom door before he pulled her close again, whispering something to her. She could barely hear him, but she had a pretty clear idea of what he wanted to say. She stepped into the bedroom and he followed her. Then he slowly started undressing her. Once she was naked, he kneeled in front of her and kissed her stomach. His tongue wandered down towards her most intimate parts.

"Well, I have to get going," Peter Matsson said, and sat up in the bed.

The magic was broken. They had lain next to each other for a while, staring at the ceiling. There was nothing to say so they had stayed silent until a moment ago, when he abruptly told her that he had to leave.

"Already?" she said, and instantly put her guard up again. Why did she react like that?

"I have to go home. I've got some stuff to do," he said cryptically. "But I'll call you later."

She wasn't going to make a scene over it. It wasn't her way of dealing with people. But for some reason, she still felt uncomfortable. Her body looked so small next to his and it scared her as much as it intrigued her. She felt a sudden desire to be small, instead of being the strong one who kept it all together. To be taken care of, instead of being the one taking care of everyone else. She knew that these desires were connected to danger, but there was also something very tempting about them.

She saw him glance at his watch. Then he stood up, got dressed, and gave her forehead a quick kiss. Something felt wrong. His behaviour baffled her.

"You're beautiful," he said, and left the bedroom. He closed the front door silently behind him, as if he didn't want anyone to hear him. But there was nobody there to hear him or see him, nobody except Sara. She suddenly felt irritated. He was the one who had come there. She quickly got out of bed and looked for a cigarette.

She couldn't find one. She hadn't smoked in ages. *Of course I don't have any cigarettes*, she mused as she reached for her phone. It was almost midnight. She decided to call anyway.

"It's me," she said. "Do you want to go for a run?"


"What's up with you today?" Rita said when they got back to Sara's house. She was out of breath.

"I just needed to blow off some steam," Sara said. "Thanks for coming with me."

She couldn't—and didn't want to—explain what was going on in her head.

Her hair was sweaty and hung like a wet curtain over her face. She had forgotten to tie it back and it kept falling into her face as she ran. Now it stuck to her face and neck, bothering her. With an irritated movement, she pulled a lock of stringy hair behind her ear.

She wouldn't see Peter Matsson again. Everything about it felt wrong. Good while it lasted, but completely wrong afterwards. *He can't possibly be good for me*, she reflected. *There must be other men. Better men. For me.*

# 45

Torsten Venngren and Sara Vallén sat in the flat across from Karlesson's and waited for something to happen. Evert Karlesson didn't seem to live a very interesting life. He got on his motorbike, drove for a while, and came back. A surveillance car followed him everywhere, except for a couple of times when they hadn't been able to keep up with him. He had taken some time off work, but he didn't seem to be doing anything special. Every day when he came home he sat down in front of his computer to watch what the surveillance unit thought to be porn. And he masturbated. Some days, multiple times a day. Then he rode off on his motorcycle and came back. Other than that, nothing happened.

Nobody else entered or left his flat. Sara suddenly heard the sound of a motor. They hadn't seen Karlesson since they missed him that Saturday. Not even in his flat.

"Did you hear that?" she asked Torsten.

"Yes, but where is it coming from? It didn't sound like it came from the courtyard next door."

They heard the sound of what they thought was a motorbike again. Sara leaned closer to the window and looked to the right. She saw the back of a black motorcycle disappear around the corner of Grönegatan, heading towards Drottensgatan.

"Was that him?" she said, and turned to Venngren.

"I'm not sure," Torsten Venngren said, and looked at his boss. He seemed disappointed. "We haven't seen him come home or leave today. It could've been someone else."

"You're right," Sara said, and stared at the corner where the motorcycle had just disappeared. She bit her lip.

"But what the heck," she said. "Do you think he's on to us? Do you think he knows he is being watched? What do you say?"

"Maybe, it's hard to know how much attention people pay to their surroundings. But it might be fair to assume that a man of his sort is more observant than most," Torsten said.

Sara nodded, her eyes fixed on Karlesson's flat.

"I want to have a look in his flat. I feel nervous about this."

She picked up her phone and called Prosecutor Baum. Torsten looked at her curiously. She moved her hands as much when she spoke on the phone as she did when she talked to someone who was standing in front of her. She listened and nodded as the person at the other end of the line spoke. Then she hung up.

"We'll wait a bit longer," she said.

Torsten felt a knot in his stomach.

"Baum thinks we'll ruin everything if we go in now without any real evidence. It's all circumstantial," Sara continued.

She took a deep breath and leaned against the wall by the window. Her body language told Torsten that she would wait there for an eternity if needed.

There was no sign of Karlesson. Not that day, and not the following day. He seemed to have gone missing, but his motorcycle was still parked in the courtyard.

# 46

He paced back and forth in the flat. He knew that they were on to him. And he knew that they were watching him. He noticed the unnatural movements behind him and in the corner of his eye. He felt them and knew that he couldn't escape their watching eyes. He desperately started packing; threw everything into a bag. He thought about packing his diving suit but decided to leave it behind. He probably wouldn't be able to dive for a while. He sighed. The plan for the summer had been to pick up diving again after a long break from the activity. But he left the diving suit on its hanger.

He snuck out of the flat, locked the door, and left the house through the basement. He exited the building a few doors further up the street, without looking back. It was dark outside and he could bike through town without being noticed. Once he got to the building, he parked his bike in the basement and made his way up to the flat without anyone seeing him. His mother hadn't lived there for years, but he had kept paying her rent—just in case he ever needed it. He did now. Nobody knew about this place. No mail was sent there and nobody came to visit. Except for the people he invited. And it was basically just one person.

He put on some coffee and sat down by the kitchen table. He stared at the clear summer sky. He felt calm.

He knew that it was all going to be okay. He would leave town as soon as he could. He would go far away, where they couldn't find him—where nobody knew who he was. He would connect with new people—people who could give him what he wanted. *Maybe Thailand*, he thought. *Or maybe the Baltics?* Thailand felt more tempting. It was warmer and people were cute and petite. Both the boys and the girls. He felt a tingle between his legs. He got up, walked into his bedroom, and reached for the box underneath the TV. He pulled out an old VHS tape. The cover gave away the content of the video. He licked his lips. He felt a pulsating feeling between his legs.

He pushed the tape into the VHS player and sat down in the armchair in front of the TV. He lifted himself up slightly and pulled down his trousers.

# 47

Sara, Rita, and Torsten stood outside Evert Karlesson's door. Sara stood to the left and Rita positioned herself behind Sara, who rang the doorbell. Not a sound was heard from the flat. They were all looking for Karlesson and his picture had been posted on the internet. Prosecutor Baum had finally agreed to approach Karlesson and allow the team to search his flat, whether he was at home or not. The waiting had started to get on everyone's nerves.

Sara rang the doorbell again and then she knocked on the door. Still nothing. She banged on the door with her fist. When nothing happened, she leaned down and looked through the letter box. There was a pile of mail still on the doormat. A stale smell found its way into her nostrils. She tried to get a better look into the flat when she spotted a pair of legs dangling from the ceiling. She flinched.

"What the . . . ?!" she screamed.

The other two stared at her.

"What?" Rita said.

"There's someone hanging from the ceiling!" Sara gasped. "We have to kick in the door. Do we have a crowbar in the car?"

"I'll check," Torsten said, and rushed off.

Rita leaned down to have a look.

"Can you see it?" Sara asked.

"Yes, shit. There goes one suspect," Rita said, and shook her head.

"Yes, what a miss. What a horrible miss." Sara shuddered. "That's why we haven't seen him for days."

Torsten came running with a crowbar and quickly got the door open.

They rushed in—and came to a halt when they saw the diving suit hanging on the coat hanger.

"But what the . . ." was all Torsten Venngren could say. He let out a quiet, bubbling giggle, which quickly turned into roars of laughter. Tears started trickling down his cheeks. The two women stared at him.

"Torsten . . ." Sara said. She didn't know what else to say. Then she started laughing too. It was liberating. Rita joined in. They laughed until they all cried. They were relieved, and the absurd situation was just too much to handle.

Once they had gathered themselves, Rita walked into one of the rooms.

"Come and look," she shouted to the others.

Her colleagues came into the room. It was full of newspapers and videos. A computer was standing on a desk. It was turned on. But there was nobody in the flat.

"Pretty much all of this is child pornography. And look at this." Rita held up a photo album. "It's full of pictures of children," she said. "Naked. Posing."

Sara felt a shiver down her spine. Bloody disgusting.

She studied the pictures and realised that they weren't real photos but cut-outs from magazines. The children looked foreign, and judging by the backgrounds, the photos weren't taken in Sweden. The Baltics, Russia, and somewhere in Asia, maybe Thailand.

Sara wanted to look through the computer, but her experience told her it was a bad idea to do so before the technicians arrived. Someone who lacked experience always risked contaminating the evidence. It was vital for the forensics team that nobody touch anything before they had examined the crime scene.


Ove Ovesson came alone.

"The others are busy somewhere else," he said, to answer Sara's silent question.

Ovesson started the computer and navigated through its content.

"Here," he said. "Do you see who this is?"

Sara and Rita leaned closer to the computer. It was a short video sequence of a girl with an erect penis in her mouth. The girl stared into the camera with empty eyes.

"Kajsa Lindahl!" Rita exclaimed.

Another girl, whose face they couldn't see, showed her vagina to the camera.

Sara looked away, put her hand on Ove's shoulder, and walked to the front door. She felt like throwing up. She found it hard to keep it together.

She called Jonny and told him to come to Grönegatan. Another unit joined them to help clear the flat of things that seemed relevant to Kajsa's murder—and to the obvious child pornography offence.

"Who is the girl whose face you can't see?" Sara asked her colleagues when she returned.

"I don't know. Maybe Josefin Elvebrandt?" Rita suggested. "It could be her, right?"

"Yes, it's a possibility. Or it could be some other girl. Whoever, really."

Sara had a look around the home of the man who was a paedophile, and probably a murderer. There wasn't a lot of furniture in the flat, only a couple of armchairs, a glass table, and an old orange sofa. A kitchen table and two chairs. A bed. Everything smelled bad. Dirty. The kitchen and the bathroom were in bad shape and truly nasty. *This place hasn't been cleaned in ages*, she thought as she wandered around the flat. She moved carefully, avoiding touching anything that could tell them who had been in the flat.

"I wonder what he gave the girls for that." Sara was mostly talking to herself, but the others could hear her.

"Well, I have no idea." Torsten shook his head. He had a hard time imagining why any healthy, young girl would agree to a thing like that.

"Money, drugs, more money?" Rita was obviously very upset. "What a creep," she said, and pulled a face. "I wonder if he's in touch with Rodney Ritger too."

Sara thought about that thing in the back of her head—the boy who kept calling—but didn't say anything. As an emergency buddy, she was bound by professional secrecy. But still . . .

"Yes, it really makes you wonder. Shouldn't there be footage of him too, in that case?" Sara said. "Please, Ove, make sure to copy the hard drive as soon as possible."

"Of course," Ove said. "I'll get it done the moment I get back to the office. I'll get my computer technician on it immediately."

"And we have to find Rodney Ritger," Sara said. "We need to interrogate him. It should have happened yesterday. Isn't it strange that the surveillance unit hasn't seen him, by the way? How is it even possible?"

Sara wasn't expecting an answer. Instead, she put on a pair of plastic gloves and helped Ovesson secure evidence.

"Ove, get over here," she called as she dug through a rubbish bin in the kitchen. "Look what I found here!"

She carefully held up a T-shirt and a pair of jeans. It looked like the clothes had just been washed, but there were stains on them that hadn't come out. The stains were brown, almost rust-coloured.

"Not a very careful man, this Karlesson," Ovesson said. "My guess—and I think it's a pretty good guess this time—is that those are bloodstains, and that the blood is Kajsa Lindahl's."

Ovesson looked satisfied. Sara was satisfied too.

"I think you might be right. And my guess is that Karlesson washed these clothes after the murder and then threw them in the trash when he realised that the stains wouldn't come out. Not very careful, indeed."

Sara put each item of clothing in a separate bag.

When Rita and Sara came back to the police station, their colleagues applauded them. It felt great. Regional Police Chief Beatrice Larsson came in and congratulated them on a job well done.

"It's not every day that we catch a paedophile. Now we just have to find him," she said, and shook Sara's and Rita's hands before she left again.

"Karlesson won't be able to stay hidden from us forever. Isn't it strange how coincidence can take you down new paths when you least expect it?" Sara said once Beatrice Larsson had left the room.

"Yes, and I must say that this feels pretty great," Rita said, "although the whole situation is obviously horrendous."

"I hope we can identify the other girl too," Sara said. "Maybe you were right when you suggested Josefin . . ." She frowned. "Because who else could it be? They were best friends. Also, I have a feeling that Josefin is hiding something important from us."

"Have we found Rodney Ritger yet?" Jörgen asked. He was standing next to them in a slightly awkward pose with one foot pressed against the shinbone of his other leg, as if he was practising his balance skills.

Sara looked at him and giggled. He was a strange man, Jörgen Berg. But she liked him. She liked her whole team a lot.

"No, not yet. But we'll find him, I promise."

Prosecutor Åke Baum decided to issue a warrant for Evert Karlesson's arrest, and Sara felt very happy about the decision. They were finally closing in on a result.

# 48

Sara held her breath and opened the monolithic doors to the beautiful white church in Dalby. It was the Nordic region's oldest remaining stone church.

She stepped inside. There was a white coffin at the front of the church and it was surrounded by more flowers than Sara had ever seen at a funeral. The air was heavy with grief. Kajsa Lindahl's parents sat in the front row, joined by Kajsa's sister and two older couples. None of them moved. Not a neck was bent, not a sound was made. All that was heard in the church was the sad melody of the organ. Sara recognised it as Tomaso Albinoni's *Adagio*.

In the middle of the ocean of youths, Josefin cried so hard that her whole body trembled—as if she was crying for every single person in the church.

After the musical piece, the minister started speaking. Her voice was gentle. She spoke about violence and the loneliness of our time. About love between people and the need for support and comfort. And she spoke about being grateful for what life gives you. For the time you get to spend together with the people you love.

A young man stood and walked up to the organ. He started singing a beautiful song. His voice was deep.

The church was full of young people. They were probably Kajsa's friends from different parts of her life—one part of which had been worse for her than the others.

Sara wished that someone in the dead girl's family would show a sign of their grief. Just as she had finished her thought, she heard a scream. Kajsa Lindahl's sister had rushed over to the white coffin and thrown herself on top of it, screaming hysterically. People started squirming in their seats, unsure of what to do about this sudden display of emotions.

The girl was still lying on top of the coffin, but she wasn't screaming anymore. The church was silent. There was no comfort to be found.

Sara had one final look at the people who had gathered to say goodbye to Kajsa. Then she left the church silently. The moment she opened the heavy church doors, fresh air hit her face. She took a deep breath and jumped into her old Saab. But for some reason, she couldn't get herself to start the engine. After a while, the church bells rang and people started exiting the church to gather on the gravelled path in front of it. Some of them wiped their tears and most of them looked relieved to leave the church, as if it had been a prison.

The Lindahl family were the last ones to walk through the church doors. They were all holding hands. Kajsa's sister looked tense. Her mascara was smeared across her face. Kajsa's parents were staring ahead with empty eyes. As if nothing could save them from the darkness now.

Sara called District Police Chief Bengt Allin. He was a man in his fifties and had been Sara's boss for many years, back when she first arrived in Malmö. If it hadn't been for him, she would probably have moved away from there a long time ago. Now Bengt had been transferred to Lund because of the reorganisation, just like Sara. Still, they hadn't seen each other for ages.

Sara had made up her mind. They had to interrogate Kajsa's classmates again.

"It'll mean a bunch of work, but we have other questions to ask them now. It's about the pornographic footage that we've found. I'll send you some material and the questions I want to ask."

"We'll take care of it. I'm sure we can get the information we need. If the students know anything, that is," Bengt Allin said.

Sara was just about to end the call when he spoke again.

"Oh, and there is one more thing. Malva Gran has taken a couple of days off, but she handed me a USB containing photos of the crime scene in Lund City Park. She forgot to send it over before and asked me to get it to you. But then I forgot too, up until now. I apologise."

"That's fine," Sara said, sounding somewhat irritated. "Send me the photos. Or no, actually, I'll swing by to get them when I'm back in Lund. And don't worry about Josefin Elvebrandt. I want to interrogate her myself."

"Okay, see you later then. You're always welcome here," Bengt said, and Sara could almost hear him smiling.

Sara carefully backed out of the parking space and drove off. She felt like an uninvited guest at the funeral—as if her presence there was inappropriate. Once she got back to Lund, she felt better. The beauty of the countryside didn't sit well with funerals. Everything looked so much sadder against the backdrop of a landscape in full bloom. She walked up the stairs and through the glass doors on the first floor of the police station.

# 49

The girl sat silently by the kitchen table. She had just returned from her best friend's funeral. Her eyes nervously wandered between Rita Anker and Sara Vallén. A tiny bead of sweat rested on her upper lip. Her gaze was unsteady.

Rita and Sara were silent. The ticking of the clock on the wall echoed throughout the kitchen.

"No," the girl said, staring straight ahead with empty eyes. "I've never heard of him. What was his name again?"

"Evert Karlesson," Sara Vallén said, and smiled. "And you're sure?"

"I have no idea who he is," Josefin Elvebrandt said, but she didn't look very confident.

"Absolutely sure?"

"Yes."

"But we know that Kajsa met with him. How come you, who are . . . were Kajsa's best friend, aren't aware of who she met?"

"We didn't spend every moment together," the girl said, staring at Sara Vallén.

"No, but as I understand it, you girls told each other everything?" Sara remained calm. The girl's body language told her more than her words.

"Yes," Josefin said. She looked down for a second, and then up again.

"But not everything. Definitely not everything."

"Okay," Sara said. "I understand. Can you tell me again about Kajsa as a person?"

"She was the nicest girl in the world. Very intelligent. Funny, exciting. Kind, always kind."

"Was she the same this year as last year?" Sara Vallén asked.

"What do you mean?" The girl was obviously suspicious now.

"I'm wondering if something might have happened to Kajsa, something that changed her," Sara Vallén proposed.

The girl studied her as if she was trying to figure out what she wanted. Then it looked as if she had made her mind up, and Sara listened carefully.

"She was sick of school," Josefin said, looking relieved for a second.

"Yes, that happens," Sara said as casually as possible. "And how did she express this?"

"That's not really something you express," Josefin said, refusing to understand the question.

"Yes, I think it is. How did she show you that she was sick of school?"

"She didn't study for the tests and she wasn't as friendly to the other kids in class. In the beginning, she was so nice and helpful, but this year she distanced herself from the rest of the class. She liked our mentor, Lena Johannesson. She did. But not the other teachers."

*Right, the mentor*, Rita thought.

"Was she in love with Martin Lingryd?" Rita asked carefully. Up until now, she had been watching the interview in silence.

"She liked him last year, but not lately. She thought he was a loser. She preferred older guys. Or not like, older. But guys in their twenties."

It was obvious that she was trying to smooth over what she had just said, but it was too late. Sara Vallén knew she had to keep the girl talking.

"So, she was mostly interested in older guys. Did she have a boyfriend?"

"No, she didn't want a boyfriend," Josefin said, and shook her head.

"Did Kajsa take any drugs?" Sara could tell that Josefin wasn't prepared for her question.

"No," she said quietly. "I'm not sure."

Sara and Rita looked at each other, satisfied with how the interview had developed. It wasn't really what was said that was important, but what was implied.

"Okay," Sara said. "I think that's all for now. Before we finish, I'll let you look at some photos. I want you to tell us what you think about them."

Rita Anker put twelve photos on the table. It was the same set of photos they had shown the curator at the botanic garden.

The girl's hand trembled as she picked up the photos one at a time. Both Sara and Rita studied her reactions carefully.

Suddenly, Josefin flinched. She immediately gathered herself, but stayed silent. Then she looked at the next photo. The photo that had made her react was a photo of a slightly younger Evert Karlesson.

Sara wrote something down in her notebook and turned to the microphone, stating that the girl had just looked at the photo without comment.

# 50

He calmly put his sneakers on. Grabbed his knife. The tool made him feel safe and strong. He was invincible. He took a detour and cut a white lilac branch off a bush. His knife could be used for many things. And nobody knew him. Nobody knew anything.

He ran. Fast, light, and with long strides. It wasn't very far to where he was going.

He felt happy, almost euphoric. And in a strange way, he felt relieved. It was time.

The entrance door was open. He walked into the basement and into the bike room. When a man entered to park his bike in the room, he leaned over another bike, pretending to fix something on it. The man muttered something and left without closing the door completely behind him.

When he heard the basement door close, the boy smashed the light in the ceiling and positioned himself in the corner—waiting for her.

# 51

Lena Johannesson felt annoyed. She knew that a bike ride would help. She walked into the basement and just as she was about to turn the corner towards the bike room, she ran into a man. He came rushing around the corner and Lena jumped and let out a surprised little scream.

"Oops," he said, and hurried past her.

She watched him as he ran up the stairs. He wasn't a neighbour. Unless he'd moved in recently, of course . . . But nobody had moved out, as far as she knew. Then again, he might have moved in with someone who was already living in the building.

She put her key in the lock and realised that the door wasn't closed properly. *Careless*, she thought. *This is how bikes get stolen.*

She tried turning on the light, but nothing happened. There was always something broken in the building. Why couldn't things just work?

Suddenly, she heard a scratching sound, as if someone was pulling something metallic against the concrete floor.

She walked backwards towards the door and the light. Then she felt someone breathing behind her, and the hair on the back of her neck stood up. She spun round and gasped, but before she could scream, a big hand was placed over her mouth. Her hair was pulled back and she could feel a man's breath on her face.

*This is where I die*, she thought.

He forced her to lie down on the ground. She was on her back now and his hand was still covering her mouth. She felt dizzy. She couldn't see anything, but felt his hand and his sweet, stale breath.

He lay down on top of her. The weight of his body was too much for her to handle, and she passed out.

When she woke up again, he was no longer lying on top of her. He had removed his hand from her mouth. She gasped for air. *Now*, she thought. *Now I have to scream*. But she couldn't make a sound.

He waved something in front of her face, something shiny. Then, everything turned black.

# 52

Olof Svensk came home around 9:30 p.m. He was surprised to find the flat quiet and dark when he opened the door. Sure, it was still light outside, but it was dark enough to at least turn a couple of lights on at home. He called out for Lena, but nobody answered him. He walked around the flat but found no sign of where she could be. Her new summer sandals were still in the hallway, so at least she wasn't out with her girlfriends. Somehow this realisation made him worry.

He kept looking for clues. She normally didn't go anywhere without telling him. They had a fight earlier that day and he thought that maybe the argument had something to do with her sudden disappearance. She had called him, upset about him working late—again. She had asked him what was the point of being a couple if they never saw each other. In a way, he understood her. But he wanted to impress his boss, and work was much more fun than being home all night.

But no, this wasn't like Lena at all.

Where could he look next? Maybe he should check the key cabinet?

The key to her bike was missing.

He stayed up waiting for her until late but decided to go to bed around midnight. He fell asleep, but woke up again at 4 a.m. Her side of the bed was still empty. He was overwhelmed with unease. *I might have to call the police,* he thought. But before he did that, he decided to call Lena's best friend, Sofia.

"What?" Sofia said over the phone. She sounded confused and it was obvious that he had woken her up.

"Hi, this is Olof," he repeated patiently.

"Are you insane?" Sofia said. "Why would you call here at 4 a.m. in the middle of the week?" She sounded confused and slightly annoyed.

"Lena is missing. She never came home last night. I thought you might know where she is?" he said, trying to sound less worried than he really was.

"No, Olof. I have no idea. When did she leave?"

"I don't know. She called me around 6 p.m., but I was working late."

He heard Sofia scoff and realised that Lena had probably shared her frustrations about their relationship with her friend.

"Did she tell you that she had received a couple of strange emails lately?" she said after a pause.

Olof felt dizzy.

"No, she hasn't mentioned it."

"I'll be over in a little bit," Sofia said, and hung up.


Olof called the hospital, and then the police. When he told the officer on the phone about the situation, he had promised to send a car over shortly. Strangely, he had asked him if Lena was suicidal. And strangely, he hadn't been able to answer him.

# 53

The bike room? What do you mean? Why would she hide out in the bike room?"

"No, that's not what I mean. That's where she keeps her bike, so I thought we should start from the beginning," Peter Matsson said, and stood up. Malva Gran followed his example.

The operator who sent them to this address had said it was probably better to check in on the caller than to ignore it. The woman was probably just annoyed with her husband and had probably left the flat to punish him, or maybe to think. Peter thought that she was out for revenge while Malva believed she just needed some time to clear her head. But they both agreed that the fact that the couple had an argument earlier that day made it all a bit more complicated.

They walked down into the basement together, unlocked the bike room, and tried turning on the light. It didn't work. Peter lit his flashlight but turned it off right away. They had both seen it.

There was a woman on the floor. Her body was twisted and the back of her head bashed in. There was blood around the woman's head and her tongue was on the floor next to her.

Malva managed to get Sofia Lärka and Olof Svensk out of the basement before they had a chance to see it.

"You need to wait here," she said as professionally as she could.

"What was that? Was that Lena?" Olof Svensk exclaimed, almost screaming. He tried to push past Malva, who blocked his way.

"You'll have to wait here for a while, Olof."

Malva turned to Sofia Lärka and asked her to take Olof away from there. Sofia was shocked. She had seen. But she understood the police officer's request and put a hand on Olof's shoulder.

"Come on, Olof. Let the officers do their job."

Olof lowered his head. Then he nodded and followed Sofia back to the flat. When they closed the door behind them, Olof Svensk sat down on the floor and cried until his big body trembled like a leaf.

"It's my fault," he whimpered through his tears.

"No, it's not your fault." Sofia Lärka struggled to keep it together, but knew she had to—for Olof. She picked up her phone, called her husband, and asked him to come over immediately.

"I'll explain later," she said, and hung up.


Once again, Sara Vallén was woken in the middle of the night.

And once again, Malva Gran and Peter Matsson were the officers at the scene. Poor souls.

She gave Matsson a pitiful smile when he came out of the basement.

"We have cordoned it off—pretty much all the way around Sofiaparken. A K-9 unit and the forensics team are on their way. Shit, Sara, what is this? What kind of maniac are we talking about here?"

Sara reacted to him calling her by her name. Maybe she was overreacting, but she felt as if the tone was a bit too intimate and she was worried that he would expose their relationship. She shot him a serious look.

He nodded as if he understood.

"What do you have so far?" Sara asked.

"The tongue is cut out and her skull is crushed, but no cuts this time. We're not sure if she was raped. We found a lilac branch in her hand. The medical examiner is having a look at her before the body is sent off for an autopsy. Her partner is in their flat. Apparently, they had an argument earlier today. He called the woman's best friend, Sofia Lärka, at around 4 a.m. She was here when we got here. She has identified the victim. Lärka's husband is also here. This is turning into a bloody tourist attraction. The victim is a teacher by the name of Lena Johannesson. Lärka tells us that she has received threatening emails lately. I can't tell you if there is a connection between her and the girl who died last week. Maybe it's a copycat."

Suddenly, everything felt too connected for Sara to be able to ignore it.

Lena Johannesson was Kajsa's mentor. She had received threats via email, just like Kajsa. The modus operandi was basically the same this time, except for the apparent lack of sexual assault. She felt angry. Jörgen Berg had never made the interrogation with Lena Johannesson happen, even though she had asked him to. Clumsy.

"Thanks, Matsson, but I don't think so. As you know, we haven't given the press any details, so there is no way that someone could know about the tongue or the lilac. I'll have a look at the victim and then talk to the partner, if possible."

*We can't rule him out as a suspect, even if it doesn't feel very likely*, she thought.

"He's in shock. Crying like a child," Peter Matsson said.

"This has to be the same perpetrator as the one who killed Kajsa Lindahl. There aren't too many people out there who cut off their victims' tongues," Sara continued as she walked down the basement stairs to have a look at the victim. Peter Matsson didn't hear Sara's last comment, but still felt just as offended as he had the first time they met.

"Oh, and when Rita and Torsten get here, ask them to come to see me up in the flat."

The medical examiner studied the dead body as if it didn't bother him at all that he was examining a dead woman with her head bashed in and her tongue cut out.

"Well, she has probably been here for a while. I find it strange that nobody has seen her until now. An incredible amount of blunt trauma. Judging by the injuries, the perpetrator has probably used a pipe of some kind. And then probably a knife, to cut the tongue out. The cut is clean and the tongue is a thick muscle. Therefore, I assume the knife must have been very sharp. There are a lot of blood vessels in the tongue. As you can see, there is a lot of blood here," he continued, and pointed at the floor.

"Yes, I can see that," Sara said. She felt as if she had seen enough.

"I'm waiting for the forensics team," the medical examiner said. "When will they be here?"

"Soon. It's best if we don't move her until they get here," Sara said. "If possible, they want to have a look at the crime scene before we touch anything."

"Okay. Have we cordoned everything off to avoid inquisitive neighbours?" he asked.

"Of course," Sara said, and left the bike room. She walked up to the victim's flat and rang the doorbell. *I wonder if she's the owner of the flat, as her name appears before his on the letter box*, Sara thought, and heard footsteps on the other side of the door.

A woman in her thirties opened the door. Her eyes were red.

Sara introduced herself and Sofia Lärka asked her to come in. She offered Sara coffee and for once, she said yes. She hadn't had time to have her morning coffee yet.

# 54

I don't really know much," Sofia said. "All I know is that Lena was pretty unhappy with Olof. She hated that he was always gone. He worked a lot. He wasn't having an affair," she added when she saw how Sara looked at her.

Sara Vallén and Sofia Lärka sat in the kitchen while Sofia's husband, Erik, sat with Olof Svensk in the living room.

"You said something about threats on her computer?" Sara said.

"Well, I don't know how serious they were, but I know she found them creepy. She actually forwarded them to me to show me. But she hasn't told Olof about them."

"We'll have to check Lena's computer to see if she saved these messages. There might be more threats on there that she hasn't told you about. The easiest thing to do is probably for me to take a copy of your phone. We'll bring the computer in anyway."

Sofia burst into tears. Sara felt that it was enough for now. She put a hand on Sofia's elbow to help her back to the room where her husband was waiting. He stood up and hugged his wife. He said nothing. *The right type*, Sara thought.

"Can I talk to you for a moment?" she asked Olof Svensk. "It won't take long."

Sofia and Erik Lärka got up and left the living room.

Sara tried to keep it short, but she had to go through the chain of events carefully. Olof Svensk started talking but cried so hard that it was difficult to make out what he was saying.

"It's my fault," he said. "My fault. If we hadn't had that argument, she wouldn't have had the idea to go on that bike ride. I'm sure of it."

His voice was full of grief as he told her what a horrible partner and human being he was. Sara tried to calm him down, but no matter how many kind words she used, he wouldn't stop blaming himself. Not even when she switched tactics and ordered him to stop.

There was no point talking to him right now. Either way, she found it hard to believe that he was the murderer. She would look into him later to be sure. And he would still have to provide a DNA sample.

"Would you like to help me?" she asked him. "I need to access your computer and look through Lena's emails. Do you think you could help me with that?"

He nodded. The inbox was empty.

"You can restore it," Olof managed to say through his tears.

"You can? I understand that you are going through something horrible here, but it's important I get to see those messages. Then I'll send a group of techs here so that they can take a copy of the computer. They will also go through Lena's belongings."

Olof Svensk worked on the computer for a while and he made it look easy, at least to Sara. Before she knew it, Lena's inbox was restored. She immediately noticed a couple of anonymous emails with very disturbing content. Sara took notes of the messages in her notebook and decided to leave the rest to the forensics team.

"Who the hell would send threats like that to Lena? Do you think it's the murderer?" Olof was pale and he clenched his jaw.

"Is it the murderer?" he asked again.

"I don't know," Sara said. "We have to look into it before I can say anything."

She turned to Olof, who was now trembling like a leaf. Sara instantly made up her mind. Physical contact usually had a calming effect on people, so she put her arms around him and held him until he stopped shaking.

"Do you have anyone who we can call for you? We can drive you to the hospital. They can help you get some sleep."

"I n-need to get out of here. Th-the hospital. Thanks," he stuttered.

# 55

How come we haven't done better than this?" Regional Police Chief Beatrice Larsson said sternly. "Another murder, probably the same perpetrator," she continued.

"Calm down," Sara Vallén said, and stood up next to her boss with her arms crossed. "How could we have stopped this murder from happening?"

"By finding the perpetrator," Beatrice Larsson said, slightly calmer. "Isn't it Evert Karlesson?"

Sara Vallén stood in front of her, radiating the type of authority that came from intelligence and competence, rather than a title. Beatrice Larsson took a step back.

"We are working on it," she said calmly. "We are working around the clock, doing everything we can. Right now, we are looking for Evert Karlesson, leaving no stone unturned. We just don't know where he is. And also, we aren't one hundred per cent sure he is our guy, even if so much points in that direction. What makes me upset is that I explicitly asked for an interrogation of Lena Johannesson. This interrogation never took place. Now we have a dead mentor who won't be able to help us solve Kajsa's murder. But I must say that it feels unlikely that Karlesson would have a relationship with Johannesson. Why would he kill her? It can't have been sexual as he is obviously attracted to children and young girls."

Beatrice nodded at Sara but didn't say anything. She left the room, muttering to herself.

Sara turned to her team and then she looked at Jörgen Berg, who was obviously ashamed.

"Well?" she said.

"I'm terribly sorry. I simply had too much to do."

"It doesn't matter now, but I assume you realise how serious this is. The interview with Lena Johannesson might have given us answers that we will now have to find ourselves."

Jörgen nodded and sighed.

If there had been tension in the group before, it was nothing compared to the tension in the room now. They all had their heads lowered, staring at the table. It looked as if nobody in the room could muster the energy to lift their gaze. They looked defeated. Rita looked calm but tired and Torsten tried to keep up morale by discussing tactics for the upcoming interrogations. Now they would have to talk to a whole apartment building—a whole block. Hundreds of people had been or would be interviewed, including Lena's partner and her closest friends and family. Uniformed officers and detectives had spent their morning knocking on doors in the area. They had all followed basic procedure when it came to door-to-door interviews. This procedure normally resulted in the answers needed for the preliminary investigation. Most of the people in the area hadn't seen or heard anything interesting, but a couple of them had shared information that could be of value. Now it was up to Torsten, Jonny, and Jörgen to interrogate these people further. Jörgen had his work cut out for him later. The documents had piled up during the day and it was hard to keep everything in order.

Rita's task was to talk to Olof and the school where Lena worked. Sara would join her. Olof had been admitted to hospital as he was simply too shocked to be on his own, according to the doctor.

"By the way, I talked to Göransson, the medical examiner," Sara said. "A cut-out tongue causes a lot of bleeding. The only reason Kajsa didn't bleed to death at the scene was that she received medical attention so quickly. Unfortunately, she died from her other injuries, but it's still relevant. In Lena's case, it's hard to say if she died from the blunt trauma to her head, or if she bled out. The object that Kajsa was beaten with was long and narrow. According to Göransson, a similar object had been used to assault Johannesson. This is just a preliminary assessment, of course. It'll be another week or so before we have all the answers. If you ask me, it doesn't really matter what she died from. Either way, she was murdered, and by the looks of it, we are looking at the same murderer as the one who killed Kajsa. But why murder Lena Johannesson—a seemingly innocent teacher? That's the question."

Everyone in the room fell silent again.

Suddenly, Sara thought about the boy who had called her at the emergency buddy centre. His whispering but enraged words echoed in her head: *Never, she won't get it. And she knows too much anyway.* She wrote his words down in her notebook.

"One thing is certain, and that is that Josefin Elvebrandt knows who Evert Karlesson is," Sara said. "She denied it during the interrogation, but she reacted when she saw the photo of him."

"Maybe this means that she is the other girl from those videos?" Torsten said.

"Yes, that seems pretty likely. What else could she be hiding? Kajsa is dead and doesn't need her loyalty anymore."

Rita looked through copies of interrogation transcripts and finally found the one from their interview with Josefin—the one with the photo line-up.

"The interrogations didn't really give us any explicit answers," she said, "but Sara made some important notes about the girl's reactions. She was very nervous to start with but gained some confidence as the interview went on."

"That doesn't have to mean that she lied though. Research tells us that we are exceptionally bad at exposing lies," Jörgen said with a little laugh.

"Yes, you're right," Sara said. "But I studied her subtle reactions, the ones that she wasn't even aware of herself. I've done my research too, you see."

They all laughed, relieved that the mood in the room was slightly less depressing.

"Okay, okay." Jörgen laughed. "I just wanted to show off my knowledge." He stood up. "Well, it's time to get back to work."

Sara raised her hand and made him sit down again.

"Josefin confirmed that Kajsa had changed during the last year. She told us that she was sick of school and acted less friendly towards her classmates. And apparently, she thought Martin Lingryd was a loser. She preferred older guys. Josefin acted somewhat strangely when this came up. Almost as if she had told us something that she shouldn't have. Many times, the things that are left unsaid are the things that give us the best clues. She wasn't a fan of us asking about drugs either. However, she mentioned that Kajsa seemed to trust her mentor, Lena Johannesson. Maybe that's our connection. Maybe she told her mentor something. Something about Karlesson. Maybe Karlesson found out?"

Sara Vallén looked down at the words in her notebook. She felt a shiver run down her spine.

"I have to think about this for a while," Sara said. I'll drive out to Ribersborg for a walk. I'll be back around lunchtime. I really need to think."

The others looked surprised.

"Can you give me a ride?" Rita asked. "I'm meeting with the firearms instructor in half an hour. This way, we don't need to take two cars."

Sara nodded.

# 56

The man was in the shower. The boy was pushed up against the wall.
"You're too tall now," the man said, obviously displeased. "It was better before."

The boy's eyes were empty. He couldn't feel pain anymore. He pressed his lips together. His ribs hurt and his back was marked by the leather belt that the man had used to punish him. He wasn't sure why he had been punished though. He always did what he was told.

"You know I love you, right?" the man said. "I'll make it good for you, afterwards."

The boy blinked. Everything was dark. Pitch black. And hate burned inside of him. It burned his brain and turned his heart into granite. *Or maybe marble?* he thought as part of him sat up in the corner of the ceiling, looking down at the rest of him. He could see it all from up there, as if the boy in the shower was someone completely different. As if it wasn't him. Now he didn't feel anything anymore—didn't care. Nothing hurt anymore, there was no pain. He was just a ghost, watching the man and the boy. He was nobody, just a body. He might as well have been dead.

When the man was done, he didn't say anything.

He pushed the boy out of the shower and kept washing off.

The boy took his clothes, got dressed, and walked towards the door. The scent of the lilacs in the vase on the kitchen table was overwhelming and made him feel nauseous. He wanted to get out of the horrible flat, away from the horrible man. Suddenly, every cell in his body ached. Just as he was about to sneak out the front door, the man came out of the bathroom.

"I'm going away soon and I'll let you know when I need your help," the man said.

The boy, who was as tall as the man, leaned over slightly as if he was expecting another lashing. The man didn't hit him again, but the boy knew that the belt could come flying through the air at any second. The boy shrugged his shoulders.

"Okay," he said, "I want to leave now."

"Go. I don't have time for you anyway," the man said. "I'll let you know when I need your help," he repeated.

The boy nodded and left quietly.

# 57

Is something bothering you?"

Rita had been wanting to ask Sara for a while now and, by the looks of it, the question caught her by surprise.

"Yes, this case is getting to me, I guess," she said unconvincingly.

"Yes, of course. But it's the same for all of us. I meant in your private life?"

Rita turned her head and smiled quickly at Sara. Then she turned her focus back to the road ahead.

"I don't know. I guess there has been some stuff going on privately. I can't tell you too much about it, but I've met someone. A man. I think I've fallen in love with him. He scares me and tempts me at the same time. I'm not sure what to do. I've decided not to see him again, and still, I can't stop thinking about him."

"So, you're hooked, even if you don't want to be?"

"Something like that. It takes a lot of energy and it's just so stupid," Sara said, and let out a growling noise.

Rita laughed.

"It really doesn't make sense that an intelligent person like you—or me for that matter—can turn into a complete idiot like this for a man."

"Yeah, you really wonder sometimes," Sara said, and took a couple of shallow breaths, followed by a couple of deep ones.

"I've even managed to promise myself not to allow him into my house, and I still let him in when he comes. The problem is that he won't stay and that he'll show up whenever he feels like it—and not as often as I would like him to. There is something strange about him. I think he's hiding something from me. But I'm not sure what."

"Maybe he is married?" Rita asked. Suddenly, she didn't sound as cheerful.

"He tells me that he got a divorce two years ago, but I'm not sure if it's true. He's acting strangely. I can't tell you what it is, but I know there is something off about him."

"It doesn't sound great. You never know with men though. Maybe he's just trying to hide the fact that he's in love with you?"

"I don't know. I doubt it. And if I'm being honest, it scares me."

Sara had decided to not tell Rita about Peter Matsson, but now she had already told her everything about him—except for his name. She must have suppressed her need to share everything with someone.

Finally, the question came: "Who is he?" Rita asked, pretending that it wasn't important.

"I can't tell you. For reasons that you've probably figured out by now."

"Oh, a colleague. I just hope that it's nobody from the old team."

"No, of course not," Sara said, feeling slightly offended.

"Okay, I won't force you to tell me who it is, I just hope that it all works out and that this whole thing won't cause you too much trouble."

Sara hesitated and looked up towards the sky to try to sort out her mind. Should she tell her friend? Maybe what really kept Sara from telling her was fear of how much—and what—Rita knew about Peter Matsson. If she told her, she would have to decide what to do next. She knew she wasn't capable of that at that moment, and it would only make her look even more stupid.

They had arrived at Davidshallstorg in Malmö. Rita stroked Sara's cheek and stepped out of the car.


The ocean breeze felt wonderful. Sara walked slowly along the water's edge. Movement had always meant power and speed to her—losing and generating energy, competing against others or yourself. She had always found it difficult to walk slowly.

*Never, she won't get it. She knows too much anyway.* The boy's words echoed in the back of Sara's mind. The connection felt clear, but she couldn't fit all the pieces of the puzzle together. The boy's hate towards the world, his dad, the "monster" and his teacher. It was too much to be a coincidence. Or was it?

Sara stopped for a second. The wind made her hair dance behind her, which felt nice. She rubbed her sore lower back for a moment, reached her arms up over her head, leaned back slightly, and stretched. She twisted her head to the right, and then to the left.

*How is it possible for a man like Evert Karlesson to just disappear?* she pondered. Malmö was a busy city full of life. But it was also full of problems like segregation, misery, and poverty. It wasn't exactly surprising that horrendous crimes like these took place in a city like Malmö. The level of frustration and aggression was high here. So, what was the difference between Malmö and Lund?

*Nothing,* she decided. People could be crazy, angry, disappointed, and feel let down everywhere. These feelings don't stem from a geographical place, but from a person's heart—or brain. *Lund,* she thought again, *is a different place than Malmö.* The vibe in Lund was different. The crimes that took place there were different from those in Malmö—crimes typical for a middle-class town. Better social control, higher level of education. Sara preferred Lund in certain ways, but she missed the ocean breeze.

*Maybe I should move to Malmö after all?* she thought. *At least the issues there are obvious and easy to spot. And then there is the ocean.*

She started thinking about her job as chief inspector and wondered how suitable she really was for the position. *Maybe I'm not as good at this as they believe I am—or, more importantly, I want to believe?* she thought. The wind was picking up now. It wasn't as warm as before. She saw the clouds sweeping in from the ocean. *Storm clouds,* she thought. She put her shoes on and pulled her sweater closer.

Sara got in the car and drove towards the police station at Davidshallstorg, where she had once started her career in southern Sweden as an investigator at the youth crime unit. *Just as beautiful as it has always been,* she thought. *Maybe I should've stayed here?* She got out of the car and as she walked up to the entrance she noticed that it was slightly warmer in the city, although the sky was almost completely covered with clouds now.

"Hey, Sara, I think it's going to rain," Rita said as she stepped out of the impressive door of the police station.

* * *

Sara drove back to Lund in silence. Rita looked at the yellow rapeseed fields on the side of the road.

"When I work as an emergency buddy, there is this boy who calls me. He isn't doing so well," Sara said, breaking the silence.

"Oh yeah?"

"He said something that I can't shake. But I might be reading too much into it."

"I'm listening," Rita said, and took her eyes off the fields.

"His father is beating him up, that much I know. But he also keeps mentioning someone who disgusts him. When I asked him if he has anyone to talk to, a teacher for example, he told me that she doesn't get it and that she already knows too much. He speaks quietly and starts stuttering when he gets upset. He is very angry, full of hate. What do you say? Could he be talking about Lena Johannesson?"

"Hard to say. And I assume he hasn't reported his dad to the police? Do you know who he is?"

"No, of course I don't. It's all anonymous. That's the point of the whole thing. And no, he has no interest in talking to the police. But do you think there could be a connection?"

"Where do these calls come from?"

"All across the country," Sara said, and the moment the words left her mouth, she felt less sure about the whole thing.

Rita chuckled.

"A lot of kids hate their teachers. I don't know. It could be connected somehow, I guess. But I mean, if the call could've come from anywhere in the country . . . Does he even have a southern accent?"

"Oh, I haven't even thought about that." Sara couldn't believe herself.

"Maybe make a mental note of it the next time he calls," Rita said.

# 58

"Evert Karlesson hasn't showed up at work, although he has run out of holiday days. His boss is pissed off," Sara told Jörgen.

She got up, twisted her hands, and started pacing back and forth. *Someone should have seen him, somewhere,* she thought to herself. She followed the movement of Jörgen's hand as he emptied his coffee cup. Her own cup was on the table in front of her, half full. She hadn't experienced any problems with gastritis for years, but now it was flaring up again. *Shit,* she thought.

"I'm going to grab another cup of coffee," Jörgen said, and nodded towards Sara's cup. "Do you want any?"

"No," she replied at the same moment as Ovesson entered the room.

"Hey, those creepy emails we found on Kajsa Lindahl's computer—they are the same ones that were sent to Lena Johannesson. And it's impossible to trace the sender."

"But we can't overlook the connection, which is a good thing."

"We are going through the rest of Lena Johannesson's computer as we speak. It looks like she's been in a chat room of some kind. But we haven't found anything relevant so far. We'll keep digging."

"And how about Karlesson's computer? Have you found anything relevant to the case? I mean, except for the pornographic content that we have already seen? Is there anything that implies he has been in contact with Kajsa Lindahl or Lena Johannesson, via email or any other way?"

"There is a mountain of photos and videos." Ovesson's tanned face turned into a disgusted grimace. "But when it comes to the threats that were sent to the two women, we haven't found anything. It seems a bit strange, if you ask me. But he has probably taken great care to cover any possible connection between himself and these women."

"Do you think he is the one who sent them those threats?"

"Maybe, but I've said it before and I'll say it again . . . Those threats feel quite juvenile and I doubt that a grown man has sent them. Evert Karlesson is our main suspect for Kajsa's murder, and by the looks of it, he also killed Lena. If a young person sent these threats, the connection between them and the two murders isn't very strong. It doesn't make sense to me."

"Yes, they are very childish and it doesn't make sense to me either," Sara said. It annoyed her that she wasn't able to piece everything together. She started pacing back and forth in the room again. Ovesson stayed where he was, seemingly unaffected by his colleague's nerves.

"Did you find any more footage of the girl whose face we couldn't see?"

"Hard to say. But it seems to be the same girls over and over again—Kajsa and the girl without a face. There are a lot of videos, and it looks like this has been going on for a couple of years. We are looking through the material. It's not an easy task, but it looks like the videos have been filmed over a period of time. The girls' bodies are developing and their hairstyles change."

"It would be great if we could identify the other girl. She could be in danger."

"You're right. I'll get back to you as soon as I have something. By the way, we've sent some evidence to the NFC as well to see if we can get some DNA. The clothes are extremely interesting and there were dirty dishes in the flat and sperm stains on the sheets. When it comes to fingerprints, we have already determined that they belong to Karlesson and an unknown person. It could be anyone. But they're not the girl's prints."

"Great," Sara said.

"Super," Ovesson added, and walked away without making a sound. Sara never could get used to how quietly Ovesson moved. Sara Vallén was loud in every way imaginable. She took up a lot of space in a room and could definitely be seen and heard. She was aware that people around her found her annoying at times.

"And what about Malva Gran's photos? Wasn't something missing in them?" Sara called out after Ovesson, who came back.

"Oh, right. I forgot to tell you. Everything looks as it should, except for that cigarette butt. It's not in Gran's photos. It must have ended up on the ground after the photo was taken and before we arrived at the scene." Ove Ovesson looked perplexed. Sara felt furious.

# 59

"Close the door please," she said, and pointed to one of the chairs on the other side of her desk.

Sara wrote the time and date on the form in front of her. She was very aware of the fact that she wasn't allowed to perform a disciplinary interview without talking to the union first, so she decided to call this something else to get around the official procedure. She crossed the word *disciplinary* off the form and simply called the meeting an interview.

"You're a smoker, Jonny," she said. You and Torsten are the only ones who smoke. And Torsten doesn't smoke at work."

Jonny instantly realised that she was giving him an opportunity to come clean.

"The cigarette butt at the crime scene. It was yours, wasn't it?"

"I didn't throw a bloody cigarette butt there!" Jonny said angrily.

"Do you think I'm stupid? I know you don't like having me as your boss, but are you insane? Are you going to ruin a whole investigation, just because you don't like me? What's the most important thing in your position? Have you forgotten?" Sara was so angry that it looked like her eyes were on fire.

"Maybe I accidentally threw it there, but I didn't mean to," he said, sounding worried.

"You do understand that what you did is very serious, right?" Sara said, locking eyes with Jonny. He nodded. She made a note in her notebook.

"I won't report this as you admit to it."

He nodded again.

She saw a glimmer of hate in his eyes. It rattled her, but she shook it off quickly.

"It's one thing if you hate me—another thing if you ruin my investigation. I don't need you to love me, or even like me, but I need you to show me respect and not put this investigation at risk. You could've ruined both my career and your own. And I want you to understand something. If you try to take me down, I'll take you down with me. As far down as I can."

Once again, Sara felt so furious that she was worried she would actually explode. The man across from her suddenly changed his attitude. The hate in his eyes was gone and now he looked scared. For some reason, it made her feel great.

Jonny Svensson looked at his hands. He was sweating.

"I didn't mean to," he said.

"What?"

"I didn't mean to put the investigation at risk," Jonny said. He still wasn't looking at the chief inspector.

"In that case, I really don't understand how you've managed to survive or keep your job within the force for all these years. To throw a cigarette butt at a crime scene is just . . . unacceptable. It would've made more sense if you had done it to deliberately sabotage me."

"I said I didn't mean to. I guess I was so annoyed with you that I didn't really think clearly as I was smoking at the crime scene. I've never done anything like it before. It was just an impulse."

"So bloody stupid," Sara said.

"Sorry," Svensson said quietly. "I'm fucking sorry. I've been feeling horrible about that bloody cigarette butt."

"Are you telling me that you've known about this the whole time?"

"I said I'm sorry."

"Yes, you did. From now on, I expect you to show your colleagues the respect that they deserve. And you better do a great job from here on out."

Jonny stood up, walked over to the door, and turned around.

"I'm sorry. I'll do the best I can," he said.

Sara looked at her colleague. Judging by his body language, she had really got through to him.

"Great," she said. "Let's move on now. It'll be okay. The important thing is that you get it. Now we can assume that we are dealing with a sole perpetrator. I hope."

When Jonny had closed the door behind him, Sara raised her desk. She felt pleased. Maybe things would be better with Jonny now. Maybe she had finally made him realise that she wouldn't tolerate him being lazy or disrespectful. Maybe this was the best thing that could have happened.

# 60

How come we haven't interrogated Rodney Ritger yet?" Baum asked, interrupting Sara, who was telling him the story about the boy who called her every week.

"Because we don't know where he is. The surveillance unit hasn't seen him. And he's not in school. And it's not like we suspected him of anything to start with. It was more a question of a routine interrogation."

Baum said nothing.

"There is a reason why the calls to the emergency buddy centre are completely anonymous. Without this principle, most of these kids wouldn't call," Sara continued.

"Yes, I understand. It's problematic," Baum said. "But, based on what you've told me, we don't have a choice. Let's hope you can find him and interrogate him. But anyway, I have come to a decision, and I've decided that the call needs to be traced."

# 61

Sara was glad that she and Göran could plan the graduation party together. They had been sitting down together all evening, without one single argument. They agreed on most things and they had even agreed to share the cost of the party.

But even if everything was peaceful between the two of them, she found it hard to relax completely. She still worried about the investigation, even if she trusted her colleagues. She just couldn't stop thinking about the case.

Now and again, she glanced at her phone. No texts and no emails. There was so much going on now. But at the same time, she couldn't let her daughters down because of a case. She should be able to dedicate at least one night to them. One single night.

Göran and Sara hadn't really talked much lately, but things had felt better between the two of them. They had a common enemy. An enemy that had come for their son.

"Thanks for a good chat tonight," Göran said as he left.

"No, thank you," she answered him from the kitchen.

When he had closed the door behind him, Sara sat down by her computer and worked until she could barely keep her eyes open. She lay down on her bed. She was exhausted but couldn't possibly go to sleep as thoughts kept racing through her head. Her mind wandered from Johannes to the murders of Kajsa Lindahl and Lena Johannesson. Then

she thought about Evert Karlesson, what had been said during the interrogations so far, and the ongoing surveillance. She got up, drank some
water, and lay down on the sofa instead. She felt uneasy and lonely.
Maybe because her children weren't home. Johannes was staying at his
father's house for the night and Klara and Bella had travelled to Poland
for a couple of days with school.

When she opened the door, he was leaning against the door post. It
smelled like he had been drinking and alarm bells instantly went off in
Sara's head. He pushed past her and grabbed her, hard. She tried to get
out of his grip, but it only made him hold her tighter. He pressed his nose
against her neck and inhaled her scent.

"Mmmm," he said, and she could feel that he was struggling to keep
his balance. But only slightly.

"Come with me." She tried to make him move in the direction of the
kitchen. He reluctantly followed her, still with his arms wrapped around
her. Although she was pretty good at judo, she wasn't as strong as him,
and now she was at a disadvantage. She didn't like it but decided to let
it go for now.

"Kiss me," he said.

"Later." She managed to get him to sit down on a chair. He let go of
her and she walked over to the sink to get him a glass of water. Now she
was in control of the situation again and instantly felt more at ease. He
was just a normal, drunken man. She was used to those after many years
on the force.

"Here, drink."

"Why?" He looked at her, and she didn't recognise the look in his
eyes. It was cloudy, yet firm. She suddenly felt scared but forced herself
to ignore it.

"So that I can kiss you," she said, trying to sound calm.

"Okay, fine. But then you'll kiss me? 'Cos I'm the only man you kiss,
right?"

"Yes, of course, only you."

*What did he want out of this?* she thought, and clenched her teeth
until they hurt.

"Right, that's what they all say," he continued. "Women always say
one thing and do another."

*This is not the time to start an argument*, she thought, and decided to avoid his comment.

"Do you want a cup of coffee?" She tried to sound as sweet as possible in an attempt not to provoke him. Didn't she recognise this pattern?

"Hell no," he said. "I want a kiss. Now."

She leaned over and kissed him.

He bit her lip.

"Ow!" she said, and instinctively slapped him on the side of his head while she pulled away from him. He grabbed her, faster than she thought he was able to, and pulled her close. He kissed her again, without biting her this time. She felt a bit calmer, but she was still anxious. He stood up. Then he pulled her close and kissed her with passion. He pressed against her and she tried to push him away, which seemed to only make him more excited. He pushed his body even closer to hers and she panicked. She forgot everything she knew about defending herself. One of his hands found her breast and he squeezed it until it hurt. She desperately tried to get away from him but the more she pulled, the harder he held her—the harder he squeezed her breast. She screamed. Then, he let go of her breast and hit her hard with his fist, right in the stomach. She gasped for air and fell backwards.

"What the fuck are you doing?" she screamed.

"You whore! Who have you been fucking? Why don't you want to fuck me?"

She stayed on the floor, curled up into a ball. Would he kick her now? She didn't answer him. She just lay there. *Brave, strong Sara*, she heard a sarcastic voice say in the back of her head. But she didn't dare move. Couldn't move.

"Answer me!" he screamed again. "Answer me, you whore! You dirty slut."

She kept quiet and clenched her jaw to stop herself from crying.

The next thing she knew, he had rushed out of the kitchen. She heard the front door slam shut so hard that it didn't close but flew open again. She slowly stood up and tiptoed into the hallway, terrified that he would be there. But the hallway was empty. She closed the door, locked it, and dropped to the floor like a sack of potatoes. Then she started crying. Her whole body trembled and her stomach started cramping. She cried until she ran out of tears.

# 62

He hasn't even touched his accounts. I asked his bank to let us know immediately if any transactions took place," Jörgen said.

"This is so strange." Sara shook her head.

"Do you think he's dead?" Rita Anker asked.

"No, why would he be?" Sara shot Rita a surprised look.

"Why not? We might be off track." Rita looked just as surprised as Sara. It wasn't like her boss to be locked into one idea like this. It was still possible that Evert Karlesson wasn't the guy they were looking for. "Maybe he is also a victim in all this?" she said.

"You might be right, but nothing really points in that direction," Sara Vallén said. That he could be a victim had never really crossed her mind. In her mind, either he was the perpetrator, or someone else was. And if it was someone else, Evert probably wasn't involved at all.

"Well, nobody has seen him and we've been looking for him for a while. He is gone without a trace. He hasn't withdrawn any money, and Jörgen told me that he hasn't been in his flat since we were there. As far as we know, he doesn't have anywhere else to stay," Rita said.

"I guess you have a point," Sara had to admit.

She looked down at the floor and reflected on everyone's shoe choices. She was wearing a pair of elegant sandals and her toenails were painted red. Rita, on the other hand, had gone for sneakers, while Jörgen had chosen a pair of horrible hiking sandals that looked like they were from the sixties. Sara's father had similar ones when she was a kid. *Why do we make the choices we do?* she thought. *Even the smallest details are choices. Why do I do what I do? And what am I going to do about Peter Matsson?* It wasn't easy as her feelings told her to stay while her intellect screamed "NO!" as loudly as it could. She held back a sigh and looked up at her colleagues. They were all staring at her. *They probably want me to say something smart now,* she thought.

"We haven't heard from forensics yet. Let's see what they say," she said. "Jörgen, reach out to Ovesson and ask how far along they are. Report back to me by 2 p.m."

"Sure," Jörgen said.

Rita scratched her head.

"Is there any reason to believe that someone other than Karlesson did this?" she asked.

"Why not Rodney Ritger?" Jonny asked on a whim.

"Rodney Ritger? Yes, he's been on my mind too. We could be looking at two perpetrators here. Zandor Mårtensson said it was possible, even if unlikely."

"Why not?" Rita Anker said, and nodded.

"Okay," Sara said. "I've actually thought about the possibility myself."

Then she told the rest of the team about the boy who kept calling her at the emergency buddy centre.

# 63

He pulled his hoodie up, walked through the basement, and exited at the back of the building. He walked across the car park and stayed close to the wall until he reached Klostergatan. He had a quick look around and crossed the road. Nobody was after him, he was sure of it.

He rounded the corner of Lilla Fiskaregatan and hurried to the bank. He snuck in through the big glass doors, walked up to the cashpoint, and withdrew money, little by little, just as he had been instructed. But when he had withdrawn a certain amount, the cashpoint refused to give him more. He wasn't sure what to do next. The money burned a hole in his pocket. Dirty money.

He picked up his phone and hit the number on speed dial.

# 64

After further interrogations with Kajsa Lindahl's parents, we have a better idea of who the girl was. They finally understood that we need all the information we can get to solve this case. Combined with previous interviews with her classmates, and Josefin Elvebrandt in particular, we now know more about Kajsa's life," Sara said. Then she turned to Torsten and asked him to tell the others about Kajsa.

"Kajsa was allegedly molested by Evert Karlesson when she attended the Ladybird Primary School twelve years ago. However, the case was dropped as Kajsa's parents saw what happened to the boy Rodney Ritger during the preliminary investigation and refused to let the same thing happen to their daughter. Very unfortunate if you ask me. The girl had a much better support system than Ritger and would most likely have been just fine. Anyway, the girl grew up and she didn't seem too affected by what had happened at her primary school. She did well in school and was athletic, friendly, happy, and open-minded. A beautiful girl, as we've all seen. She took care of how she looked but didn't seem to struggle with her appearance in the way many teenage girls do. She was easy to deal with and reliable, at least until last summer. She worked for a month, mid-June to mid-July. Then she took a trip abroad by herself. Her parents didn't like it, but she was stubborn and apparently said there was nothing they could say or do to stop her. As she had always been such a good girl, they allowed it. In the end.

"After the trip, she changed. Her mood got worse, she started to fall behind in school, and she stopped showing up to handball practice. She became rebellious towards her dad and constantly fought with her mum. Her parents were confused but assumed that it was a phase that would pass. It didn't. But they didn't ask for help, although they were worried. You can probably imagine how they feel today."

"Did they ever find out what happened in Karlesson's flat recently?" Jörgen Berg wanted to know.

"Yes, we had to tell them. It would have been revealed during the trial anyway—whenever that will take place, as we still haven't found Karlesson."

"Have they picked their own counsel?" Sara asked.

"Yes, a guy called Anders Magnusson," replied Rita.

"What?" Sara said. "Anders Magnusson, is he down south now?"

"What do you mean?" Rita gave Sara a look of surprise.

"Last time I saw him, he worked up in Stockholm. He is an old classmate of mine," Sara explained. "If it's the same guy, of course. Never mind. Please continue."

"Kajsa's mother, Margareta, thought that Kajsa might be doing drugs. Ecstasy was her guess. Mostly because it is known as a party drug. Apparently, Kajsa wasn't home much during the weekends, and she had told her parents that she liked going to techno clubs. When I asked her about Sundays, Margareta told me that all she really knew was that Kajsa normally went to a spinning class. When I told her that we think she met Karlesson on Sundays, at least a couple of times a month, she seemed surprised. But she did admit to suspecting that Kajsa had been seeing a guy. The parents hadn't thought about Karlesson since the incidents during Kajsa's primary school years."

Rita frowned. Her head was suddenly killing her.

"The father, Gunnar, didn't suspect that Kajsa was using drugs until Margareta brought it up. They asked their daughter once, but when she told them they were wrong, they left it alone. They didn't know what else to do."

"Hmm," Sara said. "It feels good that they now know what really happened, and I'm glad that we also know more about Kajsa than we did before. I think it's fair to assume that Kajsa spent those hours that we can't account for with Evert Karlesson. Also, I asked Kajsa's sister to come in for an interview later this afternoon. Maybe she'll be able to give us the final pieces of the puzzle."

"Why haven't we found that boy Ritger?" Rita asked. "I can't believe he has managed to avoid us for this long, especially now when we have surveillance on him."

"He hasn't shown up to school either, according to the principal. We have to find him, period. Keep looking," Sara said, and turned to her colleagues.

They nodded in agreement.

"We would really appreciate it if you could give us any information that you haven't shared with us previously. We know that your parents worried about Kajsa using drugs."

It looked like Magda needed a moment to decide how much she was prepared to share. Up until now, she had been leaning back in the chair, but now she straightened her back and moved to the edge of the seat. She locked eyes with Sara.

"She used ecstasy. Some guy gave it to her when she went abroad last summer. It was the first time she did any drugs, but it left her wanting more. I have no idea how she could afford it though. She didn't work and all she had was her allowance. But I think she got high often."

Sara wanted to ask Magda why she hadn't told them about this until now but stopped herself. Instead, she gave Magda an encouraging nod.

"She didn't care about school and started acting pretty shitty to everyone, to be honest. She was the worst to Mum and Dad, but she wasn't very nice to me either. I think the only one she liked was Josefin. I know her latest grades were horrible. And she met this guy one Sunday a month. I guess it was that *E* that you were asking me about before." The girl gave Sara an inquiring look and Sara nodded again.

"Yes, maybe," she answered.

"I've seen it on Kajsa's calendar but when I asked about it, she refused to answer. Who is he?"

"All we can do at the moment is speculate," Sara said to avoid answering the question.

"But he is the murderer, right?"

The girl's question took Sara by surprise.

"We don't know," she said after a couple of seconds.

"I hope you catch him and that he gets life in prison for what he did." The girl's words carried a lot of weight. "I wish we still had the death penalty and that he was sentenced to it."

"We don't know if he is the guy who did this," Sara answered, "and we do not have the death penalty. Luckily," she added.

<h1 style="text-align:center">65</h1>

It was 3:45 p.m., and Sara was waiting for her son in town. They were buying him new shoes, but she also needed to talk to him. There was something about him that she needed answers to. He was staying out late and sneaking into the house in the mornings. It worried her. Maybe it was only natural, considering it was summer. But still.

Five minutes later, she saw him walking towards her across the square. Her heart filled with pride when she saw him.

"Hi, Mum," Johannes said, and hugged her.

"Hi, baby," Sara said.

They sat down at a café. They both agreed that it was probably best to have a coffee and a cinnamon bun before shopping.

"I want to tell you something," Johannes said suddenly. "I'm seeing Josefin."

"What?"

"I had been meaning to tell you, but it ended when I was arrested for that thing with Kajsa. Obviously. When I was released, she wanted to start seeing me again."

"But, Johannes, you have to tell me stuff like this. Especially now." Sara couldn't hide the frustration in her voice. She was angry.

"I know," Johannes said, looking right at her. "But I couldn't find a good time for it. And I was scared."

"Is that why you've been staying out so late?"

"Yes," Johannes said.

"I see," Sara said, tightening her jaw.

"I'm sorry I didn't tell you," her son said, and looked down.

"It's not that, Johannes. It's just that we're in a situation now where we really don't need any more surprises."

"I know, but there is something strange about her. She doesn't want me to touch her."

The boy was obviously embarrassed and Sara placed a hand on top of his to comfort him.

"I think I know why, but I'm afraid that I can't tell you anything more. I don't want you to see Josefin right now. Okay?"

"Okay."

He was far too smart to ask more questions.

Sara suddenly felt convinced. Everything made sense now.

# 66

The man waited for the boy. He had been waiting for hours. He grew more and more irritated as the time went by. But the boy didn't show up. He called him, but he didn't answer.

*What the fuck; is the kid trying to trick me now?* he thought. *He'll regret it.*

He fired up his computer to calm down. He unzipped his jeans and pulled them down to his knees.

The man didn't hear the door open. He suddenly heard a swooshing sound and then he fell into darkness.

The eternal darkness. He would never see the white lilac that was placed in the palm of his hand.

*It's a long way between heaven and earth,* the boy thought. *But close to pain and longing.* The demons inside him were quiet now, hiding in the dark. But he knew they were there. He could feel them.

He wiped all there was to wipe. His hands were swimming in sweat inside the gloves. He let the body lie just as it had fallen—the man's zipper unzipped and his penis hanging outside of his trousers. The boy left the flat, locked the door behind him, and walked off into the night. He felt pure. It would all be over soon. That's what it felt like as he walked through the park. He headed down Maskinvägen and took a right across from the cardboard factory. Then he went down into the tunnel that led to Klostergården. He knew where he was going. His legs carried him towards the south of Lund.

# 67

Josefin sat with her hands in her lap. Her back was straight, but her gaze was lowered. Her hair was short and dark. Sara noticed that she must have cut it recently. The last time she saw the girl, her hair had been longer. Her blue eyes focused on something that the others in the room couldn't see. Her mother sat next to her, but not too close. Her face was stiff. Sara looked at the girl's face. Inspector Torsten Venngren fiddled with his iPhone to start recording. He spoke into the microphone, stating the date, time, and place for the interrogation, as well as the name of the person being interrogated.

"So, Josefin," he said gently. "We're not here to accuse you of anything. We just want to figure out why Kajsa was murdered. You understand that, right?"

Josefin nodded but didn't say anything. She had a frightened expression on her face and it looked as if she would collapse into a pile any second now. But instead, she straightened her back and looked at Torsten, who found it hard to meet her gaze. Her eyes were full of darkness and guilt. *That guilt must be unbearable to carry*, he thought. A shiver ran down his spine.

"It would be great if you could answer the questions clearly," he said. He spoke quietly, careful not to scare the girl.

"Yes," she answered. Her voice was flat and tense.

"Do you know a man called Evert Karlesson?" Torsten went straight to the point.

"Yes," the girl whispered, as if her voice had lost all of its strength.

"If you speak a bit louder, it will be easier to hear on the recording later," Sara said, and leaned over the table to put a hand on the girl's shoulder. "You don't have to be scared."

"Yes," the girl said, somewhat louder.

"How do you know him?"

The girl flinched, surprised by the direct question. She didn't answer. Torsten Venngren decided that it was probably best to tread a bit more carefully when it came to questions concerning Josefin herself.

"We know that Kajsa knew him. Do you know how?"

"He gave her ecstasy." The girl shuddered and squirmed in her chair. She looked anxious and worried. Sara remembered the video sequences and the girl without a face.

"How did she pay for it?"

The girl fell silent again. Sara saw her struggling to come up with an answer.

"With sexual favours?" Torsten asked, and hoped he hadn't been too direct.

"Yes," she said, quietly but clearly.

"Did you also know Karlesson?"

"Yes."

"In the same way?"

Josefin started crying and her thin body began to tremble. Her tears fell silently, but forcefully.

"Yes."

The answer was clear and cut through her tears. Sara and Torsten looked at each other. The girl needed to calm down. Her mother looked like she was falling into a black hole. She gasped. *Destroyed*, was the word that popped into Sara's head. She stood up, walked over to Josefin's mother, and guided her out of the room. Once the door closed behind her, the mother collapsed on the floor.

"Call Henrik," she gasped. "He has to come home."

"Of course." Sara picked up her phone and called the girl's father. She explained what had happened and let it sink in for a moment. Henrik Elvebrandt promised to be there as soon as he could.

"I think it's probably best if you wait outside for the rest of the interrogation," Sara said to Josefin's mother after hanging up.

The woman nodded. She crawled up on the sofa like a little child. Then she hugged a pillow and cried violently.

Sara went back to her colleague and Josefin Elvebrandt. She closed the door behind her.

The girl had calmed down and wanted to continue the interview.

"How often did you meet Karlesson?" Torsten Venngren braced himself after asking the question. This was not a simple interrogation.

"One Sunday a month."

"How much ecstasy did he give you for your services?"

"Different every time. But only enough for the weekends."

"Was this the only time you had sexual contact with Karlesson?"

Josefin looked at Sara. She looked tired.

"Yes," she answered.

"Was it always recorded?"

"Yes," the girl said again with the same lethargic look in her eyes.

"Did someone else participate in these meetings?"

"Yes, the man who filmed it all. He always wore a mask and a big black coat, so I don't know who he was. But I think he got ecstasy for helping out. I'm not sure, but I think so."

"Can you describe the man who was doing the filming?" Torsten asked.

"He was really tall. He felt familiar somehow, I can't explain why. I never saw his face, but I think he was young."

"Do you know if he was exploited sexually as well?" Sara had a feeling there was something there. Something that she needed to figure out.

"I'm not sure, but I got the feeling they had known each other for a long time. Don't ask me why."

"Okay, please let me know if you come to think of anything," Sara said, and gave the girl a friendly smile.

"Yes."

"Did you meet Karlesson the night that Kajsa was attacked?"

"We were there before we went to the cinema."

"Was the man who filmed you there too?"

"No, actually he wasn't, for once," Josefin said quietly.

"So, he wasn't there. Do you think Kajsa could have met him after you said goodbye to her?"

"I don't know," Josefin said. "I don't even know who he is."

"No, that's true. But you might have known who he was if you had seen his face? Maybe it's someone you know," Torsten said calmly.

"The only person I know who is that tall is Rodney in our class, but he is the nicest boy in the world."

Sara held back a gasp.

"Do you *think* that the man filming you might also have been sexually abused by Karlesson?"

The girl shrugged her shoulders.

But Sara was sure that was the case.

"Okay. How long has this been going on for?"

"One and a half years, I guess. I don't remember exactly."

"I see," Sara Vallén said. "Did anyone else know?"

"No, but I just told Johannes. I couldn't carry it inside any longer."

"I understand," Sara said, and smiled at the girl.

"Do you think that Karlesson murdered Kajsa and Lena Johannesson?" Josefin blurted out.

The directness of the question caught Sara off guard and she had to think for a while before she answered. Torsten cleared his throat. Sara gathered herself and turned to the girl.

"I honestly don't know, but it looks a bit suspicious, doesn't it?" she said, not expecting an answer.

"Yes, it does," the girl said. "He's insane. And gross." She made a disgusted face.

"Did you notice if Karlesson seemed to like a special type of flower?" Torsten asked.

"What?" the girl looked confused. "Not that I can remember."

"I think we'll end the interrogation here," Sara said. "Is it okay if we contact you again? If we have any more questions?"

Sara didn't want to dig any further into all the darkness, at least not for now. The girl looked exhausted. She needed a break. Sara would talk to the parents and contact social services to make sure she got the support she needed.

"I want to say something," the girl said suddenly. "He has ruined me. I'm ruined and it's all my fault. If I had said no, none of this would've happened. I'm dirty, and I will always be dirty. I feel like a whore. And that's what I am, right?"

"Oh, little one," Sara said, and put her hand on top of the girl's, "you're not a whore. You're a young girl who ended up in the claws of an adult man. None of this is your fault and he carries all the blame. Now you just have to find your way back to yourself. And I'll talk to your parents so that they can get you the help you'll need."

Sara remembered all the shame she had felt, all the filth she had spent years trying to wash away and all the pain she had carried inside of her for all those years. It wasn't until she had met Louise Malmberg that she had got rid of it for real. And by then, she was already an adult. All those years of shame and self-hate, for no reason. The kind of shame that clung to your inner being and slowly but steadily killed your self-esteem and caused constant suffering. She wouldn't wish it on her worst enemy.

Josefin's father entered the room. He was pale.

*Scared and angry, probably,* Sara thought.

She took the man's hand and introduced herself. Then she asked him and Josefin's mother to join her in another room. She told them as firmly as she could that she needed to talk to them both. She could tell how tense the father was and, to avoid conflict between him and his daughter, she wanted to make it very clear who was in charge.

"I will contact social services as your daughter will need a lot of support. I won't press charges at the moment. Josefin is going through something very difficult and I don't want to put her through that. Right now, Inspector Venngren is asking Josefin to hand over all her drugs. I advise you to keep an eye on her. And let the professionals do their job as they are working with her. You need to make sure that she sees a therapist as well."

Josefin's parents listened. Neither of them said anything, but the dad looked a bit calmer now. As if he wasn't as angry anymore. The mother looked tired and confused.

Finally, Josefin's mother said, "Of course we'll make sure she gets all the help she needs. How will we find a good therapist?"

"There are plenty of good ones. Talk to social services, they will guide you in the right direction," replied Sara.

The girl's parents' faces were pale, but they managed to nod as Sara told them what she needed them to do.

Torsten and Sara left the Elvebrandt family and drove to Byggmästare-gatan. Josefin had given them a couple of ecstasy pills. The girl had wept as she told them that she had never intended to go to Karlesson again after what had happened to Kajsa. She was terrified of him. *Poor child,* Torsten Venngren thought to himself.

"Who is the guy with the camera?" he suddenly said.

"Someone who enjoys watching, I think."

"You're probably right. But who is he?"

"No idea."

Sara lost herself in her own thoughts. Her nails kept getting shorter.

"Stop biting your nails," Torsten said, and grabbed her hand. "It's nasty."

Sara sighed. As if she didn't know that.

"Yeah, yeah," she said, and kept biting. "Where is Karlesson hiding?"

"If we knew that, the case would have been solved by now." Venngren smiled bitterly.

# 68

The NFC got back to us," Jörgen Berg said as soon as they had stepped into the police station.

"And?" They both looked expectantly at Jörgen.

"They have identified DNA in the flat. The same DNA that we found on Kajsa Lindahl."

"Karlesson," Torsten and Sara said at the same time.

"We couldn't get any DNA from Lena Johannesson. On the other hand, the modus operandi tells us that it might be the same perp in both cases. Just as expected, there was DNA in the flat that matched Kajsa's, as well as DNA that probably belongs to the other girl in the footage."

"Josefin Elvebrandt," Sara and Torsten said in unison.

"Oh, okay," Jörgen said, and stared at them. "What do you guys know that I don't?"

"We'll tell you later," Sara said. "Please continue."

"And there is DNA from another, unknown person. A fourth person."

"The man with the camera!" Sara and Torsten exclaimed.

"What?!"

"We'll tell you later," Sara repeated. "Let's gather the team. We need to go through the case again now while we have all this new information. And by the way, did you hear anything from the US service provider regarding the owner of the IP address? We need to know who sent those messages to Lena Johannesson." Sara felt like a nag, but she was frustrated with how slowly everything moved because of all the bureau-cratic red tape.

"No, but I called them and they have promised to get back to me by tomorrow."

"I have to say it, but they are moving bloody slowly on this," Sara said, deciding to display her irritation for everyone to see. She hated it when things were out of her control.

"Yes, but we'll have our answer by tomorrow. I assume they came from Karlesson's computer. Maybe Lena Johannesson knew about him too? Maybe she knew too much, or suspected something? Maybe Kajsa told her? Maybe she had told Karlesson that she was planning on telling Johannesson?"

It was impossible to answer any of the questions at this point, so they all stayed silent.

Sara gathered her team: Rita Anker, Jonny Svensson, Torsten Venngren, Jörgen Berg, and Ove Ovesson. She gave them an update about every-thing that had come to the surface during the day.

"I can smell the end of this case," she said, and felt surprisingly invigo-rated. The circumstantial evidence wasn't circumstantial anymore.

# 69

Emergency buddy, this is Sara."

"Hi, it's me." The boy's voice made Sara's heart skip a beat. She looked at her watch and made a note of the time.

"Hi, how are you?" Sara listened carefully, ready to pick up on every word, every nuance.

"My dad is gone, at least for now. I'm fine. But I did something bad. Something mean."

"I'm sure it's not that bad," Sara said.

"What would you know about it?" the boy screamed into the phone.

"You're right. I don't know anything about it. So, what did you do?"

"I hurt someone," he whispered.

"How?" Sara held her breath and did her best not to annoy the boy.

"I won't tell you," he said quietly.

"Okay. Do you want to talk about it anyway?"

Sara's heart was beating in her chest. Her intuition had been right. She waited.

"No, not really. I'm just worried, that's all."

"Why?"

"I don't want to get caught. I only did what was right. You should get rid of useless people like that."

Sara did her best to hide what she really felt.

"What do you mean?" she finally said. "Get rid of, how?"
"There are many ways. Goodbye, we won't talk again," the boy said.
"No, wait, you won't hurt yourself, right?" she shouted.
"Nope," he said, and hung up.

# 70

Sara called her team to another meeting, although it was late.

When they arrived at the station, she was waiting for them in the conference room.

"The boy's call came from a phone owned by a Wilkinsson. He lives on Hårlemans Väg 4, here in Lund. So, it didn't come from Ritger's flat."

"But didn't Kajsa's parents tell us that Karlesson used to go by another name?" Jörgen said, and started searching through his notes.

"Yes, that's right," Torsten said, and scratched his unshaven chin.

Jörgen stood up and left the room. He returned with a laptop in his hand. They were all waiting silently. Sara felt frustrated that this hadn't been brought up earlier.

"The problem is that he called from a mobile phone, so he could've called from anywhere. Not necessarily from there," Jörgen said.

Rita rolled her eyes. "No shit, Sherlock."

"We still have to go there though. Who is Wilkinsson?" Sara turned to Jörgen.

"It's a woman, born 1935. Hold on . . ."

Jörgen's fingers moved swiftly across the keyboard.

"She is registered at another address too. By the looks of it, it's a nursing home. And, she has a son called Evert Karlesson. Bingo," Jörgen said, and clapped his hands together.

"Then that's probably where Karlesson is hiding. How come we didn't know about this earlier?" The tone of Sara's voice was sharp as a knife and even Jonny straightened his back. None of them knew what to say.

They all stood up at the same time and the room filled with the scraping sound of chairs being pushed away from the table. Nobody said anything.

# 71

They rang the doorbell to Wilkinsson's flat on the third floor. Nobody came to open it. Sara put her ear against the door but couldn't hear a thing.

She leaned down to look through the letter box. She was overcome by an eerie sensation of déjà vu. The flat seemed empty.

The locksmith was waiting at the bottom of the stairs. Sara waved him over.

From the hallway, they could see straight into the living room. There was a man's body on the floor. Sara rushed over. The back of the man's head was crushed. She turned the body over. It was Evert Karlesson. He was obviously dead.

"What the . . ." Sara and Rita looked at each other, and then at the body again. The others were standing in the hallway with their mouths wide open.

"Rodney Ritger," Rita said.

Sara pulled out her phone and called the operations centre to tell them she wanted to put out an APB on Rodney Ritger.

"I'll send you a photo of the boy shortly," she said, and described him quickly over the phone.

The medical examiner looked at the bashed-in skull and then at the limp penis hanging outside the victim's trousers.

He shook his head. "Well, would you look at that."

The coroner parked his car outside the house.

Two men walked into the flat and put the body in a body bag before carrying it out to the car. The forensics team trod carefully through the flat. They all wore white rubber gloves. There was a vase of thirsty lilacs on a table.

Ovesson approached Sara and shook his head, just as the medical examiner had done.

"Not a trace, it's all wiped clean. At least so far," he said.

"Yes, but you might still be able to find something," said Sara. "I'm convinced it's the boy who keeps calling the emergency buddy centre, and that his name is Rodney Ritger."

"It sure looks that way," Ovesson said solemnly.

# 72

The boy walked along Lund's smaller side streets. He was on his way to Nilstorp—a neighbourhood on the south side of town. He had been there many times before. He had stood outside the house, staring in through the windows. The lights in there always looked so warm and inviting. *She isn't like Kajsa—cold and mean like a shark*, he thought. Kajsa had always had sharp teeth and cold eyes. But she had paid. She denied him but gave herself to that monster for some drugs. Josefin, on the other hand, had a warm smile. Her eyes looked like deep wells. She was always kind to him. She always offered to help him. With homework, maths, and reading. But there was something smug about her, as if she thought that she was better than him. He couldn't let her think that, so he always declined her offers. None of them were better than him. They were the ones who had given their bodies to that monster for a small portion of drugs. The monster had used them and without them knowing it, he had watched it all. But the monster had paid too, he had punished him. For all those years. All the suffering.

# 73

When Sara and Baum met him in the corridor, Jörgen Berg jumped up and down like an impatient child.

"We've heard from the American service provider. The messages came from a man named Conrad Ritger, or at least from a computer owned by him. The address is Lilla Gråbrödersgatan in Lund."

"Rodney Ritger is definitely suspected on probable cause," Baum said. "Great job."

"Great. Then we'll change the status of the APB to *suspected on probable cause,*" Sara said, turning to the prosecutor.

He nodded.

"Change it," Sara ordered Jörgen.

# 74

He arrived at Plommonvägen and stood outside the house. He felt braver than usual and took a couple of steps into the garden. Once again, all those years of trying to avoid his father came in handy. He silently walked up to the house and tried to look inside—a hard thing to do if you wanted to stay unnoticed. He didn't have to get on his tiptoes to see. On the contrary, he was tall and almost had to crouch down to get a good look. He walked over to the side of the house where he could hide in the bushes next to the house wall and avoid the neighbours' prying eyes. One of the windows was partly covered by blinds. He peeked in and saw Josefin walking around in panties and a T-shirt. She had no makeup on and it looked as if she was ready to go to bed.

She sat down by a computer next to the wall. *I wonder why she hasn't placed her computer by the window?* he thought as he studied her carefully. She flinched and screamed something, and a second later, her parents came rushing into the room. They stared at the screen and started debating something. They were almost screaming, but the boy couldn't hear what they were saying. They all left the room and he could get a better look at the screen.

The boy smiled. She had finally received his email. He looked at the screen again and felt pleased with his message: "You'll soon be dead too," it said. He clenched his teeth to hold back the laughter that bubbled up inside him. But then he suddenly felt regret. He wanted her to fear him, but he also wanted her to like him. He didn't really want to hurt her. He wanted her to save him.

He stayed by the window as he saw a car approach the house and park on the driveway. At first, he couldn't see what type of car it was as the headlights blinded him. A moment later, he saw two uniformed police officers step out of the car and walk into the girl's room. They looked at the screen and took notes as the girl and her parents kept talking. They all looked very upset. The girl anxiously looked around the room, but as the light was switched on, she couldn't see anything but darkness and the bushes outside the window. One of the officers moved towards the window and turned his head to his colleagues to say something. The other officer turned the lights off in the bedroom. Before the police officer made it to the window, the boy had taken a step to the side. Now he was moving quickly away from the window along the house wall. *That was close*, he thought.

He waited for the police to leave before he sneaked back to the girl's window. Now she had pulled the blinds all the way down and he couldn't see anything at all. He sat down in the cool grass and decided that he was going to stay there. Nobody was looking for him, and, if they were, they wouldn't look there. After a while, he fell asleep with his head resting against the wall's rough tile surface.

# 75

When the boy woke up, it was light outside. His neck felt stiff and he lay down again, using his backpack as a pillow. The bag contained some of his few belongings. He fell asleep again and woke up to the sun shining and the birds chirping happily in the bush next to him.

The boy realised that it was time to find another hiding place. The risk of the girl's family seeing him here was significant. He had a look around and realised that there was a garden shed behind the house. He decided to sneak in there. Those sheds were always full of crap, and you always stored whatever you used in the front. He could crawl in and hide in the back. They probably wouldn't look there, at least not for a good while. He crawled along the house and over to the garden shed.

Luckily, the door was unlocked, so he crept in. Just as he had thought, the shed was full of stuff. At the front, he saw a barbecue, some plastic garden furniture and a couple of rakes and shovels. In the back, the family had lined up their skis, skates, and other things that were only used in the winter. He crawled in behind the garden furniture and found a blanket that had been thrown on top of a wooden chest. He put the blanket down on the floor behind the chest and leaned his backpack against the wall. He pulled out the bloody pipe from the backpack and hid it among the clutter on the shed's floor. He was relieved to finally get rid of it. He lay down and fell asleep again. He had no idea what time it was, but he was pretty sure that it was still too early for him to be awake.

# 76

Everyone was looking for Rodney Ritger. Sara didn't need to join the search for now. They had enough people on it. If they found him, they would let her know. Instead, she decided to join a judo class. She hadn't attended one in a while.

"Do you want me to drive you home?" the instructor asked her when they were done.

"That would be really nice of you," Sara answered, glad that she didn't have to ask. She was relieved not to have to take the train.

He talked the whole way home and Sara did her best to listen. But mostly, she tried to sort out the emotions that rushed through her head. Anger, disappointment, and hatred mixed with the irrational feelings she had felt so many times in her professional life when it came to domestic abuse cases—feelings like hope, love, and passion. *Powerless is a good way to describe it*, she thought. *Completely powerless while facing yourself.*

She shook her head and her instructor glanced at her.

"Why are you shaking your head?" he asked.

"Nothing special. I'm just thinking about some stuff," she said, realising that the instructor had probably just said something she hadn't heard.

"You act like you're in love," he said. "When you're in love, you can't hear or see anything else. Right?"

"No, that's not it," Sara said, and it was true. She was confused and had no idea which feeling was the dominant one. He smiled again and shrugged his shoulders.

"Whatever you say. I get that you don't want to share your personal life with me," he said with a sparkle in his eye. "But I see what I see." He ended the discussion and parked outside her house.

"Thanks for the ride," Sara said. Then she spotted a man standing next to her door. It was Peter Matsson and he was leaning against the doorframe. He didn't move a muscle. She stepped out of the car and was just about to close the door when the instructor smiled at her again.

"My pleasure," he said, before adding: "And hey, I told you so!"

"Stop it," she said with a crooked smile. "Bye!"

He drove off. Sara walked over to the door. Peter Matsson barely looked at her. She had been excited when she first saw him, but now she felt nervous and scared. Still, she put her key in the lock and opened the door. She walked into the dark and empty house and Matsson followed her. Once they had entered the house, he pushed her. She wasn't prepared and fell forwards. *Not again*, she thought. To her surprise, she found herself staying on the floor. She didn't stand up, didn't defend herself. She let it happen. He started kicking her. Most of his kicks landed across her back and some of them hit her chest and stomach. She tried to curl up to protect herself. He was silent but kept kicking. Suddenly, he started screaming, just like he had the last time, calling her whore, skank, trash, and slut.

"You whore! You're not only seeing *one* other man!" he screamed. "I knew it, I knew it. And who is this guy? Do I need to *kill* him?" He hissed the last part of the sentence through clenched teeth. Then he leaned over and grabbed her arms. He pulled her up to her feet, but she crouched down. He stopped kicking her and started punching her upper body with his fists. She didn't try to defend herself. She just took it. Without a word.

He grabbed her long hair and pulled her head back. She heard a cracking sound from her neck. Then he slammed her head into the wall. He pulled her hair again and it hurt like hell. Then he punched her, right in her face. She could hear her nose break. Finally, she screamed.

He pushed her to the floor again and rushed out of the house. He slammed the door behind him. She stayed on the floor. She was so ashamed that she couldn't get up. She felt paralysed. And the sadness was merciless.

She stayed on the floor for a long time. After a while, she managed to get up and into the bathroom. Her nose was swollen and crooked. She put a hand over the base of her nose and twisted it into place. It was extremely swollen and blood squirted out of it. She grabbed some toilet paper and pressed it against her nose, but it was bleeding so heavily that the paper was soaked in blood before she could reach for more.

All she could think about was how grateful she was that her children hadn't been home. How grateful she was that they hadn't seen this.

She picked up her phone and called the hospital. The nurse told her to call a taxi and come in immediately.

They looked at her nose and made sure it would heal correctly. Then they gave her something to stop the bleeding. They also asked her what had happened. The doctor told her that her face had taken quite the beating and when she pulled Sara's shirt up to listen to her heart and lungs, Sara pulled away.

"Now, you'll have to tell me what happened to you," she said. "This hasn't happened because of a little accident."

"I'm a boxer," Sara lied. "I think we played a bit too rough this time."

"Hmm," the doctor said, and continued her examination. Sara screamed when the doctor touched her ribs.

"You have a broken rib," she said, "but we can't really do much about that. You'll have to stay still, that's all you can do. I'll recommend that you go on sick leave for at least a week. And I think you should see our therapist."

"No," Sara said. "I don't need to go on sick leave. I'm in the middle of a huge investigation and I don't need to see a therapist. This will heal on its own. I've been boxing, that's all."

"It's up to you," the doctor said. "But feel free to contact me if you need me, or the therapist. You don't look great, I must say."

Sara thanked the doctor and left the hospital. She needed to get out of there. She wanted to work but realised that it was probably best to wait until the morning—at least. Her whole body was in pain. But most painful of all was her soul and her self-esteem. *How could I let him do this to me?* she thought, blaming herself. *And twice—or had it been three times now? What's wrong with me?*

She took a taxi as she didn't want anyone to see her in the state she was in. She knew that everyone who saw her would think of her as a poor assault victim, and the thought of that made her feel cold inside. She felt a shiver down her spine.

She came home and lay down on the bed. *I just need some rest*, she thought, and fell asleep.

Sara woke up in the middle of the night, covered in sweat. Her body hurt so much that she thought she would pass out. *Judo is nothing compared to this*, she groaned inwardly. Sweat poured down her face and made her pillow wet. She turned the pillow over and lay down again. She stared at the ceiling for the rest of the night. She couldn't even muster the energy to go and take a painkiller. She didn't want to see her face in the mirror.

She dreaded the way she would look. It hurt when she cried. Everything hurt.

"You fucker," she said. "I'll kill you."

In a way she hoped that he would come back to apologise. Then she would fight back. Then she would kill him.

# 77

Sara heard the key in the door. At first, she felt terrified, but then she decided to get ready. Was he trying to break in? She grabbed a knife from the kitchen drawer and turned the lights off. She stood next to the kitchen table, ready to fight.

"Mum?" she heard Bella's voice, "where are you?"

Sara turned the lights on in the kitchen again. *Jesus, the thought, how could I forget about the kids?*

"I'm in here," she answered, realising that she would have to explain to her kids why she looked the way she did. She tried to pull herself together and come up with a lie. But she decided she had to tell them the truth. *It was what it was*, she thought.

Johannes, Bella, and Klara stepped into the kitchen together. As soon as they saw their mother, they stopped. They all stared at her.

Klara whimpered while Bella looked down at the floor. Johannes looked furious.

She walked towards them, hunched over from pain. She tried to lift her arms to hug them all, but her arms refused to obey. They hurt too much.

"What happened to you, Mum?" Bella's question hit Sara like a thunderbolt. It felt like her daughter saw right through her. She knew that a man had done this.

Klara cried and hid in her younger brother's embrace. Johannes was quiet, outraged.

Sara stroked her children's faces, one after the other.

"Let's sit down for a while," she said. "I'll tell you what happened to me, and I promise to tell you the truth."

The children helped her to the kitchen table and she sat down—slowly. They all wanted to sit close to her, as if they wanted to protect her. All at once, she felt infinitely grateful that they had come home, even if she knew that she would have to tell them the truth.

She spent an hour telling them her story, comforting them, and trying to keep Johannes calm. She had never seen him like this before. Her daughters did their best to help their mother calm him down. He finally understood that there was nothing he could do and that it was up to his mum to deal with Peter Matsson.

The girls didn't want to let go of their mother. When they went to bed, the sun had started to rise and there wasn't a cloud in the sky. It was painfully beautiful. Sara's daughters lay down on the bed next to her. The boy pulled his mattress into Sara's bedroom and lay down on the floor next to her bed. They were all overcome by fear. The children fell asleep after a while, but Sara couldn't close her eyes.

# 78

She was lying on her back with her daughters right next to her. She didn't dare to move—scared of the pain and scared of waking them up, now that they had finally fallen asleep.

It was just past 7 a.m. when she heard a quiet knock on the door. *Now*, she thought, *now I'll kill you, you devil.* She quickly realised that it would be impossible. She could barely move. Let alone kill someone. She slowly got out of bed, walked over to the door, and looked out through the little window next to it before she carefully opened it. A woman dressed in an elegant summer dress stood on the stairs. Sara looked down to try to hide her injuries as best she could.

The woman offered her hand—a slender hand with perfect nails. Her face was pale and her skin looked like porcelain. Sara took the woman's hand, still with her head down—staring at her feet.

"My name is Linda Matsson," the woman said. "I can see that Peter has been here."

Sara was baffled. She looked up at the woman, surprise written all over her face.

"What?" she said, sounding like an idiot.

"I'm married to Peter Matsson," the woman explained. "I came here to warn you, but I can see that it's already too late. At least, judging by the way you look." The woman was still holding Sara's hand in hers.

Sara pulled her hand away as if the woman had burned her. The sudden movement made her chest hurt.

"Can I come in?"

Sara took a step to the side and let the woman into the house.

"Do you have any coffee?"

"Yes," was all Sara could bring herself to say. She showed her into the kitchen and the woman sat down by the kitchen table. Sara closed the door behind them. *I hope the kids don't wake up*, she thought, and was reminded of all the anxiety and fear she had caused them.

"I always know about Peter's affairs. He tells me about them. To torture me. What he doesn't know is that I don't care anymore. He can beat me and tell me whatever he wants, I can't feel a thing anymore. But I wanted to warn you. I was hoping I wouldn't be too late. But I obviously was."

"Yes, but in a way, you weren't," Sara answered. She sounded tired.

"I can see that he really got you good this time. That means he has hit you before. He always starts out more carefully, before he escalates things." The woman stroked Sara's hands. "You're in pain. And your nose is broken. What are you going to do?"

"Kill him," Sara said, and smiled sadly at the woman. Her mouth was swollen now too, and it felt as if her upper lip had grown into her nose. She couldn't breathe through it and was forced to breathe through her open mouth. Everything hurt.

"Yes," the woman said, "I've had the same idea many times. I guess I don't have it in me, I'm afraid. But you could always go to the police. I never did. I've always convinced myself to feel sorry for him. And because he's on the force, he'll be punished extra hard. For some strange reason, I cared more about that than my own well-being."

Sara was shocked but admired the woman on the other side of the table. She was sitting there, completely still, with a cup of coffee in her hand. She had a sip of the hot drink as if nothing could touch her.

"But maybe *you* can kill him," the woman said quietly. Her voice was full of irony.

"No, I don't think so," Sara replied. "I don't really want to, I guess that's just something you say. But I'll do something."

Linda Matsson didn't seem to care about Sara's presence, not really. She had a long monologue inside her, and she needed to let it out. Sara let her speak without interruptions. Linda told her about how she had met Peter Matsson when she was still a young woman. She was nineteen. He was twenty-five. He was wonderful. The most beautiful man on the planet, she couldn't get enough of him. He was tall, strong, and handsome. In the beginning, he was thoughtful and generous with both compliments and gifts. After a while, he grew aggressive and suspicious. He started watching her every step and wanted her to tell him about everything she did. He slapped her for the first time after they had been together for six months. It scared her, but she had forgiven him as he had been drinking. He was also terribly sorry afterwards. During the days that followed, his touch had been kinder and gentler than ever.

"That was the first time," Linda said, nodding to confirm her own words. "After about a month, he hit me again. This time he wasn't drunk. He was upset about me coming home late after a party at work." The woman told her story methodically. She paused abruptly for a while, as if she was trying to organise her inner chaos. Then she continued. She had been a bit tipsy herself that time after the work party, and afterwards, she thought that maybe she had provoked him. At least that's what he said. It continued after that. Month after month, year after year. It got worse and worse. Also, he had caused friction within her own family and now they didn't even come to visit anymore. She was constantly sad and never found enough energy to get herself out of the situation. She had never pressed charges against him, although he had broken her nose at one point and her left arm at another. The staff at the hospital recognised her as she came in from time to time. Each time, they wanted her to see a therapist. And each time, they tried to make her tell them what had really happened. But she refused. She didn't dare tell them. She felt too embarrassed.

Sara listened to the woman for over an hour without saying a word. Her phone rang at one point, but Sara ignored it as she didn't want to interrupt her. Even if she was hurting—both physically and mentally—she knew that her pain was nothing compared to what the woman in front of her was going through. She decided that this had to end. She would report him. She had to. She couldn't possibly do anything else. She had to end the suffering for herself, and for this woman, before it was too late.

Linda Matsson suddenly stopped talking. Her monologue had come to an end. All that was left was a big black hole. Her eyes were empty.

She kept moving her lips as if she was still talking, without making a sound.

"I'll report him," Sara said, "I will. I hope that you will consider doing the same. I think that's the only way we can stop him. We can be strong together."

"Nothing can stop a man like him." The woman ran her hands across the tablecloth. Sara placed her hands on top of them.

"Yes. *We* can stop him. There is no other way. It's the only right thing to do."

"You report him if you want, I need to go home." She stood up and pushed the chair in under the table. With her head still high, she made her way to the front door again, followed by Sara. Before she left, she turned around.

"Nothing can stop a man like him," she repeated.

Linda opened the door, stepped outside, and turned to Sara again. "But now you know," she said. "Now you know what you can expect. If you stop him now, you might still have a chance. Otherwise, you won't." Then she left.

Sara sat down in the kitchen again. She felt confused, sad, and very angry. She called her old colleague, Marie Tengerby, in Malmö, telling her that she would come in to file a report. She pointed out that her visit concerned a private matter. After her appointment in Malmö, she would go to work. "And I request Anders Magnusson to be my solicitor," she added.

# 79

When Sara stepped into the conference room, the others fell silent. Their otherwise alert and strong chief inspector moved slowly and hunched over from the pain. Her entire face was swollen, not just her nose. Her lips were almost double their normal size.

"What the fuck," Rita cursed. "What happened to you? Who did this? Was it him?"

"I'll tell you about it later, not now. Now we have to work. We have to put an end to this hell."

"What happened to you?" Beatrice Larsson exclaimed when she entered the room. "You've reported this, right?"

"Of course. Now I'm just working on a plan to kill the guy who did it," Sara said with an ironic, and swollen, smile on her face.

"I'll send you on sick leave right away," Beatrice Larsson said.

"Nope," insisted Sara. "No way. I'll lead this investigation even if it takes me years. I'll finish it!"

She didn't even realise that she was shouting. Her face hurt and she grimaced. The others didn't say a word.

"Can I continue now?" Sara said to her boss, who nodded and left the room. Quickly.

# 80

I don't want to be under surveillance my whole life, like some prisoner," Josefin Elvebrandt said dramatically to her parents. She had regained some of her optimism, relieved to finally share the burden that she had carried all alone for over a year. She had got over the worst grief after Kajsa's death, just like young people always find a way to move on. At least that was what the girl's parents thought. All they could see was the defiant look in their daughter's eyes. They couldn't see the fear that lurked under the surface, the fear that she was struggling to keep under control.

"It's just for a short while," they told her. "You'll have to get used to it for now. Rather a prisoner than dead. Until they find Kajsa's murderer—who is probably the same person who sent you that threat—you'll have to find a way to deal with this."

Josefin's parents didn't even dare mention his name. They had a feeling that doing so was enough to make him appear. Feelings of anxiety and worry hung like a wet blanket over the household. Josefin went back into her room and slammed the door behind her. She was still sceptical. She just couldn't picture her sweet and slightly awkward classmate as Kajsa's murderer. Or Lena Johannesson's. But then again, Lena had always been a pain to Rodney. She had been on his case, constantly. She always told him how horrible he was doing and how shitty his life was going to turn out. She never stopped nagging him and some days she completely ignored him. *Maybe he did murder Lena after all?* she considered. But then he must have murdered Kajsa as well. It didn't make sense. Why would he have done that? Because she was hot, cool, athletic, and liked by everyone?

Then she remembered. Kajsa told her that Rodney had tried to get closer to her and that she didn't like it. But she had never been scared of him. He had only made her feel uncomfortable. She hadn't been able to explain why. As Josefin remembered this, she realised something horrendous: Rodney Ritger must have been the guy behind the camera in Karlesson's flat. He must know that disgusting creep that fed them ecstasy in exchange for sexual favours. She had never had to be close to him, not really. She hadn't been forced to do what Kajsa did. But now it felt obvious that the guy behind the camera was Rodney Ritger. She had never seen his face, but his height, his body, the big hands—they all matched Rodney's appearance. They had discussed it multiple times, but none of them had been able to figure out who the person holding the camera was—even if they both thought that he had somehow felt familiar. They had talked about it so many times. Now she knew. But why would he want to murder them? And could he really murder *her*? She had always been so helpful and kind to him. Kajsa was more of a bully. Maybe that's why he had picked her? Josefin's head was spinning as she sat in her bedroom. A bedroom decorated in black and pink. A bedroom that suddenly reeked of fear.

She didn't say anything to her parents. Everything about the situation was taboo. Their girl—their young and innocent girl—had turned into a prostitute in front of their eyes. None of them could bring themselves to talk about it. Josefin suddenly felt angrier than ever before. She expressed her guilt, which in fact was the most terrible guilt a human being could carry, by defying them. And by defying the terror she felt—because she had never been this scared before. He was out to get her too—Rodney. She couldn't believe it. But it was true. She felt trapped in her fear and in the knowledge that there was nothing she could do.

"Can you at least ask the security guards to stay away from the back of the house while I sunbathe? It's creepy having them around," she said. Her parents looked at each other.

"Fine, I guess it should be fine during the day," her father said. "I'll ask them to be a bit more discreet." Each time he thought about what his beautiful daughter had done, he felt her shame and couldn't look into her eyes. He felt as if her eyes were windows into the world that she had been living in lately. It was a world that he didn't dare or want to see.

Josefin grabbed a lounge chair and dragged it into the sun. She shot an irritated glance at the security guards, who were now standing at the side of the house, trying to be a bit less visible. *Discreet . . . yeah, right*, she thought. *About as discreet as a whale in a swimming pool.* She scoffed, lay down, picked up her book, and started reading. After a while, the security guards disappeared to the front of the house and Josefin removed her bikini top.

*Nice*, she thought, *finally some privacy.* She felt safe as long as the sun was up. It was worse during the nights.

# 81

The boy stood by the window in the garden shed. He looked at the girl in the lounge chair and squinted his eyes to see better through the dust-covered glass. The boy had seen the security guards and swore silently at them. They were standing at the side of the house now, looking at the girl. He smiled when they disappeared to the front of the house. He wasn't sure how long it had been since he had sneaked into the shed, but it felt like an eternity. One night he had slipped out and made his way over to the petrol station to get something to eat. Two chocolate bars and two litres of Coca-Cola. He assumed that people were looking for him by now, so he took great care, moving as silently and discreetly as he could. The boy wasn't sure what the police knew, but he was worried enough to stay out of sight during the day. He waited patiently and knew that he would have to be ready to leave as soon as he was done with what he came here to do. He wasn't scared. Just a bit worried.

Sometimes he fell asleep. He didn't care if it was night or day. He dreamt about his father, towering over him with clenched fists—ready to punch. But then, suddenly, he was dead. Another dream was even more terrifying. He was playing Russian roulette—even if the game looked somewhat different in his dream. Huge spiders and beetles hid behind a trapdoor in the ceiling. A voice asked him questions. If he couldn't answer, the trapdoor would open and the gigantic bugs would rain down on him. The voice asked what his name was. He couldn't answer and the trapdoor opened. The bugs fell down onto him and he woke himself up screaming, trembling with fear. He didn't sleep any more that night.

When the sun had come up again, he fell asleep until he heard voices outside. It was the girl's mother, talking to a neighbour on the other side of the fence.

"I heard someone scream last night, did you hear it?"

"No," the girl's mother said, "I didn't hear anything. I slept like a baby for the first time since Josefin received that threat."

"Maybe I imagined it," the neighbour said, "but I was sure that I heard it last night."

The boy didn't move. He had to be more careful. That could've gone badly. Really badly.

# 82

Night came, but it wasn't dark yet. *Summer is so strange like that*, he thought, and couldn't wait to get out. When evening came, you had to wait for hours for the dark to catch up. And when morning came, it had already been light for hours.

He knew that he would probably have to leave the shed later that day and find a new place to hide. When all was done, he would disappear for good. Maybe he would go to his mum's, maybe somewhere else. Either she would come with him willingly, or he would force her—Josefin with the golden hair.

When it was finally dark outside, he made his way over to the hedge. He had found a clearing in it the night before. Now he walked through it, as silently as he could. On the other side of the hedge, he stumbled over a cat that hissed at him with its back arched and its fur standing on end. It didn't run but stayed like that, ready to attack. The boy stopped and waited. He wasn't sure what to do next. Cats were nothing like him. They were unpredictable and couldn't be trusted. His father had always told him that. *It takes one to know one*, the boy thought. His father had always been unpredictable, unreliable, and mean. A devil. The cat was black and the boy decided that it was probably the devil himself disguised as a cat. He aimed a kick at the cat and sent it flying through the air. "You had it coming," the boy whispered. The cat landed on its feet a bit further away. *That's what cats do*, the boy thought. The injured animal limped over to a bush and took cover underneath it. It meowed and moaned for a while and then it lay down. The boy walked over to it. The cat's breath was shallow, and after a while, it fell silent. The boy leaned over it and felt its warm fur. He ran his fingers over its chest. It felt strange. The cat's heart beat fast underneath the thick fur. He could feel it. He grabbed the cat's neck and squeezed. After a while, it stopped breathing—just as its heart stopped beating.

He kicked the cat again and kept moving silently along the hedge. Then he crossed another garden and kept walking towards Sankt Lars Park.

His heart raced. He felt aroused. A bit further into the park, he stumbled upon a construction trailer. He broke into it. The trailer had everything he could ever need. A little kitchen, a table, a couple of chairs, and a bed. He lay down on the bed and fell asleep. His heart calmed down. His penis went flaccid again. He wasn't aroused anymore.

# 83

The boy woke himself up, screaming in his sleep. *Not again*, he thought as his heart threatened to jump out of his chest. The dream about the bugs had returned. It scared him half to death. He was too terrified to go back to sleep and decided to leave the construction trailer. He walked back to Plommonvägen, where he would be close to people again. The dark construction trailer scared him. He felt trapped, like in a prison. The fact that he felt that way amazed him. The trailer wasn't any scarier than the other places he had been hiding lately. He had been trapped for most of his life, surrounded by darkness. Trapped in his flat, his room, and the basement. In his own darkness. In his eternal longing.

Once again, he crossed garden after garden via the hedges that separated the houses from each other until he made it to his old hiding place—the garden shed behind Josefin Elvebrandt's house. He crept back into the shed, where he knew that nobody would look. He felt safer in there and decided to stay. He still had some chocolate and a couple of sips of Coca-Cola left from his visit to the petrol station. Even if he knew that the area was being watched—and basically a minefield for him—he was happy about his return to the shed. Once again, he could relax. Now he was hoping that he would get to see Josefin back in the lounge chair later that day. Maybe he would even be brave enough to step out of the shed. He knew he could fool the security guards. He was way smarter than they were. He inhaled the familiar scent of the moist wooden floor and fell asleep on the blanket.

# 84

Sara had gone to see Beatrice Larsson to tell her the truth about her injuries. Beatrice had agreed with her when she said that Peter Matsson should be killed. In the midst of all the misery, they had laughed about it until Sara had to bend over from the pain. It was a bizarre situation.

"But seriously," her boss said once they had calmed down, "you need to report him. Even if his wife won't do the same, it will be hard for him to explain all your injuries. He might go to prison for this. And he will probably lose his job. As you understand, I will do everything in my power to make him pay for this. And I'm here for you if you need me—anytime."

Sara's laughter was replaced by tears. This time, she couldn't stop herself. An ounce of kindness and her wall broke down. Beatrice Larsson stood up, hugged her carefully, and stroked her hair.

"What are your children saying about this? Have you told them?"

"Yes, I told them everything. And I feel so bad for them. They won't leave the house while I'm home. They're so scared he will be back. I feel horrible," Sara cried.

"It'll be okay. It'll be okay."

"Yes, I guess it will," Sara said, and wiped her tears. On the way to her office, she ran into a frustrated Jonny Svensson.

"How hard can it be for the bloody surveillance unit to find this kid?" he said.

Sara felt that she really didn't have the energy to deal with Jonny Svensson, so she kept walking towards Torsten's office.

Torsten was crouching over a tall stack of documents, and judging by his posture, he was tired.

"Well, there isn't a lot of progress happening here, to be honest," he said. "We haven't found the boy."

He held up a bunch of documents.

"This is the medical report. It's pretty straightforward. Nothing strange about it, really."

Sara nodded carefully. Any movement bigger than a wink hurt like hell. Her face was sore and her ribs were aching, just like her stomach. Every little thing she did caused her excruciating pain.

Suddenly, a thought popped into Sara's head, and all at once, everything made sense. "I think I know where he is," she said.

# 85

*Lund is a beautiful, calm place*, Sara thought as she, Rita, Jonny, and Torsten drove towards the south of the town. Lund was full of beautiful houses, as well as a couple of bigger apartment complexes on the outskirts of town. The city centre consisted of old and well-kept buildings that made the old town feel genuine. People walked slowly along the streets—in and out of the little shops. Then they made their way to the little cafés along the narrow streets, or to the restaurants surrounding the two squares—Stortorget and Mårtenstorget. *People here live in harmony with their hometown,* Sara thought. Still, it had always been hard for her to find her place in Lund. But just as she had often felt like a stranger, Göran had always felt right at home—something that had caused many arguments between them. She was a social person and very interested in making new friends, but ever since she had arrived in Lund, she had felt like people were sceptical towards her. Göran, on the other hand, had grown up in Lund and didn't think there was anything sceptical about the people there at all. Sara had struggled from time to time and was grateful for her friendly neighbours. Without them, she would have felt completely alone. But despite all this, she loved Lund. As time went on, she had made it her home. *Everything is better than being homeless,* she thought, and smiled.

Jonny's phone rang.

"A tip," he said after hanging up. "Rodney was spotted close to Plommonvägen this morning."

"I knew it," Sara said.

"Someone saw him sneaking along some hedges. Apparently, the caller found his cat dead in the bushes close by, just minutes after. The cat had nasty injuries. But then again, it could have been hit by a car and then made its way to the bushes to die in peace. At least the person who called in the tip was sure he saw Rodney Ritger close by. I assume he knows the kid. Because we haven't gone public with his name yet—only a description of him—right?"

"Yes," Sara said, "that's right. But as you know, this kid is pretty easy to spot."

"That's true," Jonny said, and shrugged his shoulders.

Torsten sighed, thinking how they were always one step behind.

Sara felt grateful they had placed security guards outside Josefin Elve-brandt's house. Who knew what might happen to her otherwise? She was really concerned. How had the kid managed to avoid them for this long? He must have realised that the police were on to him. Or else he might as well have stayed home, right? She realised that they had under-estimated him. Just because he wasn't very socially adept, it didn't mean he was an idiot. *What a miss*, she thought. *What a bloody miscalculation.*

Sara felt heavy and her whole body wanted to sink down into the car seat. Once they'd parked on Plommonvägen, she could barely get out of the car.

Jonny was the first one to step out of the car, unusually alert. Maybe because the other three officers seemed so tired. Torsten Venngren opened the rear door and put his feet on the asphalt with great effort.

"Do you really believe we're on the right track here?" he said hesi-tantly. "Why would Rodney Ritger hang around here, now that we have placed security outside Josefin's house?"

"I don't know," Sara said. She was feeling hesitant too. Jonny was the only one who seemed to be in a good mood. It was as if he was hoping that this would be the moment when he could finally show people what he was made of.

An arsehole like Rodney Ritger would be punished for his crimes—no doubt about it. Jonny Svensson would make sure of it, and he was sur-prised to see how lacklustre his colleagues seemed about it. He pointed to the hedge that ran along the back of the houses on Plommonvägen.

"These security guards must be bloody amateurs," he said as he nodded towards the hedge and pointed out all the gaps. "Anyone can sneak through here if this hedge is left unattended."

Sara called Jörgen and asked for details of the neighbour who had contacted them about the cat. He gave her a phone number and she called the man, who told her he had heard a sound that reminded him of an angry cat. As his family owned a cat, he had gone outside to check it out. He spotted a tall, broad-shouldered young man sneaking along the hedge. Then the man found his dead cat. Something had made him feel very uneasy—then he remembered the news about the wanted youth. As the guy he saw was so big—which matched the description of the youth in question—he concluded he must be the one the police were looking for. So, he called them. In any case, his cat was dead. "Sad, but true," as the man put it.

Sara asked the neighbour when this had taken place. He told her it had happened the night before and apologised for not thinking about it until now. *Not good*, thought Sara. She turned to her colleagues; they all knew that Rodney could be far away by now. The tip didn't tell them much, except that they had been right about Josefin Elvebrandt. It was obvious that she could be in danger here.

The man told her that the boy had walked towards Malmövägen.

"Okay," Torsten said. "I guess we can always take a look in the park in that direction. Who knows, maybe that's where he's hiding?"

Sara received another call from Berg, who told her about a tip that had come in days before but that had somehow fallen between the cracks. Someone had seen an unusually large young man in Lund Cathedral. The sexton had apparently called it in one evening. Also, the petrol station by the south entrance to Lund had a customer who fitted the description of Ritger. Apparently, they didn't think anything strange about it when he first came in but reflected on it the morning after.

"They were terribly sorry about it, but I must admit that I got a bit upset," Jörgen Berg said.

As they approached Sankt Lars Park, they passed a construction trailer. By the looks of it, it wasn't being used right then. They parked the car and started walking around the area with no apparent plan. Sara called the operations centre to ask them to get a K-9 unit ready, in case they might need it. The operator promised to get back to her as soon as one was ready.

Sara walked along the park's main path. She saw the construction trailer they had passed by earlier in the car. The door was open. *Strange,* she thought. *Shouldn't that be closed?* Then it hit her. It was so obvious. She rushed over to the trailer and immediately saw that it had been broken into. She called back to the operations centre.

"I need a dog here, *now,*" she ordered. "There has been a break-in in a construction trailer. There is a chance that the murderer has been here." Her heart started to beat faster. The operator immediately radioed all available units. The K-9 unit responded right away, as well as a couple of other units that were close by.

They all showed up at the park within minutes. The forensics team were on their way too. Sara hoped that this would lead to a resolution before something else happened. She already knew that the boy wasn't in the trailer, but he couldn't be too far away now. Everybody spread out in the area, some on foot and some in cars. Sara ordered a couple of officers to check the blocks surrounding the park.

The dog sniffed in and around the trailer and picked up a scent almost immediately. The dog handler told Sara this meant that someone had been in there quite recently. Then the dog took off through the park with the experienced dog handler close behind.

*Finally*, Sara thought.

She was in constant contact with the operations centre, but a colleague had also given her a radio. The dog followed the scent across Malmövägen and towards Nilstorp, which was the area where Josefin lived. Then it stopped. The dog had lost the trail, confused by the various scents in the surroundings of other dogs and people.

But Sara had enough information to glean that the boy was headed towards Plommonvägen again, which told her that he was interested in Josefin. This obviously meant that Josefin was in a dangerous position, but Sara didn't feel too worried—they were on his heels. As long as the security guards outside her house were awake, he wouldn't be able to do anything.

She gathered her team and they all headed back towards Josefin's house. She told the operator at the operations centre about their plan and informed him that she wanted all the other units to keep looking in Sankt Lars Park. He could still be there, after all.

# 86

The boy moved silently in the garden shed. He wanted to get out of there. He wanted to look at Josefin. *I'll risk it*, he thought, and opened the door. It squeaked a little, but if he pushed it down while he opened it, he could stop it from making too much sound.

He crept over to Josefin's window. The blinds were open and she was moving around in there. It was a warm day and she probably wanted to go outside to enjoy the summer. She left her room and he couldn't see her.

He could hear the door to the deck open. He made his way to the side of the house. Josefin was standing on the deck with a cup in one hand and a sandwich in the other.

The boy realised how hungry he was. He would have done almost anything for a sandwich and a cup of chocolate milk, or coffee. He tried to pick up a scent from her cup to figure out what was in it. All he'd had to eat and drink in the past few days was chocolate and some Coca-Cola. No wonder he was hungry.

The girl sat down in what looked like a very comfortable chair. It was obvious she was enjoying the moment, yet he couldn't understand how someone who had sold her soul and body to a monster like Evert Karlesson could enjoy anything whatsoever. *The devil must have taken her*, he thought as he watched her. He was overcome by hate and jealousy.

He both admired and envied the beautiful creature who was sunbathing on the deck.

She was wearing a summer dress and her naked legs looked smooth. Slightly tanned. Her face was sun-kissed and her skin reminded him of peaches. He wanted to touch it. He wanted to place his face close to hers and smell her. He wanted to feel her hair tickle his cheeks and touch her with his lips. Desire washed over him. He found it hard to contain his excitement. His erection grew but he didn't dare move, terrified that she would discover him. He fought with his own conflicting feelings. He loved and hated the girl at the same time.

She looked up as if she had heard something. As if she felt someone's presence. Then a guy who seemed familiar somehow came walking through the front gate. *He must be from school or something*, the boy thought. And then he remembered. *Shit*, he thought, and quickly backed away, holding his breath. He closed his eyes and counted. *One, two, three, four, five, six, seven, eight, nine—ten.*

He opened his eyes again and there she was, with that guy. Right in front of him. They had discovered him. Neither of them said anything. The guy looked like he was about to pass out. Josefin was staring at him. Her eyes were wide open and he couldn't tell if she was surprised or terrified.

He handed her a white lilac branch. She took it and stared at the flower as if she wasn't sure how to interpret the gesture. He quickly reached out for her and grabbed her wrist. He pulled her close and placed a knife against her throat.

Her male friend didn't move a muscle.

"Are your p-parents home?" he stuttered. She shook her head.

"But you've got security guards by the entrance door, right?" he continued.

She nodded.

"Just be quiet now," he said, and his stutter was suddenly less noticeable. He kept talking to her as he pulled her backwards around the corner of the house and into the back garden. Josefin's male friend followed them but stopped at the corner.

"What do you want?" she whispered.

He held the knife against her throat with one hand and stroked her cheek with the other. She wasn't moving. *Firm as a rock*, he thought. He pressed his nose against her. She smelled nice. Her skin was hot and it almost felt like she had a fever. He kept stroking her cheek and his fingers wandered up to her hair and down to her shoulders. His fingers were exploring her. He couldn't stop. His breathing became heavier and he felt desire spread through his body again.

"You're not like Kajsa," he said. His stutter was gone now.

She nodded, scared to do anything else.

"She thought that she could fool me. She didn't know that I had seen everything. You don't know it either, but I was the one filming you when you were with Karlesson, the monster. And Kajsa always moaned and made sounds when he was doing his thing. But I could see that you were only faking it."

It was clear the boy was aroused by the situation and that the girl was petrified.

"Yes," she whimpered. "I was faking it."

"And she wanted nothing to do with me. She never wanted to have anything to do with me, even if she was a whore. For that reason, she had to die. And for being a dirty whore, she had to be cleansed. That's why I killed her. But you're not trash. You're pure and beautiful."

He kept stroking her and realised that he had forgotten about the guy standing a bit further away. He looked at him, relieved to see that he was still completely paralysed.

"Johannes," he said. "Your name is Johannes. Your mother is with the police."

Johannes didn't move. He was petrified. The shiny knife against Josefin's neck terrified him. Thoughts were racing through his head. He was standing too far away from them to reach her in time.

"And that fucking bitch knew too much. She was also trash. A disgusting, fat whore. It felt so good getting rid of them. And now they can never say anything again. Never speak again. Speech is silver, silence is golden. Nobody can talk without a tongue. And she really got what she deserved."

He giggled. Josefin bit her lip until it started bleeding. Then he slapped her across the face. The skin on her cheek stung. She instinctively raised her hand to her face and gasped for air, but there was none. She couldn't breathe. Not a sound, not a movement.

"You're also trash. You've sold your soul to the devil," the boy said, and grinned at her. She looked past him.

"And I spilled it all out over her face, the devil's face. You don't understand, but she couldn't scream. She couldn't do shit. The bitch couldn't do shit either. She tried, but you know, I'm stronger than the devil. And nobody—nobody—can buy me. They were also frightened by the emails I sent them, just like you. I scared you, right? I enjoy fighting with the devil's tools," he continued. "I'm terribly sorry, but I won everything. They won nothing. Do you want to win, beautiful little Josefin?"

Josefin wasn't sure if she was dreaming when he started singing. A lullaby. All she knew was that he was crazy and that he was going to kill her. His hands trembled as they stroked her skin—his hands, all over her.

# 87

Sara stopped the car outside Josefin Elvebrandt's home on Plommon-vägen. They stepped out and walked slowly towards the house.

"We have no idea what this guy is capable of," Sara whispered. "He is probably here. Where else would he have gone?"

"Are you worried?" Jonny Svensson whispered back to her.

"No, not really. But it's probably best we don't announce that we are here, if you know what I mean? I'll talk to the security guards."

Sara walked up to the two men standing by the front door.

"Have you guys seen anything?"

"No, but then again, they've told us not to go to the back of the house. Apparently, we bothered the girl," replied a tall, chubby security guard.

"What?" Sara stared at them. "Are you insane? There are multiple ways to get into the house from the back. Didn't you understand your assignment?" She was overcome by rage as she stared at the wide-eyed security guards.

"What?" the chubby guard said. "We're just following orders."

"Well, I definitely haven't given you those orders," Sara said through clenched teeth.

She turned to her colleagues and informed them about the so-called orders to stay away from the back of the house.

"Who the fuck gave them that order?" Rita hissed, clearly upset.

"We'll find out later," Sara whispered. "Let's go to the back of the house. God bless us all." She glanced up at the sky and prayed for good luck.

They started moving slowly towards the back of the house, staying close to the wall. Torsten had gone to the car to inform the duty officer that they were going in. They couldn't wait for backup. The duty officer wasn't happy about it, but he had no option other than to concede.

"There's nothing you can do about it," Torsten Venngren said. "There's no time. We have no idea if he is here, or if he is about to do something. We can't wait, full stop."

# 88

Please, Rodney," Josefin pleaded. She was almost choking from his strong arm around her throat.

She felt dizzy. *I need to stay cool,* she thought. *I don't want to die* was another thought that played on repeat in the back of her head. She glanced over at Johannes, who was standing a bit closer now. *Johannes will save me,* she thought.

Rodney was so excited now that he could barely contain it. Although his plan had been to control himself, he simply couldn't. His hands took on a life of their own, his body wanted to be close to her.

Josefin could feel how aroused he was through the fabric of their clothes. She thought about Kajsa's face. Pictured her friend in the hospital bed, connected to all those machines. She blinked to get rid of the tears that were welling up in her eyes, but before she knew it she was crying and a sobbing sound rose from her throat. She couldn't help it.

"B-be quiet," he said, stuttering again. "I'll kill you if you make a sound."

And she believed him. Panic washed over her, and her heart was beating so hard it felt like it was going to explode in her chest.

"Be quiet," he repeated. "If I die, you die."

The girl was shaking and she suddenly became very aware of how tiny her body was compared to his. He stroked her cheek awkwardly. "You'll be okay. Neither of us is going to die. But you have to come with me. We're getting out of here together, you and me. We're going far away, where nobody can find us."

He didn't even notice that she wasn't listening to him anymore. She stood there passively in his embrace and her tears had stopped falling. Her body was trembling like a leaf. But other than that, she was paralysed, silent, and deaf. Not a word, not a tear, not a movement. The scent of the lilac was overwhelming.

# 89

Johannes noticed that Rodney was so focused on Josefin that he seemed to have forgotten he was there.

He started moving closer to them, a couple of steps at a time. He was only a couple of metres away from them now. Rodney whispered something into Josefin's ear with his eyes fixed on her.

Then, suddenly, Rodney looked up.

"Back off!" he screamed. "Back off!"

Johannes didn't back off, but he stopped moving forwards.

He waited for his opportunity.

Then in an instant, what felt like an ocean of police officers surrounded them.

Rodney looked at all the guns pointing at him. *They can't kill me, I've got the devil in my grip*, he thought. He felt confused. They were all devils.

Sara and Rita spotted Johannes at the same time. He was standing close to Rodney Ritger. Sara waved at Johannes to get him to back off. But he refused.

"I'm closer," he mouthed at her.

Sara could see it too but kept waving her hand.

# 90

Let the girl go and nobody will get hurt," Sara said as calmly as she could. She managed to keep her voice steady even if she could feel fear wrapping around her like a hissing snake.

The other officers started shouting at Rodney. They all had their guns aimed at him. Sara turned to her colleagues and shot them a look that could kill. They stopped shouting. There was no time to wait for backup or the mediator, and she knew that she had to find another way to resolve the situation. None of them had expected this. Now they were on their own.

They were all staring at the boy, who was holding a knife pressed against the girl's throat. Her eyes were wide open and she was frozen. His face didn't move. Rodney didn't seem to hear what they said to him. He was staring into space. Sara noticed that his arms were covered in bruises and, judging by their yellow hue, they were at least a couple of days old. One of the boy's cheeks was covered in a bruise of similar colour.

Sara turned to him again and spoke calmly.

"If you let her go now, maybe we can talk about this," she said.

He didn't answer. The air was silent. Completely silent. Everyone knew that this could end in a number of ways. Sara stood there with her broken nose and her cracked rib and experienced the girl's fear as if it was her own.

"Everything will be okay," Sara said, turning to Josefin.

Jonny Svensson tried to determine if he could make it to Rodney and neutralise him before he could hurt the girl. Maybe he could fire a well-aimed shot, right in his forehead?

Torsten Venngren aimed his gun at Rodney, knowing that he would never use it.

Sara kept talking to Rodney, who suddenly started moving forwards with Josefin as a shield. She realised that he couldn't hear her. He moved in a trance. Sara felt that she was losing control of the situation. *But I have to find a way to get him under control. I just have to.* She noticed that Johannes was standing even closer to Rodney now. She had no idea how to get him to move away without Rodney realising how close he was. Sara saw the look on her son's face and knew that he wasn't going to move. It frightened her.

Suddenly, Rodney tried to say something, but all that was left in his mouth were a bunch of stuttering sounds. Sara and the others looked inquiringly at him. He pushed Josefin in front of him and tried to speak again. None of the officers understood a word. Then Sara remembered that Rodney stuttered.

She focused her eyes on him. He was only a couple of metres away from them now.

"I know you're trying to tell us something," she said calmly, "but you have to try to say it in a way that we can understand. Maybe it's easier if you focus on one word at a time?"

"I . . ." he said, followed by a couple of stuttering sounds.

"You . . ." Sara said, trying to help him. "You want something?"

The boy nodded, but he was still staring into space.

"Ge-ge-ge . . ." he continued. Sara tried to figure out what it was that he wanted.

"Get?" she suggested.

Rodney nodded and the penny dropped. He wanted to get out of there. As a free man. She understood that now.

"You want to get out of here," Sara continued, and he nodded again. Rodney was so close to Sara now that she would be able to reach him if she took three steps forwards. But Josefin was in her way. Rodney looked confused, as if he wasn't sure what to do. Sara didn't dare to move. What would he do to the girl if she did? She felt her body tensing, like a frightened animal.

Suddenly, Johannes threw himself at Rodney with a loud roaring sound. But he was too far away from him to get his hands on him.

Rodney screamed, pulled the knife across Josefin's neck and let go of her. The white lilac fell out of her hand and landed on the grass. Rodney lunged at Johannes with the knife and Johannes jumped to the side. Jonny Svensson decided to throw himself into the situation and his sudden movement made Sara lose her balance. Her gun flew out of her hand and into the air. The gun and Jonny landed on the ground at the same time. Sara saw the boy reaching for the gun and closing his hand around it.

For a split second, everything was still. Sara stared at her gun in Rodney's hand and froze. Her brain refused to function.

With a sweeping motion, the boy placed the gun against his temple.

Then he pulled the trigger. The sound was merciless. Sara watched it all happen in slow motion, as if she was watching it from above. Still, she reacted instinctively. She threw herself forwards to stop what had already happened.

The boy fell to the ground with a thump. The horror of the sight was reflected in the faces of the officers surrounding the boy.

Everything was silent.

Sara felt an ice-cold wave wash over her. She froze. Everything stopped and the silence was as merciless as the sound of the gunshot. A couple of seconds passed by and nobody moved. Torsten Venngren was the first one to shake off the shock, and he rushed over to the girl. They could hear the ambulance in the distance. Venngren took off his shirt and pressed it against the girl's neck.

Sara Vallén sat down and took the boy in her arms, rocking him back and forth like a baby. She didn't care about the blood, or about the hole in his head. He was only a child. Nobody moved.

The boy was holding Josefin's white lilac.

# 91

They would never forget that day.

They were sitting around the conference table. Exhausted. She allowed them time to gather their thoughts. Their minds were probably spinning, just like hers.

She carried the blame for the boy's death. It was her gun and she had lost control of it. She couldn't stop thinking about the fact that she had let him get his hands on her weapon. Her brain refused to accept it, but she knew that it was exactly what had happened. Johannes wasn't doing so well, but she knew he would be okay. He was getting help. And Josefin was alive. The knife hadn't cut deep enough to damage any major blood vessels. She had told Johannes that it was mostly thanks to him. He had forced Rodney out of his trance by lunging at him like he did. They would be okay. It would just take time.

Then she thought about Peter Matsson. She had really felt like killing him, but she realised that it was just something she needed to feel to get through it all. He would be punished anyway. Her children's fear had made them cling to her like a second skin and it had been hard to deal with at first. After a while, she had managed to convince them that it wasn't their job to protect her—that she could take care of herself, after all. She knew that they would carry their fear with them for a long time, but she also knew that it would pass eventually. Matsson was out in the cold, although his wife was still with him. She hadn't been able to summon up enough strength to report him, or leave him. Sara missed love but realised that love wasn't synonymous with Peter Matsson. She knew that it would be hard to look at him during the trial. He would make her feel like a traitor.

Outside of this nightmare, the summer was beautiful. Sara's nose was still swollen, yellow and blue, and a hard bump had formed on the ridge of her nose. The rest of her face had taken on a golden colour. She had picked out a white dress. She wanted to dress up a little to make herself look better, but also to celebrate that summer was finally here. The case was solved and she could move on from it. She wasn't sure if they had actually solved it or if it had solved itself in the end—but she knew that it was worth a beautiful summer dress, either way. She had painted her lips red and the night before, she had done her absolute best to make her nails look fantastic. She had soaked her feet in a wonderful foot bath. Göran had come to her house and her children had told him what had happened to her. When he stood there in the doorway and saw her broken face, he had taken her in his arms. He had grieved with her and been furious for her sake. His tears and his anger had warmed her heart. There was something between them after all. Something good. She felt relieved and allowed herself to let her shoulders drop. *This will be a nice summer,* she thought. *I'll feel better every day. It'll be nice to have some time off and some rest. And it'll be nice to have dinner with Anders Magnusson. He'll have to deal with me as I am.*

Sara forced herself to snap out of her daydreaming and return to reality. She scrunched her aching nose for a second and started reading a document. Then she put the paper down and looked at her colleagues.

"I want you to know that you all did a good job, regardless of how things ended. It's not one person's fault that Rodney Ritger is dead. If anyone carries blame for his death, it's me. Let us all be happy that the girl is alive. That's our reward." Sara stood up. She had her summer vacation to look forward to. When she got back from it, the trial would start. *But that's a chapter for another time.* She turned to her colleagues and wished them all a wonderful summer.

"Try to leave this all behind you now and don't think about it too much," she said before walking out the door, knowing that they would all do the opposite. She closed the door behind her. She didn't turn around. There was nothing that couldn't wait until later.

*Finally*, she thought as she opened the police station door and stepped out into the beautiful summer's day.

# THANK YOU

*White Lilac* was not created by accident. After almost twenty years working as a police officer, I have learned a lot about human beings and seen first-hand how life can change people and affect their journey. I have wanted to present perspectives on evil that differ from the usual and convey what all those years on the force have taught me—that actions themselves can be evil, not the people behind them. I am convinced people are born good.

I want to thank my beloved husband, Torgny, and my amazing children, Anna and Mika, for their patience. I also want to thank my dear friends and old colleagues for answering all of my questions—good and bad. Thanks to my beloved mother and a posthumous thanks to my beloved stepfather, Hompe, for all their faith in me.

Finally, all characters appearing in this work are fictitious and any resemblance to real persons, living or dead, is purely coincidental. However, there are of course fragments of everyone I know in each character.

Cecilia Sahlström
Lund, 10 April 2017

# ABOUT THE AUTHOR

Cecilia Sahlström is a popular Swedish crime writer based in Lund, in southern Sweden. Sahlström worked in the police force for twenty years before becoming a writer. Her first novel, *White Lilac*, has been praised for its gritty realism and authentic portrayal of police investigations.

# DISCOVER
# *STORIES UNBOUND*

PodiumAudio.com